THE MAN WHO WOULD BE KING
AND OTHER STORIES

THE MAN WHO WOULD BE KING
AND OTHER STORIES

RUDYARD KIPLING

This edition published in 2019 by Arcturus Publishing Limited
26/27 Bickels Yard, 151–153 Bermondsey Street,
London SE1 3HA

Typesetting by Palimpsest Book Production Limited

Cover design: Peter Ridley
Cover illustration: Peter Gray
Design: Beatriz Custodio

AD006023UK

Printed in the UK

CONTENTS

CONTENTS

INTRODUCTION

Rudyard Kipling was born in December 1865 in Bombay, India. His father, John Lockwood Kipling, was a professor of architectural sculpture and his mother was described by her contemporaries as a lively, entertaining woman. The family had moved to India earlier in 1865, and they adapted well to the culture and climate of the subcontinent, soon considering themselves 'Anglo-Indians' – a dual identity that Kipling was never able to shake.

At the age of five, like many children in his situation, Kipling was sent to Britain for his education. There, he was housed with foster parents in Southsea, Portsmouth. It was an unhappy experience for the young boy. The cruelty of his foster parents and, later, the challenge of the military education provided at the United Services College at Westward Ho! in Devon made life in England difficult for Kipling.

By 1882, he was only too happy to return to India, where his father found him a job as an editor with the *Civil and Military Gazette* in Lahore. During his free time, Kipling began to write poetry and short stories. It was not long before they appeared in print. Also at this time, Kipling wrote his first collection of verse, *Departmental*

Ditties, which was published in 1886. Kipling developed an insatiable appetite for writing. Between 1886 and 1887 he wrote no fewer than 39 stories for the *Gazette*, many of which were included in his collection *Plain Tales from the Hills*. And several more collections followed.

In 1889, he returned to England once more. This time it was a rather more pleasant experience for Kipling. He met and fell in love with an American, Caroline Balestier. After they were married in 1892, the couple moved to Vermont to live close to Caroline's family estate. It was during this period that Kipling turned to longer fiction and produced some of his best-known work. In 1894 and 1895 came the two *Jungle Books*; in 1901, he wrote his masterful novel *Kim*, and a year later he released his classic children's work, the *Just So Stories*.

Kipling's political views were deeply conservative and strongly imperialist, much to the chagrin of many contemporary liberals. His writing achieved great success in his own lifetime, as he received the Nobel Prize for Literature in 1907, but as views began to change in the run-up to World War I and during the conflict, Kipling was unable to recover the almost universal popularity he had enjoyed during the 1890s. After the death of his son in 1915, he became more inward-looking and his stories took on a melancholy tone. Kipling died in 1936 after a long and accomplished career as one of Britain's foremost writers.

This collection includes nine of Rudyard Kipling's best stories which show the exceptional range of his imagination, his ability to create atmosphere and a truly compelling variety of characters.

The Man
Who Would
Be King

'BROTHER TO A PRINCE AND FELLOW TO a beggar if he be found worthy.'

The Law, as quoted, lays down a fair conduct of life, and one not easy to follow. I have been fellow to a beggar again and again under circumstances which prevented either of us finding out whether the other was worthy. I have still to be brother to a Prince, though I once came near to kinship with what might have been a veritable King and was promised the reversion of a Kingdom — army, law-courts, revenue and policy all complete. But, today, I greatly fear that my King is dead, and if I want a crown I must go and hunt it for myself.

The beginning of everything was in a railway train upon the road to Mhow from Ajmir. There had been a deficit in the Budget, which necessitated travelling, not Second-class, which is only half as dear as First-class, but by Intermediate, which is very awful indeed. There are no cushions in the Intermediate class, and the population are either Intermediate, which is Eurasian, or native, which for a long night journey is nasty; or Loafer, which is amusing though intoxicated. Intermediates do not patronize refreshment-rooms. They carry their food in bundles and pots, and buy sweets from the native sweetmeat-sellers, and drink the roadside water. That is why in the hot weather Intermediates are taken out of the carriages dead, and in all weathers are most properly looked down upon.

My particular Intermediate happened to be empty till I reached Nasirabad, when a huge gentleman in shirt-sleeves entered, and, following the custom of Intermediates, passed the time of day. He was a wanderer and a vagabond like myself, but with an educated taste for whiskey. He told tales of things he had seen and done, of out-of-the-way corners of the Empire into which he had penetrated, and of adventures in which he risked his life for a few days' food. 'If India was filled with men like you and me, not knowing more than the crows where they'd get their next day's rations, it isn't seventy millions of revenue the land would be paying – it's seven hundred million,' said he; and as I looked at his mouth and chin I was disposed to agree with him. We talked politics – the politics of Loaferdom that sees things from the underside where the lath and plaster is not smoothed off – and we talked postal arrangements because my friend wanted to send a telegram back from the next station to Ajmir, which is the turning-off place from the Bombay to the Mhow line as you travel westward. My friend had no money beyond eight annas which he wanted for dinner, and I had no money at all, owing to the hitch in the Budget before mentioned. Further, I was going into a wilderness where, though I should resume touch with the Treasury, there were no telegraph offices. I was, therefore, unable to help him in any way.

'We might threaten a Station-master, and make him send a wire on tick,' said my friend, 'but that'd mean inquiries for you and for me, and I've got my hands full these days. Did you say you are travelling back along this line within any days?'

'Within ten,' I said.

'Can't you make it eight?' said he. 'Mine is rather urgent business.'

'I can send your telegram within ten days if that will serve you,' I said.

'I couldn't trust the wire to fetch him now I think of it. It's this way. He leaves Delhi on the 23rd for Bombay. That means he'll be running through Ajmir about the night of the 23rd.'

'But I'm going into the Indian Desert,' I explained.

'Well and good,' said he. 'You'll be changing at Marwar Junction to get into Jodhpore territory – you must do that – and he'll be coming through Marwar Junction in the early morning of the 24th by the Bombay Mail. Can you be at Marwar Junction on that time? 'Twon't be inconveniencing you because I know that there's precious few pickings to be got out of these Central India States – even though you pretend to be correspondent of the Backwoodsman.'

'Have you ever tried that trick?' I asked.

'Again and again, but the Residents find you out, and then you get escorted to the Border before you've time to get your knife into them. But about my friend here. I must give him a word o' mouth to tell him what's come to me or else he won't know where to go. I would take it more than kind of you if you was to come out of Central India in time to catch him at Marwar Junction, and say to him: – 'He has gone South for the week.' He'll know what that means. He's a big man with a red beard, and a great swell he is. You'll find him sleeping like a gentleman with all his luggage round him in a second-class compartment. But don't you be afraid. Slip down the window, and say: – 'He has gone South for the week,' and he'll tumble. It's only cutting your time of stay in those parts by two days. I ask you as a stranger – going to the West,' he said with emphasis.

'Where have you come from?' said I.

'From the East,' said he, 'and I am hoping that you will give him the message on the Square – for the sake of my Mother as well as your own.'

Englishmen are not usually softened by appeals to the memory of their mothers, but for certain reasons, which will be fully apparent, I saw fit to agree.

'It's more than a little matter,' said he, 'and that's why I ask you to do it – and now I know that I can depend on you doing it. A second-class carriage at Marwar Junction, and a red-haired man asleep in it. You'll be sure to remember. I get out at the next station, and I must hold on there till he comes or sends me what I want.'

'I'll give the message if I catch him,' I said, 'and for the sake of your Mother as well as mine I'll give you a word of advice. Don't try to run the Central India States just now as the correspondent of the Backwoodsman. There's a real one knocking about here, and it might lead to trouble.'

'Thank you,' said he simply, 'and when will the swine be gone? I can't starve because he's ruining my work. I wanted to get hold of the Degumber Rajah down here about his father's widow, and give him a jump.'

'What did he do to his father's widow, then?'

'Filled her up with red pepper and slippered her to death as she hung from a beam. I found that out myself and I'm the only man that would dare going into the State to get hush-money for it. They'll try to poison me, same as they did in Chortumna when I went on the loot there. But you'll give the man at Marwar Junction my message?'

He got out at a little roadside station, and I reflected. I had heard, more than once, of men personating correspondents of newspapers and bleeding small Native States with threats of exposure, but I had never met any of the caste before. They lead a hard life, and generally die with great suddenness. The Native States have a wholesome horror of English newspapers, which may throw light on their peculiar methods of government, and do their best to choke correspondents with champagne, or drive them out of their mind with four-in-hand barouches.

They do not understand that nobody cares a straw for

the internal administration of Native States so long as oppression and crime are kept within decent limits, and the ruler is not drugged, drunk, or diseased from one end of the year to the other. Native States were created by Providence in order to supply picturesque scenery, tigers and tall-writing. They are the dark places of the earth, full of unimaginable cruelty, touching the Railway and the Telegraph on one side, and, on the other, the days of Harun-al-Raschid. When I left the train I did business with divers Kings, and in eight days passed through many changes of life. Sometimes I wore dress-clothes and consorted with Princes and Politicals, drinking from crystal and eating from silver. Sometimes I lay out upon the ground and devoured what I could get, from a plate made of a flapjack, and drank the running water, and slept under the same rug as my servant. It was all in a day's work.

Then I headed for the Great Indian Desert upon the proper date, as I had promised, and the night Mail set me down at Marwar Junction, where a funny little, happy-go-lucky, native managed railway runs to Jodhpore. The Bombay Mail from Delhi makes a short halt at Marwar. She arrived as I got in, and I had just time to hurry to her platform and go down the carriages. There was only one second-class on the train. I slipped the window and looked down upon a flaming red beard, half covered by a railway rug. That was my man, fast asleep, and I dug him gently in the ribs. He woke with a grunt and I saw his face in the light of the lamps. It was a great and shining face.

'Tickets again?' said he.

'No,' said I. 'I am to tell you that he is gone South for the week. He is gone South for the week!'

The train had begun to move out. The red man rubbed his eyes. 'He has gone South for the week,' he repeated. 'Now that's just like his impudence. Did he say that I was to give you anything? – 'Cause I won't.'

'He didn't,' I said and dropped away, and watched the red lights die out in the dark. It was horribly cold because the wind was blowing off the sands. I climbed into my own train – not an Intermediate Carriage this time – and went to sleep.

If the man with the beard had given me a rupee I should have kept it as a memento of a rather curious affair. But the consciousness of having done my duty was my only reward.

Later on I reflected that two gentlemen like my friends could not do any good if they foregathered and personated correspondents of newspapers, and might, if they 'stuck up' one of the little rat-trap states of Central India or Southern Rajputana, get themselves into serious difficulties. I therefore took some trouble to describe them as accurately as I could remember to people who would be interested in deporting them; and succeeded, so I was later informed, in having them headed back from the Degumber borders.

Then I became respectable, and returned to an Office where there were no Kings and no incidents except the daily manufacture of a newspaper. A newspaper office seems to attract every conceivable sort of person, to the prejudice of discipline. Zenana-mission ladies arrive, and beg that the Editor will instantly abandon all his duties to describe a Christian prize-giving in a back-slum of a perfectly inaccessible village; Colonels who have been overpassed for commands sit down and sketch the outline of a series of ten, twelve, or twenty-four leading articles on Seniority versus Selection; missionaries wish to know why they have not been permitted to escape from their regular vehicles of abuse and swear at a brother-missionary under special patronage of the editorial We; stranded theatrical companies troop up to explain that they cannot pay for their advertisements, but on their return from New Zealand or Tahiti will do so with interest; inventors of patent punkah-pulling machines, carriage couplings and unbreakable swords and axle-trees call with specifications in their pockets and hours at their disposal; tea-companies enter and elaborate their prospectuses with the office pens; secretaries of ball-committees clamour to have the glories of their last dance more fully expounded; strange ladies rustle in and say: – 'I want a hundred lady's cards printed at once, please,' which is manifestly part of an Editor's duty; and every dissolute ruffian that ever tramped the Grand Trunk Road makes it his business to ask for employment as a proof-reader. And, all the time, the telephone-bell is ringing madly, and Kings are being killed on the Continent, and Empires are saying, 'You're another,' and Mister Gladstone is calling down brimstone upon the British Dominions, and the little black copy-boys are whining, 'kaa-pi chayha-yeh' (copy wanted) like tired bees, and most of the paper is as blank as Modred's shield.

But that is the amusing part of the year. There are other six months wherein none ever come to call, and the thermometer walks inch by inch up to the top of the glass, and the office is darkened to just above reading light, and the press machines are red-hot of touch, and nobody writes anything but accounts of amusements in the Hill-stations or obituary notices. Then the telephone becomes a tinkling terror, because it tells you of the sudden deaths of men and women that you knew intimately, and the prickly-heat covers you as with a garment, and you sit down and write: – 'A slight increase of sickness is reported from the Khuda Janta Khan District. The outbreak is purely sporadic in its nature, and, thanks to the energetic efforts of the District authorities, is now almost at an end. It is, however, with deep regret we record the death, etc.'

Then the sickness really breaks out, and the less recording and reporting the better for the peace of the subscribers. But the Empires and the Kings continue to divert themselves as selfishly as before, and the foreman thinks that a daily paper really ought to come out once in twenty-four hours, and all the people at the Hill-stations in the middle of their amusements say: – 'Good gracious! Why can't the paper be sparkling? I'm sure there's plenty going on up here.'

That is the dark half of the moon, and, as the advertisements say, 'must be experienced to be appreciated.'

It was in that season, and a remarkably evil season, that the paper began running the last issue of the week on Saturday night, which is to say Sunday morning, after the custom of a London paper. This was a great convenience, for immediately after the paper was put to bed, the dawn would lower the thermometer from 96° to almost 84°

for almost half an hour, and in that chill − you have no idea how cold is 84° on the grass until you begin to pray for it − a very tired man could set off to sleep ere the heat roused him.

One Saturday night it was my pleasant duty to put the paper to bed alone. A King or courtier or a courtesan or a community was going to die or get a new Constitution, or do something that was important on the other side of the world, and the paper was to be held open till the latest possible minute in order to catch the telegram. It was a pitchy black night, as stifling as a June night can be, and the loo, the red-hot wind from the westward, was booming among the tinder-dry trees and pretending that the rain was on its heels. Now and again a spot of almost boiling water would fall on the dust with the flop of a frog, but all our weary world knew that was only pretence. It was a shade cooler in the press-room than the office, so I sat there, while the type ticked and clicked, and the night-jars hooted at the windows, and the all but naked compositors wiped the sweat from their foreheads and called for water. The thing that was keeping us back, whatever it was, would not come off, though the loo dropped and the last type was set, and the whole round earth stood still in the choking heat, with its finger on its lip, to wait the event. I drowsed, and wondered whether the telegraph was a blessing, and whether this dying man, or struggling people, was aware of the inconvenience the delay was causing. There was no special reason beyond the heat and worry to make tension, but, as the clock-hands crept up to three o'clock and the machines spun their fly-wheels two and three times to see that all was in order, before I said the word that would set them off, I could have shrieked aloud.

Then the roar and rattle of the wheels shivered the quiet into little bits. I rose to go away, but two men in white clothes stood in front of me. The first one said: – 'It's him!' The second said – 'So it is!' And they both laughed almost as loudly as the machinery roared, and mopped their foreheads. 'We see there was a light burning across the road and we were sleeping in that ditch there for coolness, and I said to my friend here, the office is open. Let's come along and speak to him as turned us back from the Degumber State,' said the smaller of the two. He was the man I had met in the Mhow train, and his fellow was the red-bearded man of Marwar Junction. There was no mistaking the eyebrows of the one or the beard of the other.

I was not pleased, because I wished to go to sleep, not to squabble with loafers. 'What do you want?' I asked.

'Half an hour's talk with you cool and comfortable, in the office,' said the red-bearded man. 'We'd like some drink – the Contrack doesn't begin yet, Peachey, so you needn't look – but what we really want is advice. We don't want money. We ask you as a favour, because you did us a bad turn about Degumber.'

I led from the press-room to the stifling office with the maps on the walls, and the red-haired man rubbed his hands. 'That's something like,' said he. 'This was the proper shop to come to. Now, Sir, let me introduce to you Brother Peachey Carnehan, that's him, and Brother Daniel Dravot, that is me, and the less said about our professions the better, for we have been most things in our time. Soldier, sailor, compositor, photographer, proof-reader, street-preacher, and correspondents of the Backwoodsman when we thought the paper wanted one. Carnehan is sober, and so am I. Look at us first and see that's sure. It will save you cutting into my talk. We'll take one of your cigars apiece, and you shall see us light.' I watched the test. The men were absolutely sober, so I gave them each a tepid peg.

'Well and good,' said Carnehan of the eyebrows, wiping the froth from his mustache. 'Let me talk now, Dan. We have been all over India, mostly on foot. We have been boiler-fitters, engine-drivers, petty contractors, and all that, and we have decided that India isn't big enough for such as us.'

They certainly were too big for the office. Dravot's beard seemed to fill half the room and Carnehan's shoulders the other half, as they sat on the big table. Carnehan continued: – 'The country isn't half worked out because they that governs it won't let you touch it. They spend all their blessed time in governing it, and you can't lift a spade, nor chip a rock, nor look for oil, nor anything like that without all the Government saying – 'Leave it alone and let us govern.' Therefore, such as it is, we will let it alone, and go away to some other place where a man isn't crowded and can come to his own. We are not little men, and there is nothing that we are afraid of except Drink, and we have signed a Contrack on that. Therefore, we are going away to be Kings.'

'Kings in our own right,' muttered Dravot.

'Yes, of course,' I said. 'You've been tramping in the

sun, and it's a very warm night, and hadn't you better sleep over the notion? Come tomorrow.'

'Neither drunk nor sunstruck,' said Dravot. 'We have slept over the notion half a year, and require to see Books and Atlases, and we have decided that there is only one place now in the world that two strong men can Sar-a-whack. They call it Kafiristan. By my reckoning its the top right-hand corner of Afghanistan, not more than three hundred miles from Peshawar. They have two and thirty heathen idols there, and we'll be the thirty-third. It's a mountainous country, and the women of those parts are very beautiful.'

'But that is provided against in the Contrack,' said Carnehan. 'Neither Women nor Liquor, Daniel.'

'And that's all we know, except that no one has gone there, and they fight, and in any place where they fight a man who knows how to drill men can always be a King. We shall go to those parts and say to any King we find – 'D'you want to vanquish your foes?' and we will show him how to drill men; for that we know better than anything else. Then we will subvert that King and seize his Throne and establish a Dynasty.'

'You'll be cut to pieces before you're fifty miles across the Border,' I said. 'You have to travel through Afghanistan to get to that country. It's one mass of mountains and peaks and glaciers, and no Englishman has been through it. The people are utter brutes, and even if you reached them you couldn't do anything.'

'That's more like,' said Carnehan. 'If you could think us a little more mad we would be more pleased. We have come to you to know about this country, to read a book about it, and to be shown maps. We want you to tell us that we are fools and to show us your books.' He turned to the bookcases.

'Are you at all in earnest?' I said.

'A little,' said Dravot, sweetly. 'As big a map as you have got, even if it's all blank where Kafiristan is, and any books you've got. We can read, though we aren't very educated.'

I uncased the big thirty-two-miles-to-the-inch map of India, and two smaller Frontier maps, hauled down volume INF-KAN of the Encyclopædia Britannica, and the men consulted them.

'See here!' said Dravot, his thumb on the map. 'Up to Jagdallak, Peachey and me know the road. We was there with Roberts's Army. We'll have to turn off to the right at Jagdallak through Laghmann territory. Then we get among the hills – fourteen thousand feet – fifteen thousand – it will be cold work there, but it don't look very far on the map.'

I handed him Wood on the Sources of the Oxus. Carnehan was deep in the Encyclopædia.

'They're a mixed lot,' said Dravot, reflectively; 'and it won't help us to know the names of their tribes. The more tribes the more they'll fight, and the better for us. From Jagdallak to Ashang. H'mm!'

'But all the information about the country is as sketchy and inaccurate as can be,' I protested. 'No one knows anything about it really. Here's the file of the United Services' Institute. Read what Bellew says.'

'Blow Bellew!' said Carnehan. 'Dan, they're an all-fired lot of heathens, but this book here says they think they're related to us English.'

I smoked while the men pored over Raverty, Wood, the maps and the Encyclopædia.

'There is no use your waiting,' said Dravot, politely. 'It's about four o'clock now. We'll go before six o'clock if you want to sleep, and we won't steal any of the papers. Don't you sit up. We're two harmless lunatics, and if you come, tomorrow evening, down to the Serai we'll say goodbye to you.'

'You are two fools,' I answered. 'You'll be turned back at the Frontier or cut up the minute you set foot in Afghanistan. Do you want any money or a recommendation down-country? I can help you to the chance of work next week.'

'Next week we shall be hard at work ourselves, thank you,' said Dravot. 'It isn't so easy being a King as it looks. When we've got our Kingdom in going order we'll let you know, and you can come up and help us to govern it.'

'Would two lunatics make a Contrack like that!' said Carnehan, with subdued pride, showing me a greasy half-sheet of note-paper on which was written the following. I copied it, then and there, as a curiosity: –

This Contract between me and you persuing witnesseth in the name of God – Amen and so forth.

(One) That me and you will settle this matter together:
i.e., to be Kings of Kafiristan.
(Two) That you and me will not while this matter is being settled, look at any Liquor, nor any Woman black, white or brown, so as to get mixed up with one or the other harmful.

(Three) That we conduct ourselves with Dignity and
     Discretion, and if one of us gets into trouble the
     other will stay by him.
Signed by you and me this day.
     Peachey Taliaferro Carnehan.
     Daniel Dravot.
     Both Gentlemen at Large.

'There was no need for the last article,' said Carnehan,
blushing modestly; 'but it looks regular. Now you know
the sort of men that loafers are – we are loafers, Dan, until
we get out of India – and do you think that we could sign
a Contrack like that unless we was in earnest? We have
kept away from the two things that make life worth having.'

'You won't enjoy your lives much longer if you are
going to try this idiotic adventure. Don't set the office
on fire,' I said, 'and go away before nine o'clock.'

I left them still poring over the maps and making notes
on the back of the 'Contrack.' 'Be sure to come down
to the Serai tomorrow,' were their parting words.

The Kumharsen Serai is the great four-square sink of
humanity where the strings of camels and horses from
the North load and unload. All the nationalities of Central
Asia may be found there, and most of the folk of India
proper. Balkh and Bokhara there meet Bengal and Bombay,
and try to draw eye-teeth. You can buy ponies, turquoises,
Persian pussy-cats, saddle-bags, fat-tailed sheep and musk
in the Kumharsen Serai, and get many strange things for
nothing. In the afternoon I went down there to see
whether my friends intended to keep their word or were
lying about drunk.

A priest attired in fragments of ribbons and rags stalked up to me, gravely twisting a child's paper whirligig. Behind him was his servant, bending under the load of a crate of mud toys. The two were loading up two camels, and the inhabitants of the Serai watched them with shrieks of laughter.

'The priest is mad,' said a horse-dealer to me. 'He is going up to Kabul to sell toys to the Amir. He will either be raised to honour or have his head cut off. He came in here this morning and has been behaving madly ever since.'

'The witless are under the protection of God,' stammered a flat-cheeked Usbeg in broken Hindi. 'They foretell future events.'

'Would they could have foretold that my caravan would have been cut up by the Shinwaris almost within shadow of the Pass!' grunted the Eusufzai agent of a Rajputana trading-house whose goods had been feloniously diverted into the hands of other robbers just across the Border, and whose misfortunes were the laughing-stock of the bazar. 'Ohé, priest, whence come you and whither do you go?'

'From Roum have I come,' shouted the priest, waving his whirligig; 'from Roum, blown by the breath of a hundred devils across the sea! O thieves, robbers, liars, the blessing of Pir Khan on pigs, dogs, and perjurers! Who will take the Protected of God to the North to sell charms that are never still to the Amir? The camels shall not gall, the sons shall not fall sick, and the wives shall remain faithful while they are away, of the men who give me place in their caravan. Who will assist me to slipper the

King of the Roos with a golden slipper with a silver heel? The protection of Pir Kahn be upon his labors!' He spread out the skirts of his gaberdine and pirouetted between the lines of tethered horses.

'There starts a caravan from Peshawar to Kabul in twenty days, Huzrut,' said the Eusufzai trader. 'My camels go therewith. Do thou also go and bring us good luck.'

'I will go even now!' shouted the priest. 'I will depart upon my winged camels, and be at Peshawar in a day! Ho! Hazar Mir Khan,' he yelled to his servant 'drive out the camels, but let me first mount my own.'

He leaped on the back of his beast as it knelt, and turning round to me, cried: – 'Come thou also, Sahib, a little along the road, and I will sell thee a charm – an amulet that shall make thee King of Kafiristan.'

Then the light broke upon me, and I followed the two camels out of the Serai till we reached open road and the priest halted.

'What d'you think o' that?' said he in English. 'Carnehan can't talk their patter, so I've made him my servant. He makes a handsome servant. 'Tisn't for nothing that I've been knocking about the country for fourteen years. Didn't I do that talk neat? We'll hitch on to a caravan at Peshawar till we get to Jagdallak, and then we'll see if we can get donkeys for our camels, and strike into Kafiristan. Whirligigs for the Amir, O Lor! Put your hand under the camel-bags and tell me what you feel.'

I felt the butt of a Martini, and another and another.

'Twenty of 'em,' said Dravot, placidly.

'Twenty of 'em, and ammunition to correspond, under the whirligigs and the mud dolls.'

'Heaven help you if you are caught with those things!'
I said. 'A Martini is worth her weight in silver among
the Pathans.'

'Fifteen hundred rupees of capital – every rupee we
could beg, borrow, or steal – are invested on these two
camels,' said Dravot. 'We won't get caught. We're going
through the Khaiber with a regular caravan. Who'd touch
a poor mad priest?'

'Have you got everything you want?' I asked, overcome
with astonishment.

'Not yet, but we shall soon. Give us a momento of
your kindness, Brother. You did me a service yesterday,
and that time in Marwar. Half my Kingdom shall you
have, as the saying is.' I slipped a small charm compass
from my watch-chain and handed it up to the priest.

'Good-by,' said Dravot, giving me his hand cautiously.
'It's the last time we'll shake hands with an Englishman
these many days. Shake hands with him, Carnehan,' he
cried, as the second camel passed me.

Carnehan leaned down and shook hands. Then the
camels passed away along the dusty road, and I was left
alone to wonder. My eye could detect no failure in the
disguises. The scene in the Serai attested that they were
complete to the native mind. There was just the chance,
therefore, that Carnehan and Dravot would be able to
wander through Afghanistan without detection. But,
beyond, they would find death, certain and awful death.

Ten days later a native friend of mine, giving me the
news of the day from Peshawar, wound up his letter with:
– 'There has been much laughter here on account of a
certain mad priest who is going in his estimation to sell

petty gauds and insignificant trinkets which he ascribes as great charms to H. H. the Amir of Bokhara. He passed through Peshawar and associated himself to the Second Summer caravan that goes to Kabul. The merchants are pleased because through superstition they imagine that such mad fellows bring good-fortune.'

The two then, were beyond the Border. I would have prayed for them, but, that night, a real King died in Europe, and demanded an obituary notice.

★　★　★　★　★

The wheel of the world swings through the same phases again and again. Summer passed and winter thereafter, and came and passed again. The daily paper continued and I with it, and upon the third summer there fell a hot night, a night-issue, and a strained waiting for something to be telegraphed from the other side of the world, exactly as had happened before. A few great men had died in the past two years, the machines worked with more clatter, and some of the trees in the Office garden were a few feet taller. But that was all the difference.

I passed over to the press-room, and went through just such a scene as I have already described. The nervous tension was stronger than it had been two years before, and I felt the heat more acutely. At three o'clock I cried, 'Print off,' and turned to go, when there crept to my chair what was left of a man. He was bent into a circle, his head was sunk between his shoulders, and he moved his feet one over the other like a bear. I could hardly see whether he walked or crawled – this rag-wrapped, whining cripple who addressed me by name, crying that he was come back. 'Can you give me a drink?' he whimpered. 'For the Lord's sake, give me a drink!'

I went back to the office, the man following with groans of pain, and I turned up the lamp.

'Don't you know me?' he gasped, dropping into a chair, and he turned his drawn face, surmounted by a shock of gray hair, to the light.

I looked at him intently. Once before had I seen eyebrows that met over the nose in an inch-broad black band, but for the life of me I could not tell where.

'I don't know you,' I said, handing him the whiskey. 'What can I do for you?'

He took a gulp of the spirit raw, and shivered in spite of the suffocating heat. 'I've come back,' he repeated; 'and I was the King of Kafiristan – me and Dravot – crowned Kings we was! In this office we settled it – you setting there and giving us the books. I am Peachey – Peachey Taliaferro Carnehan, and you've been setting here ever since – O Lord!'

I was more than a little astonished, and expressed my feelings accordingly.

'It's true,' said Carnehan, with a dry cackle, nursing his feet which were wrapped in rags. 'True as gospel. Kings we were, with crowns upon our heads – me and Dravot – poor Dan – oh, poor, poor Dan, that would never take advice, not though I begged of him!'

'Take the whiskey,' I said, 'and take your own time. Tell me all you can recollect of everything from beginning to end. You got across the border on your camels, Dravot dressed as a mad priest and you his servant. Do you remember that?'

'I ain't mad – yet, but I will be that way soon. Of course I remember. Keep looking at me, or maybe my words will go all to pieces. Keep looking at me in my eyes and don't say anything.'

I leaned forward and looked into his face as steadily as I could. He dropped one hand upon the table and I grasped it by the wrist. It was twisted like a bird's claw, and upon the back was a ragged, red, diamond-shaped scar.

'No, don't look there. Look at me,' said Carnehan.

'That comes afterwards, but for the Lord's sake don't distrack me. We left with that caravan, me and Dravot, playing all sorts of antics to amuse the people we were with. Dravot used to make us laugh in the evenings when all the people was cooking their dinners – cooking their dinners, and ... what did they do then? They lit little fires with sparks that went into Dravot's beard, and we all laughed – fit to die. Little red fires they was, going into Dravot's big red beard – so funny.' His eyes left mine and he smiled foolishly.

'You went as far as Jagdallak with that caravan,' I said at a venture, 'after you had lit those fires. To Jagdallak, where you turned off to try to get into Kafiristan.'

'No, we didn't neither. What are you talking about? We turned off before Jagdallak, because we heard the roads was good. But they wasn't good enough for our two camels – mine and Dravot's. When we left the caravan, Dravot took off all his clothes and mine too, and said we would be heathen, because the Kafirs didn't allow Mohammedans to talk to them. So we dressed betwixt and between, and such a sight as Daniel Dravot I never saw yet nor expect to see again. He burned half his beard, and slung a sheep-skin over his shoulder, and shaved his head into patterns. He shaved mine, too, and made me wear outrageous things to look like a heathen. That was in a most mountaineous country, and our camels couldn't go along any more because of the mountains. They were tall and black, and coming home I saw them fight like wild goats – there are lots of goats in Kafiristan. And these mountains, they never keep still, no more than the goats. Always fighting they are, and don't let you sleep at night.'

'Take some more whiskey,' I said, very slowly. 'What did you and Daniel Dravot do when the camels could go no further because of the rough roads that led into Kafiristan?'

'What did which do? There was a party called Peachey Taliaferro Carnehan that was with Dravot. Shall I tell you about him? He died out there in the cold. Slap from the bridge fell old Peachey, turning and twisting in the air like a penny whirligig that you can sell to the Amir – No; they was two for three ha'pence, those whirligigs, or I am much mistaken and woful sore. And then these camels were no use, and Peachey said to Dravot – "For the Lord's sake, let's get out of this before our heads are chopped off," and with that they killed the camels all among the mountains, not having anything in particular to eat, but first they took off the boxes with the guns and the ammunition, till two men came along driving four mules. Dravot up and dances in front of them, singing, – "Sell me four mules." Says the first man, – "If you are rich enough to buy, you are rich enough to rob;" but before ever he could put his hand to his knife, Dravot breaks his neck over his knee, and the other party runs away. So Carnehan loaded the mules with the rifles that was taken off the camels, and together we starts forward into those bitter cold mountainous parts, and never a road broader than the back of your hand.'

He paused for a moment, while I asked him if he could remember the nature of the country through which he had journeyed.

'I am telling you as straight as I can, but my head isn't as good as it might be. They drove nails through it to make me hear better how Dravot died. The country was mountainous and the mules were most contrary, and the inhabitants was dispersed and solitary. They went up and up, and down and down, and that other party Carnehan, was imploring of Dravot not to sing and whistle so loud, for fear of bringing down the tremenjus avalanches. But Dravot says that if a King couldn't sing it wasn't worth being King, and whacked the mules over the rump, and never took no heed for ten cold days. We came to a big level valley all among the mountains, and the mules were near dead, so we killed them, not having anything in special for them or us to eat. We sat upon the boxes, and played odd and even with the cartridges that was jolted out.

'Then ten men with bows and arrows ran down that valley, chasing twenty men with bows and arrows, and the row was tremenjus. They was fair men – fairer than you or me – with yellow hair and remarkable well built.

Says Dravot, unpacking the guns – "This is the beginning of the business. We'll fight for the ten men," and with that he fires two rifles at the twenty men and drops one of them at two hundred yards from the rock where we was sitting. The other men began to run, but Carnehan and Dravot sits on the boxes picking them off at all ranges, up and down the valley. Then we goes up to the ten men that had run across the snow too, and they fires a footy little arrow at us. Dravot he shoots above their heads and they all falls down flat. Then he walks over them and kicks them, and then he lifts them up and shakes hands all around to make them friendly like. He calls them and gives them the boxes to carry, and waves his hand for all the world as though he was King already. They takes the boxes and him across the valley and up the hill into a pine wood on the top, where there was half a dozen big stone idols. Dravot he goes to the biggest – a fellow they call Imbra – and lays a rifle and a cartridge at his feet, rubbing his nose respectful with his own nose, patting him on the head, and saluting in front of it. He turns round to the men and nods his head, and says, – "That's all right. I'm in the know too, and these old jim-jams are my friends." Then he opens his mouth and points down it, and when the first man brings him food, he says – "No"; and when the second man brings him food, he says – "No"; but when one of the old priests and the boss of the village brings him food, he says – "Yes"; very haughty, and eats it slow. That was how we came to our first village, without any trouble, just as though we had tumbled from the skies. But we tumbled from one of those damned rope-bridges, you see, and you couldn't expect a man to laugh much after that.'

'Take some more whiskey and go on,' I said. 'That was the first village you came into. How did you get to be King?'

'I wasn't King,' said Carnehan. 'Dravot he was the King, and a handsome man he looked with the gold crown on his head and all. Him and the other party stayed in that village, and every morning Dravot sat by the side of old Imbra, and the people came and worshipped. That was Dravot's order. Then a lot of men came into the valley, and Carnehan and Dravot picks them off with the rifles before they knew where they was, and runs down into the valley and up again the other side, and finds another village, same as the first one, and the people all falls down flat on their faces, and Dravot says, – "Now what is the trouble between you two villages?" and the people points to a woman, as fair as you or me, that was carried off, and Dravot takes her back to the first village and counts up the dead – eight there was. For each dead man Dravot pours a little milk on the ground and waves his arms like a whirligig and, "That's all right," says he. Then he and Carnehan takes the big boss of each village by the arm and walks them down into the valley, and shows them how to scratch a line with a spear right down the valley, and gives each a sod of turf from both sides o' the line. Then all the people comes down and shouts like the devil and all, and Dravot says, – "Go and dig the land, and be fruitful and multiply," which they did, though they didn't under-stand. Then we asks the names of things in their lingo

– bread and water and fire and idols and such, and Dravot leads the priest of each village up to the idol, and says he must sit there and judge the people, and if anything goes wrong he is to be shot.

'Next week they was all turning up the land in the valley as quiet as bees and much prettier, and the priests heard all the complaints and told Dravot in dumb show what it was about. "That's just the beginning," says Dravot. "They think we're gods." He and Carnehan picks out twenty good men and shows them how to click off a rifle, and form fours, and advance in line, and they was very pleased to do so, and clever to see the hang of it. Then he takes out his pipe and his baccy-pouch and leaves one at one village, and one at the other, and off we two goes to see what was to be done in the next valley. That was all rock, and there was a little village there, and Carnehan says, – "Send 'em to the old valley to plant," and takes 'em there and gives 'em some land that wasn't took before. They were a poor lot, and we blooded 'em with a kid before letting 'em into the new Kingdom. That was to impress the people, and then they settled down quiet, and Carnehan went back to Dravot who had got into another valley, all snow and ice and most mountainous. There was no people there and the Army got afraid, so Dravot shoots one of them, and goes on till he finds some people in a village, and the Army explains that unless the people wants to be killed they had better not shoot their little matchlocks; for they had matchlocks. We makes friends with the priest and I stays there alone with two of the Army, teaching the men how to drill, and a thundering big Chief comes across the snow with kettledrums and horns twanging, because he heard there was a new god kicking about. Carnehan sights for the brown of the men half a mile across the snow and wings one of them. Then he sends a message to the Chief that, unless he wished to be killed, he must come and shake hands with me and leave his arms behind. The Chief comes alone first, and Carnehan shakes hands with him and whirls his arms about, same as Dravot used, and very much surprised that Chief was, and strokes my eyebrows. Then Carnehan goes alone to the Chief, and asks him in dumb show if he had an enemy he hated. "I have," says the Chief. So Carnehan weeds out the pick of his men, and sets the two of the Army to show them drill and at the end of two weeks the men can manoeuvre about as well as Volunteers. So he marches with the Chief to a great big plain on the top of a mountain, and the Chiefs men rushes into a village and takes it; we three Martinis firing into the brown of the enemy. So we took that village too, and I gives the Chief a rag from my coat and says, "Occupy till I come": which was scriptural. By way of a reminder, when me and the Army was eighteen hundred yards away, I drops a bullet near him standing on the snow, and all the people falls flat on their faces. Then I sends a letter to Dravot, wherever he be by land or by sea.'

At the risk of throwing the creature out of train I interrupted, – 'How could you write a letter up yonder?'

'The letter? – Oh! – The letter! Keep looking at me between the eyes, please. It was a string-talk letter, that we'd learned the way of it from a blind beggar in the Punjab.'

I remember that there had once come to the office a blind man with a knotted twig and a piece of string which he wound round the twig according to some cypher of his own. He could, after the lapse of days or hours, repeat the sentence which he had reeled up. He had reduced the alphabet to eleven primitive sounds; and tried to teach me his method, but failed.

'I sent that letter to Dravot,' said Carnehan; 'and told him to come back because this Kingdom was growing too big for me to handle, and then I struck for the first valley, to see how the priests were working. They called the village we took along with the Chief, Bashkai, and the first village we took, Er-Heb. The priest at Er-Heb was doing all right, but they had a lot of pending cases about land to show me, and some men from another village had been firing arrows at night. I went out and looked for that village and fired four rounds at it from a thousand yards. That used all the cartridges I cared to spend, and I waited for Dravot, who had been away two or three months, and I kept my people quiet.

'One morning I heard the devil's own noise of drums and horns, and Dan Dravot marches down the hill with his Army and a tail of hundreds of men, and, which was the most amazing – a great gold crown on his head. "My Gord, Carnehan," says Daniel, "this is a tremenjus business, and we've got the whole country as far as it's worth having. I am the son of Alexander by Queen Semiramis, and you're my younger brother and a god too! It's the biggest thing we've ever seen. I've been marching and fighting for six weeks with the Army, and every footy little village for fifty miles has come in rejoiceful; and more than that, I've got the key of the whole show, as you'll see, and I've got a crown for you! I told 'em to make two of 'em at a place called Shu, where the gold lies in the rock like suet in mutton. Gold I've seen, and turquoise I've kicked out of the cliffs, and there's garnets in the sands of the river, and here's a chunk of amber that a man brought me. Call up all the priests and, here, take your crown."

'One of the men opens a black hair bag and I slips the crown on. It was too small and too heavy, but I wore it for the glory. Hammered gold it was – five pound weight, like a hoop of a barrel.

'"Peachey," says Dravot, "we don't want to fight no more. The Craft's the trick so help me!" and he brings forward that same Chief that I left at Bashkai – Billy Fish we called him afterwards, because he was so like Billy Fish that drove the big tank-engine at Mach on the Bolan in the old days. "Shake hands with him," says Dravot, and I shook hands and nearly dropped, for Billy Fish gave me the Grip. I said nothing, but tried him with the Fellow Craft Grip. He answers, all right, and I tried the Master's Grip, but that was a slip. "A Fellow Craft he is!" I says to Dan. "Does he know the word?" "He does," says Dan, "and all the priests know. It's a miracle! The Chiefs and the priest can work a Fellow Craft Lodge in a way that's very like ours, and they've cut the marks on the rocks, but they don't know the Third Degree, and they've come to find out. It's Gord's Truth. I've known these long years that the Afghans knew up to the Fellow Craft Degree, but this is a miracle. A god and a Grand-Master of the Craft am I, and a Lodge in the Third Degree I will open, and we'll raise the head priests and the Chiefs of the villages."

"'It's against all the law," I says, "holding a Lodge without warrant from any one; and we never held office in any Lodge.'

"'It's a master-stroke of policy," says Dravot. "It means running the country as easy as a four-wheeled bogy on a down grade. We can't stop to enquire now, or they'll turn against us. I've forty Chiefs at my heel, and passed and raised according to their merit they shall be. Billet these men on the villages and see that we run up a Lodge of some kind. The temple of Imbra will do for the Lodge-room. The women must make aprons as you show them. I'll hold a levee of Chiefs tonight and Lodge tomorrow."

'I was fair rim off my legs, but I wasn't such a fool as not to see what a pull this Craft business gave us. I showed the priests' families how to make aprons of the degrees, but for Dravot's apron the blue border and marks was made of turquoise lumps on white hide, not cloth. We took a great square stone in the temple for the Master's chair, and little stones for the officers' chairs, and painted the black pavement with white squares, and did what we could to make things regular.

'At the levee which was held that night on the hillside with big bonfires, Dravot gives out that him and me were gods and sons of Alexander, and Past Grand-Masters in the Craft, and was come to make Kafiristan a country where every man should eat in peace and drink in quiet, and specially obey us. Then the Chiefs come round to shake hands, and they was so hairy and white and fair it was just shaking hands with old friends. We gave them names according as they was like men we had known in India – Billy Fish, Holly Dilworth, Pikky Kergan that was Bazar-master when I was at Mhow, and so on, and so on.

'The most amazing miracle was at Lodge next night. One of the old priests was watching us continuous, and I felt uneasy, for I knew we'd have to fudge the Ritual, and I didn't know what the men knew. The old priest was a stranger come in from beyond the village of Bashkai. The minute Dravot puts on the Master's apron that the girls had made for him, the priest fetches a whoop and a howl, and tries to overturn the stone that Dravot was sitting on. "It's all up now," I says. "That comes of meddling with the Craft without warrant!" Dravot never winked an eye, not when ten priests took and tilted over the Grand-Master's chair – which was to say the stone of Imbra. The priest begins rubbing the bottom end of it to clear away the black dirt, and presently he shows all the other priests the Master's Mark, same as was on Dravot's apron, cut into the stone. Not even the priests of the temple of Imbra knew it was there. The old chap falls flat on his face at Dravot's feet and kisses 'em. "Luck again," says Dravot, across the Lodge to me, "they say it's the missing Mark that no one could understand the why of. We're more than safe now." Then he bangs the butt of his gun for a gavel and says: – "By virtue of the authority invested in me by my own right hand and the help of Peachey, I declare myself Grand-Master of all Freemasonry in Kafiristan in this the Mother Lodge o' the country, and King of Kafiristan equally with Peachey!" At that he puts on his crown and I puts on mine – I was doing Senior Warden – and we opens the Lodge in most ample form. It was a amazing miracle! The priests moved in Lodge through the first two degrees almost without telling, as if the memory was coming back to them. After that, Peachey and Dravot raised such as was worthy – high priests and Chiefs of far-off villages. Billy Fish was the first, and I can tell you we scared the soul out of him. It was not in any way according to Ritual, but it served our turn. We didn't raise more than ten of the biggest men because we didn't want to make the Degree common. And they was clamoring to be raised.

'"In another six months," says Dravot, "we'll hold another Communication and see how you are working." Then he asks them about their villages, and learns that they was fighting one against the other and were fair sick and tired of it. And when they wasn't doing that they was fighting with the Mohammedans. "You can fight those when they come into our country," says Dravot. "Tell off every tenth man of your tribes for a Frontier guard, and send two hundred at a time to this valley to be drilled. Nobody is going to be shot or speared any more so long as he does well, and I know that you won't cheat me because you're white people – sons of Alexander – and not like common, black Mohammedans. You are my people and by God," says he, running off into English at the end – "I'll make a damned fine Nation of you, or I'll die in the making!"

'I can't tell all we did for the next six months because Dravot did a lot I couldn't see the hang of, and he learned their lingo in a way I never could. My work was to help the people plough, and now and again to go out with some of the Army and see what the other villages were doing, and make 'em throw rope-bridges across the ravines which cut up the country horrid. Dravot was very kind to me, but when he walked up and down in the pine wood pulling that bloody red beard of his with both fists I knew he was thinking plans I could not advise him about, and I just waited for orders.

'But Dravot never showed me disrespect before the people. They were afraid of me and the Army, but they loved Dan. He was the best of friends with the priests and the Chiefs; but any one could come across the hills with a complaint and Dravot would hear him out fair, and call four priests together and say what was to be done. He used to call in Billy Fish from Bashkai, and Pikky Kergan from Shu, and an old Chief we called Kafuzelum – it was like enough to his real name – and hold councils with 'em when there was any fighting to be done in small villages. That was his Council of War, and the four priests of Bashkai, Shu, Khawak, and Madora was his Privy Council. Between the lot of 'em they sent me, with forty men and twenty rifles, and sixty men carrying turquoises, into the Ghorband country to buy those hand-made Martini rifles, that come out of the Amir's workshops at Kabul, from one of the Amir's Herati regiments that would have sold the very teeth out of their mouths for turquoises.

'I stayed in Ghorband a month, and gave the Governor the pick of my baskets for hush-money, and bribed the colonel of the regiment some more, and, between the two and the tribes-people, we got more than a hundred hand-made Martinis, a hundred good Kohat Jezails that'll throw to six hundred yards, and forty manloads of very bad ammunition for the rifles. I came back with what I had, and distributed 'em among the men that the Chiefs sent in to me to drill. Dravot was too busy to attend to those things, but the old Army that we first made helped me, and we turned out five hundred men that could drill, and two hundred that knew how to hold arms pretty straight. Even those cork-screwed, hand-made guns was a miracle to them. Dravot talked big about powder-shops and factories, walking up and down in the pine wood when the winter was coming on.

"'I won't make a Nation,' says he. "I'll make an Empire! These men aren't niggers; they're English! Look at their eyes – look at their mouths. Look at the way they stand up. They sit on chairs in their own houses. They're the Lost Tribes, or something like it, and they've grown to be English. I'll take a census in the spring if the priests don't get frightened. There must be a fair two million of 'em in these hills. The villages are full o' little children. Two million people – two hundred and fifty thousand fighting men – and all English! They only want the rifles and a little drilling. Two hundred and fifty thousand men, ready to cut in on Russia's right flank when she tries for India! Peachey, man," he says, chewing his beard in great hunks, "we shall be Emperors – Emperors of the Earth! Rajah Brooke will be a suckling to us. I'll treat with the Viceroy on equal terms. I'll ask him to send me twelve picked English – twelve that I know of – to help us govern a bit. There's Mackray, Sergeant-pensioner at Segowli – many's the good dinner he's given me, and his wife a pair of trousers. There's Donkin, the Warder of Tounghoo Jail; there's hundreds that I could lay my hand on if I was in India. The Viceroy shall do it for me. I'll send a man through in the spring for those men, and I'll write for a dispensation from the Grand Lodge for what I've done as Grand-Master. That – and all the Sniders that'll be thrown out when the native troops in India take up the Martini. They'll be worn smooth, but they'll do for fighting in these hills. Twelve English, a hundred thousand Sniders run through the Amir's country in driblets – I'd be content with twenty thousand in one year – and we'd be an Empire. When everything was ship-shape, I'd hand over the crown – this crown I'm wearing now – to Queen Victoria on my knees, and she'd say: – 'Rise up, Sir Daniel Dravot.' Oh, its big! It's big, I tell you! But there's so much to be done in every place – Bashkai, Khawak, Shu, and everywhere else."

"'What is it?" I says. "There are no more men coming in to be drilled this autumn. Look at those fat, black clouds. They're bringing the snow."

"'It isn't that," says Daniel, putting his hand very hard on my shoulder; "and I don't wish to say anything that's against you, for no other living man would have followed me and made me what I am as you have done. You're a first-class Commander-in-Chief, and the people know you; but – it's a big country, and somehow you can't help me, Peachey, in the way I want to be helped."

"'Go to your blasted priests, then!' I said, and I was sorry when I made that remark, but it did hurt me sore to find Daniel talking so superior when I'd drilled all the men, and done all he told me.

"'Don't let's quarrel, Peachey," says Daniel without cursing. "You're a King too, and the half of this Kingdom is yours; but can't you see, Peachey, we want cleverer men than us now – three or four of 'em that we can scatter about for our Deputies? It's a hugeous great State, and I can't always tell the right thing to do, and I haven't time for all I want to do, and here's the winter coming on and all." He put half his beard into his mouth, and it was as red as the gold of his crown.

"'I'm sorry, Daniel,' says I. "I've done all could. I've drilled the men and shown the people how to stack their oats better, and I've brought in those tinware rifles from Ghorband – but I know what you're driving at. I take it Kings always feel oppressed that way."

"'There's another thing too,' says Dravot, walking up and down. "The winter's coming and these people won't be giving much trouble, and if they do we can't move about. I want a wife."

"'For Gord's sake leave the women alone!' I says. "We've both got all the work we can, though I am a fool. Remember the Contrack, and keep clear o' women."

"'The Contrack only lasted till such time as we was Kings; and Kings we have been these months past,' says Dravot, weighing his crown in his hand. "You go get a wife too, Peachey – a nice, strappin', plump girl that'll keep you warm in the winter. They're prettier than English girls, and we can take the pick of 'em. Boil 'em once or twice in hot water, and they'll come as fair as chicken and ham."

"'Don't tempt me!' I says. "I will not have any deal-ings with a woman not till we are a dam' side more settled than we are now. I've been doing the work o' two men, and you've been doing the work o' three. Let's lie off a bit, and see if we can get some better tobacco from Afghan country and run in some good liquor; but no women."

"'Who's talking o' women?" says Dravot. "I said wife – a Queen to breed a King's son for the King. A Queen out of the strongest tribe, that'll make them your blood-brothers, and that'll lie by your side and tell you all the people thinks about you and their own affairs. That's what I want."

"'Do you remember that Bengali woman I kept at Mogul Serai when I was plate-layer?" says I. "A fat lot o' good she was to me. She taught me the lingo and one or two other things; but what happened? She ran away with the Station Master's servant and half my month's pay. Then she turned up at Dadur Junction in tow of a half-caste, and had the impidence to say I was her husband – all among the drivers of the running-shed!"

"'We've done with that," says Dravot. "These women are whiter than you or me, and a Queen I will have for the winter months."

"'For the last time o' asking, Dan, do not," I says. "It'll only bring us harm. The Bible says that Kings ain't to waste their strength on women, 'specially when they've got a new raw Kingdom to work over."

"'For the last time of answering, I will," said Dravot, and he went away through the pine-trees looking like a big red devil. The low sun hit his crown and beard on one side, and the two blazed like hot coals.

'But getting a wife was not as easy as Dan thought. He put it before the Council, and there was no answer till Billy Fish said that he'd better ask the girls. Dravot damned them all round. "What's wrong with me?" he shouts, standing by the idol Imbra. "Am I a dog or am I not enough of a man for your wenches? Haven't I put the shadow of my hand over this country? Who stopped the last Afghan raid?" It was me really, but Dravot was too angry to remember. "Who bought your guns? Who repaired the bridges? Who's the Grand-Master of the sign cut in the stone?" and he thumped his hand on the block that he used to sit on in Lodge, and at Council, which opened like Lodge always. Billy Fish said nothing and no more did the others. "Keep your hair on, Dan," said I; "and ask the girls. That's how it's done at home, and these people are quite English."

"'The marriage of a King is a matter of State," says Dan, in a white-hot rage, for he could feel, I hope, that he was going against his better mind. He walked out of the Council-room, and the others sat still, looking at the ground.

"'Billy Fish," says I to the Chief of Bashkai, "what's the difficulty here? A straight answer to a true friend." "You know," says Billy Fish. "How should a man tell you who know everything? How can daughters of men marry gods or devils? It's not proper."

'I remembered something like that in the Bible; but if, after seeing us as long as they had, they still believed we were gods it wasn't for me to undeceive them.

"'A god can do anything," says I. "If the King is fond of a girl he'll not let her die." "She'll have to," said Billy Fish. "There are all sorts of gods and devils in these mountains, and now and again a girl marries one of them and isn't seen any more. Besides, you two know the Mark cut in the stone. Only the gods know that. We thought you were men till you showed the sign of the Master."

"'I wished then that we had explained about the loss of the genuine secrets of a Master-Mason at the first go-off; but I said nothing. All that night there was a blowing of horns in a little dark temple half-way down the hill, and I heard a girl crying fit to die. One of the priests told us that she was being prepared to marry the King.

"'I'll have no nonsense of that kind," says Dan. "I don't want to interfere with your customs, but I'll take my own wife. "The girl's a little bit afraid," says the priest. "She thinks she's going to die, and they are a-heartening of her up down in the temple."

"'Hearten her very tender, then," says Dravot, "or I'll hearten you with the butt of a gun so that you'll never want to be heartened again." He licked his lips, did Dan, and stayed up walking about more than half the night, thinking of the wife that he was going to get in the morning. I wasn't any means comfortable, for I knew that dealings with a woman in foreign parts, though you was a crowned King twenty times over, could not but be risky. I got up very early in the morning while Dravot was asleep, and I saw the priests talking together in whispers, and the Chiefs talking together too, and they looked at me out of the corners of their eyes.

"'What is up, Fish?" I says to the Bashkai man, who was wrapped up in his furs and looking splendid to behold.

"'I can't rightly say," says he; "but if you can induce

the King to drop all this nonsense about marriage, you'll be doing him and me and yourself a great service."

"'That I do believe," says I. "But sure, you know, Billy, as well as me, having fought against and for us, that the King and me are nothing more than two of the finest men that God Almighty ever made. Nothing more, I do assure you."

"'That may be," says Billy Fish, "and yet I should be sorry if it was." He sinks his head upon his great fur cloak for a minute and thinks. "King," says he, "be you man or god or devil, I'll stick by you today. I have twenty of my men with me, and they will follow me. We'll go to Bashkai until the storm blows over."

'A little snow had fallen in the night, and everything was white except the greasy fat clouds that blew down and down from the north. Dravot came out with his crown on his head, swinging his arms and stamping his feet, and looking more pleased than Punch.

"'For the last time, drop it, Dan," says I in a whisper. "Billy Fish here says that there will be a row."

"'A row among my people!" says Dravot. "Not much. Peachy, you're a fool not to get a wife too. Where's the girl?" says he with a voice as loud as the braying of a jackass. "Call up all the Chiefs and priests, and let the Emperor see if his wife suits him."

'There was no need to call any one. They were all there leaning on their guns and spears round the clearing in the centre of the pine wood. A deputation of priests went down to the little temple to bring up the girl, and the horns blew up fit to wake the dead. Billy Fish saunters round and gets as close to Daniel as he could, and behind him stood his twenty men with matchlocks. Not a man of them under six feet. I was next to Dravot, and behind me was twenty men of the regular Army. Up comes the girl, and a strapping wench she was, covered with silver and turquoises but white as death, and looking back every minute at the priests.

'"She'll do," said Dan, looking her over. "What's to be afraid of, lass? Come and kiss me." He puts his arm round her. She shuts her eyes, gives a bit of a squeak, and down goes her face in the side of Dan's flaming red beard.

'"The slut's bitten me!" says he, clapping his hand to his neck, and, sure enough, his hand was red with blood. Billy Fish and two of his matchlock-men catches hold of Dan by the shoulders and drags him into the Bashkai lot, while the priests howls in their lingo, – "Neither god nor devil but a man!" I was all taken aback, for a priest cut at me in front, and the Army behind began firing into the Bashkai men.

'"God A-mighty!" says Dan. "What is the meaning o' this?"

'"Come back! Come away!" says Billy Fish. "Ruin and Mutiny is the matter. We'll break for Bashkai if we can."

'I tried to give some sort of orders to my men – the men o' the regular Army – but it was no use, so I fired into the brown of 'em with an English Martini and drilled three beggars in a line. The valley was full of shouting, howling creatures, and every soul was shrieking, "Not a god nor a devil but only a man!" The Bashkai troops stuck to Billy Fish all they were worth, but their matchlocks wasn't half as good as the Kabul breech-loaders, and four of them dropped. Dan was bellowing like a bull, for he was very wrathy; and Billy Fish had a hard job to prevent him running out at the crowd. '"We can't stand," says Billy Fish. "Make a run for it down the valley! The whole place is against us." The matchlock-men ran, and we went down the valley in spite of Dravot's protestations. He was swearing horribly and crying out that he was a King. The priests rolled great stones on us, and the regular Army fired hard, and there wasn't more than six men, not counting Dan, Billy Fish, and Me, that came down to the bottom of the valley alive.

'Then they stopped firing and the horns in the temple blew again. "Come away – for Gord's sake come away!" says Billy Fish. "They'll send runners out to all the villages before ever we get to Bashkai. I can protect you there, but I can't do anything now."

'My own notion is that Dan began to go mad in his head from that hour. He stared up and down like a stuck pig. Then he was all for walking back alone and killing the priests with his bare hands; which he could have done. "An Emperor am I," says Daniel, "and next year I shall be a Knight of the Queen."

'"All right, Dan," says I; "but come along now while there's time."

'"It's your fault," says he, "for not looking after your Army better. There was mutiny in the midst, and you didn't know – you damned engine-driving, plate-laying, missionary's-pass-hunting hound!" He sat upon a rock and called me every foul name he could lay tongue to. I was too heart-sick to care, though it was all his foolishness that brought the smash.

"'I'm sorry, Dan," says I, "but there's no accounting for natives. This business is our Fifty-Seven. Maybe we'll make something out of it yet, when we've got to Bashkai."

"'Let's get to Bashkai, then," says Dan, "and, by God, when I come back here again I'll sweep the valley so there isn't a bug in a blanket left!"

'We walked all that day, and all that night Dan was stumping up and down on the snow, chewing his beard and muttering to himself.

"'There's no hope o' getting clear," said Billy Fish. "The priests will have sent runners to the villages to say that you are only men. Why didn't you stick on as gods till things was more settled? I'm a dead man," says Billy Fish, and he throws himself down on the snow and begins to pray to his gods.

'Next morning we was in a cruel bad country – all up and down, no level ground at all, and no food either. The six Bashkai men looked at Billy Fish hungry-wise as if they wanted to ask something, but they said never a word. At noon we came to the top of a flat mountain all covered with snow, and when we climbed up into it, behold, there was an army in position waiting in the middle!

"'The runners have been very quick," says Billy Fish, with a little bit of a laugh. "They are waiting for us."

'Three or four men began to fire from the enemy's side, and a chance shot took Daniel in the calf of the leg. That brought him to his senses. He looks across the snow at the Army, and sees the rifles that we had brought into the country.

"'We're done for," says he. "They are Englishmen, these people, – and it's my blasted nonsense that has brought you to this. Get back, Billy Fish, and take your men away; you've done what you could, and now cut for it. Carnehan," says he, "shake hands with me and go along with Billy. Maybe they won't kill you. I'll go and meet 'em alone. It's me that did it. Me, the King!"

"'Go!' says I. "Go to Hell, Dan. I'm with you here. Billy Fish, you clear out, and we two will meet those folk."

"'I'm a Chief," says Billy Fish, quite quiet. "I stay with you. My men can go."

'The Bashkai fellows didn't wait for a second word but ran off, and Dan and Me and Billy Fish walked across to where the drums were drumming and the horns were horning. It was cold-awful cold. I've got that cold in the back of my head now. There's a lump of it there.'

The punkah-coolies had gone to sleep. Two kerosene lamps were blazing in the office, and the perspiration poured down my face and splashed on the blotter as I leaned forward. Carnehan was shivering, and I feared that his mind might go. I wiped my face, took a fresh grip of the piteously mangled hands, and said: – 'What happened after that?'

The momentary shift of my eyes had broken the clear current.

'What was you pleased to say?' whined Carnehan. 'They took them without any sound. Not a little whisper all along the snow, not though the King knocked down the first man that set hand on him – not though old Peachey fired his last cartridge into the brown of 'em. Not a single solitary sound did those swines make. They just closed up, tight, and I tell you their furs stunk. There was a man called Billy Fish, a good friend of us all, and they cut his throat, Sir, then and there, like a pig; and the King kicks up the bloody snow and says: – "We've had a dashed fine run for our money. What's coming next?" But Peachey, Peachey Taliaferro, I tell you, Sir, in confidence as betwixt two friends, he lost his head, Sir. No, he didn't neither. The King lost his head, so he did, all along o' one of those cunning rope-bridges. Kindly let me have the paper-cutter, Sir. It tilted this way. They marched him a mile across that snow to a rope-bridge over a ravine with a river at the bottom. You may have seen such. They prodded him behind like an ox. "Damn your eyes!" says the King. "D'you suppose I can't die like a gentleman?" He turns to Peachey – Peachey that was crying like a child. "I've brought you to this, Peachey," says he. "Brought you out of your happy life to be killed in Kafiristan, where you was late Commander-in-Chief of the Emperor's forces. Say you forgive me, Peachey." "I do," says Peachey. "Fully and freely do I forgive you, Dan." "Shake hands, Peachey," says he. "I'm going now." Out he goes, looking neither right nor left, and when he was plumb in the middle of those dizzy dancing ropes, "Cut, you beggars," he shouts; and they cut, and old Dan fell, turning round and round and round, twenty thousand miles, for he took half an hour to fall till he struck the water, and I could see his body caught on a rock with the gold crown close beside.

'But do you know what they did to Peachey between two pine-trees? They crucified him, sir, as Peachey's hands will show. They used wooden pegs for his hands and his feet; and he didn't die. He hung there and screamed, and they took him down next day, and said it was a miracle that he wasn't dead. They took him down – poor old Peachey that hadn't done them any harm – that hadn't done them any…'

He rocked to and fro and wept bitterly, wiping his eyes with the back of his scarred hands and moaning like a child for some ten minutes.

'They was cruel enough to feed him up in the temple, because they said he was more of a god than old Daniel that was a man. Then they turned him out on the snow, and told him to go home, and Peachey came home in about a year, begging along the roads quite safe; for Daniel Dravot he walked before and said: – "Come along, Peachey. It's a big thing we're doing." The mountains they danced at night, and the mountains they tried to fall on Peachey's head, but Dan he held up his hand, and Peachey came along bent double. He never let go of Dan's hand, and he never let go of Dan's head. They gave it to him as a present in the temple, to remind him not to come again, and though the crown was pure gold, and Peachey was starving, never would Peachey sell the same. You knew Dravot, sir! You knew Right Worshipful Brother Dravot! Look at him now!'

He fumbled in the mass of rags round his bent waist; brought out a black horsehair bag embroidered with silver thread; and shook therefrom on to my table – the dried, withered head of Daniel Dravot! The morning sun that had long been paling the lamps struck the red beard and blind sunken eyes; struck, too, a heavy circlet of gold studded with raw turquoises, that Carnehan placed tenderly on the battered temples.

'You behold now,' said Carnehan, 'the Emperor in his habit as he lived – the King of Kafiristan with his crown upon his head. Poor old Daniel that was a monarch once!'

I shuddered, for, in spite of defacements manifold, I recognized the head of the man of Marwar Junction. Carnehan rose to go. I attempted to stop him. He was not fit to walk abroad. 'Let me take away the whiskey, and give me a little money,' he gasped. 'I was a King once. I'll go to the Deputy Commissioner and ask to set in the Poor-house till I get my health. No, thank you, I can't wait till you get a carriage for me. I've urgent private affairs – in the south – at Marwar.'

He shambled out of the office and departed in the direction of the Deputy Commissioner's house. That day at noon I had occasion to go down the blinding hot Mall, and I saw a crooked man crawling along the white dust of the roadside, his hat in his hand, quavering dolorously after the fashion of street-singers at Home. There was not a soul in sight, and he was out of all possible earshot of the houses. And he sang through his nose, turning his head from right to left: –

'The Son of Man goes forth to war,
    A golden crown to gain;
His blood-red banner streams afar –
    Who follows in his train?'

I waited to hear no more, but put the poor wretch into my carriage and drove him off to the nearest missionary for eventual transfer to the Asylum. He repeated the hymn twice while he was with me whom he did not in the least recognize, and I left him singing to the missionary.

Two days later I inquired after his welfare of the Superintendent of the Asylum.

'He was admitted suffering from sun-stroke. He died early yesterday morning,' said the Superintendent. 'Is it true that he was half an hour bareheaded in the sun at midday?'

'Yes,' said I, 'but do you happen to know if he had anything upon him by any chance when he died?'

'Not to my knowledge,' said the Superintendent.

And there the matter rests.

THE PHANTOM 'RICKSHAW

May no ill dreams disturb my rest,
Nor Powers of Darkness me molest.
                              – Evening Hymn.

O NE OF THE FEW ADVANTAGES THAT INDIA has over England is a great Knowability. After five years' service a man is directly or indirectly acquainted with the two or three hundred Civilians in his Province, all the Messes of ten or twelve Regiments and Batteries, and some fifteen hundred other people of the non-official caste. In ten years his knowledge should be doubled, and at the end of twenty he knows, or knows something about, every Englishman in the Empire, and may travel anywhere and everywhere without paying hotel-bills.

Globe-trotters who expect entertainment as a right, have, even within my memory, blunted this open-heartedness, but none the less today, if you belong to the Inner Circle and are neither a Bear nor a Black Sheep, all houses are open to you, and our small world is very, very kind and helpful.

Rickett of Kamartha stayed with Polder of Kumaon some fifteen years ago. He meant to stay two nights, but was knocked down by rheumatic fever, and for six weeks disorganised Polder's establishment, stopped Polder's work, and nearly died in Polder's bedroom. Polder behaves as though he had been placed under eternal obligation by Rickett, and yearly sends the little Ricketts a box of presents and toys. It is the same everywhere. The men who do not take the trouble to conceal from you their opinion that you are an incompetent ass, and the women who blacken your character and misunderstand your wife's amusements, will work themselves to the bone in your behalf if you fall sick or into serious trouble.

Heatherlegh, the Doctor, kept, in addition to his regular practice, a hospital on his private account – an arrangement of loose boxes for Incurables, his friend called it – but it was really a sort of fitting-up shed for craft that had been damaged by stress of weather. The weather in India is often sultry, and since the tale of bricks is always a fixed quantity, and the only liberty allowed is permission to work overtime and get no thanks, men occasionally break down and become as mixed as the metaphors in this sentence.

Heatherlegh is the dearest doctor that ever was, and his invariable prescription to all his patients is, 'lie low, go slow, and keep cool.' He says that more men are killed by overwork than the importance of this world justifies. He maintains that overwork slew Pansay, who died under his hands about three years ago. He has, of course, the right to speak authoritatively, and he laughs at my theory that there was a crack in Pansay's head and a little bit of the Dark World came through and pressed him to death. 'Pansay went off the handle,' says Heatherlegh, 'after the stimulus of long leave at Home. He may or he may not have behaved like a blackguard to Mrs. Keith-Wessington. My notion is that the work of the Katabundi Settlement ran him off his legs, and that he took to brooding and making much of an ordinary P. & O. flirtation. He certainly was engaged to Miss Mannering, and she certainly broke off the engagement. Then he took a feverish chill and all that nonsense about ghosts developed. Overwork started his illness, kept it alight, and killed him poor devil. Write him off to the System – one man to take the work of two and a half men.'

I do not believe this. I used to sit up with Pansay sometimes when Heatherlegh was called out to patients, and I happened to be within claim. The man would make me most unhappy by describing in a low, even voice, the procession that was always passing at the bottom of his bed. He had a sick man's command of language. When he recovered I suggested that he should write out the whole affair from beginning to end, knowing that ink might assist him to ease his mind. When little boys have learned a new bad word they are never happy till they have chalked it up on a door. And this also is Literature.

He was in a high fever while he was writing, and the blood-and-thunder Magazine diction he adopted did not calm him. Two months afterward he was reported fit for duty, but, in spite of the fact that he was urgently needed to help an undermanned Commission stagger through a deficit, he preferred to die; vowing at the last that he was hag-ridden. I got his manuscript before he died, and this is his version of the affair, dated 1885:

My doctor tells me that I need rest and change of air. It is not improbable that I shall get both ere long – rest that neither the red-coated messenger nor the midday gun can break, and change of air far beyond that which any homeward-bound steamer can give me. In the mean-time I am resolved to stay where I am; and, in flat defiance of my doctor's orders, to take all the world into my confidence. You shall learn for yourselves the precise nature of my malady; and shall, too, judge for yourselves whether any man born of woman on this weary earth was ever so tormented as I.

Speaking now as a condemned criminal might speak ere the drop-bolts are drawn, my story, wild and hideously improbable as it may appear, demands at least attention. That it will ever receive credence I utterly disbelieve. Two months ago I should have scouted as mad or drunk the man who had dared tell me the like. Two months ago I was the happiest man in India. Today, from Peshawur to the sea, there is no one more wretched. My doctor and I are the only two who know this. His explanation is, that my brain, digestion, and eyesight are all slightly affected; giving rise to my frequent and persistent 'delusions.' Delusions, indeed! I call him a fool; but he attends me still with the same unwearied smile, the same bland professional manner, the same neatly trimmed red whiskers, till I begin to suspect that I am an ungrateful, evil-tempered invalid. But you shall judge for yourselves.

Three years ago it was my fortune – my great misfortune – to sail from Gravesend to Bombay, on return from long leave, with one Agnes Keith-Wessington, wife of an officer on the Bombay side. It does not in the least concern you to know what manner of woman she was. Be content with the knowledge that, ere the voyage had ended, both she and I were desperately and unreasoningly in love with one another. Heaven knows that I can make the admission now without one particle of vanity. In matters of this sort there is always one who gives and another who accepts. From the first day of our ill-omened attachment, I was conscious that Agnes's passion was a stronger, a more dominant, and – if I may use the expression – a purer sentiment than mine. Whether she recognised the fact then, I do not know. Afterward it was bitterly plain to both of us.

Arrived at Bombay in the spring of the year, we went our respective ways, to meet no more for the next three or four months, when my leave and her love took us both to Simla. There we spent the season together; and there my fire of straw burned itself out to a pitiful end with the closing year. I attempt no excuse. I make no apology. Mrs. Wessington had given up much for my sake, and was prepared to give up all. From my own lips, in August, 1882, she learned that I was sick of her presence, tired of her company, and weary of the sound of her voice. Ninety-nine women out of a hundred would have wearied of me as I wearied of them; seventy-five of that number would have promptly avenged themselves by active and obtrusive flirtation with other men. Mrs. Wessington was the hundredth. On her neither my openly expressed aversion nor the cutting brutalities with which I garnished our interviews had the least effect.

'Jack, darling!' was her one eternal cuckoo cry: 'I'm sure it's all a mistake – a hideous mistake; and we'll be good friends again some day. Please forgive me, Jack, dear.'

I was the offender, and I knew it. That knowledge transformed my pity into passive endurance, and, eventually, into blind hate – the same instinct, I suppose, which prompts a man to savagely stamp on the spider he has but half killed. And with this hate in my bosom the season of 1882 came to an end.

Next year we met again at Simla – she with her monotonous face and timid attempts at reconciliation, and I with loathing of her in every fibre of my frame. Several times I could not avoid meeting her alone; and on each occasion her words were identically the same. Still the unreasoning wail that it was all a 'mistake'; and still the hope of eventually 'making friends.' I might have seen had I cared to look, that that hope only was keeping her alive. She grew more wan and thin month by month. You will agree with me, at least, that such conduct would have driven any one to despair. It was uncalled for; childish; unwomanly. I maintain that she was much to blame. And again, sometimes, in the black, fever-stricken night-watches, I have begun to think that I might have been a little kinder to her. But that really is a 'delusion.' I could not have continued pretending to love her when I didn't; could I? It would have been unfair to us both.

Last year we met again – on the same terms as before. The same weary appeal, and the same curt answers from my lips. At least I would make her see how wholly wrong and hopeless were her attempts at resuming the old relationship. As the season wore on, we fell apart – that is to say, she found it difficult to meet me, for I had other and more absorbing interests to attend to. When I think it over quietly in my sick-room, the season of 1884 seems a confused nightmare wherein light and shade were fantastically intermingled – my courtship of little Kitty Mannering; my hopes, doubts, and fears; our long rides together; my trembling avowal of attachment; her reply; and now and again a vision of a white face flitting by in the 'rickshaw with the black and white liveries I once watched for so earnestly; the wave of Mrs. Wessington's gloved hand; and, when she met me alone, which was but seldom, the irksome monotony of her appeal. I loved Kitty Mannering; honestly, heartily loved her, and with my love for her grew my hatred for Agnes. In August Kitty and I were engaged. The next day I met those accursed 'magpie' jhampanies at the back of Jakko, and, moved by some passing sentiment of pity, stopped to tell Mrs. Wessington everything. She knew it already.

'So I hear you're engaged, Jack dear.' Then, without a moment's pause: 'I'm sure it's all a mistake – a hideous mistake. We shall be as good friends some day, Jack, as we ever were.'

My answer might have made even a man wince. It cut

the dying woman before me like the blow of a whip. 'Please forgive me, Jack; I didn't mean to make you angry; but it's true, it's true!'

And Mrs. Wessington broke down completely. I turned away and left her to finish her journey in peace, feeling, but only for a moment or two, that I had been an unutterably mean hound. I looked back, and saw that she had turned her 'rickshaw with the idea, I suppose, of overtaking me.

The scene and its surroundings were photographed on my memory. The rain-swept sky (we were at the end of the wet weather), the sodden, dingy pines, the muddy road, and the black powder-riven cliffs formed a gloomy background against which the black and white liveries of the jhampanies, the yellow-paneled 'rickshaw and Mrs. Wessington's down-bowed golden head stood out clearly. She was holding her handkerchief in her left hand and was leaning hack exhausted against the 'rickshaw cushions. I turned my horse up a bypath near the Sanjowlie Reservoir and literally ran away. Once I fancied I heard a faint call of 'Jack!' This may have been imagination. I never stopped to verify it. Ten minutes later I came across Kitty on horseback; and, in the delight of a long ride with her, forgot all about the interview.

A week later Mrs. Wessington died, and the inexpressible burden of her existence was removed from my life. I went Plainsward perfectly happy. Before three months were over I had forgotten all about her, except that at times the discovery of some of her old letters reminded me unpleasantly of our bygone relationship. By January I had disinterred what was left of our correspondence from among my scattered belongings and had burned it. At the beginning of April of this year, 1885, I was at Simla – semi-deserted Simla – once more, and was deep in lover's talks and walks with Kitty. It was decided that we should be married at the end of June. You will understand, therefore, that, loving Kitty as I did, I am not saying too much when I pronounce myself to have been, at that time, the happiest man in India.

Fourteen delightful days passed almost before I noticed their flight. Then, aroused to the sense of what was proper among mortals circumstanced as we were, I pointed out to Kitty that an engagement ring was the outward and visible sign of her dignity as an engaged girl; and that she must forthwith come to Hamilton's to be measured for one. Up to that moment, I give you my word, we had completely forgotten so trivial a matter. To Hamilton's we accordingly went on the 15th of April, 1885. Remember that – whatever my doctor may say to the contrary – I was then in perfect health, enjoying a well-balanced mind and an absolute tranquil spirit. Kitty and I entered Hamilton's shop together, and there, regardless of the order of affairs, I measured Kitty for the ring in the presence of the amused assistant. The ring was a sapphire with two diamonds. We then rode out down the slope that leads to the Combermere Bridge and Peliti's shop.

While my Waler was cautiously feeling his way over the loose shale, and Kitty was laughing and chattering at my side – while all Simla, that is to say as much of it as had then come from the Plains, was grouped round the Reading-room and Peliti's veranda, – I was aware that some one, apparently at a vast distance, was calling me by my Christian name. It struck me that I had heard the voice before, but when and where I could not at once determine. In the short space it took to cover the road between the path from Hamilton's shop and the first plank of the Combermere Bridge I had thought over half a dozen people who might have committed such a solecism, and had eventually decided that it must have been singing in my ears. Immediately opposite Peliti's shop my eye was arrested by the sight of four jhampanies in 'magpie' livery, pulling a yellow-paneled, cheap, bazar 'rickshaw. In a moment my mind flew back to the previous season and Mrs. Wessington with a sense of irritation and disgust. Was it not enough that the woman was dead and done with, without her black and white servitors re-appearing to spoil the day's happiness? Whoever employed them now I thought I would call upon, and ask as a personal favor to change her jhampanies' livery. I would hire the men myself, and, if necessary, buy their coats from off their backs. It is impossible to say here what a flood of undesirable memories their presence evoked.

'Kitty,' I cried, 'there are poor Mrs. Wessington's jham-panies turned up again! I wonder who has them now?'

Kitty had known Mrs. Wessington slightly last season, and had always been interested in the sickly woman.

'What? Where?' she asked. 'I can't see them anywhere.'

Even as she spoke her horse, swerving from a laden mule, threw himself directly in front of the advancing 'rickshaw. I had scarcely time to utter a word of warning when, to my unutterable horror, horse and rider passed through men and carriage as if they had been thin air.

'What's the matter?' cried Kitty; 'what made you call

out so foolishly, Jack? If I am engaged I don't want all creation to know about it. There was lots of space between the mule and the veranda; and, if you think I can't ride – There!'

Whereupon wilful Kitty set off, her dainty little head in the air, at a hand-gallop in the direction of the Bandstand; fully expecting, as she herself afterward told me, that I should follow her. What was the matter? Nothing indeed. Either that I was mad or drunk, or that Simla was haunted with devils. I reined in my impatient cob, and turned round. The 'rickshaw had turned too, and now stood immediately facing me, near the left railing of the Combermere Bridge.

'Jack! Jack, darling!' (There was no mistake about the words this time: they rang through my brain as if they had been shouted in my ear.) 'It's some hideous mistake, I'm sure. Please forgive me, Jack, and let's be friends again.'

The 'rickshaw-hood had fallen back, and inside, as I hope and pray daily for the death I dread by night, sat Mrs. Keith-Wessington, handkerchief in hand, and golden head bowed on her breast.

How long I stared motionless I do not know. Finally, I was aroused by my syce taking the Waler's bridle and asking whether I was ill. From the horrible to the commonplace is but a step. I tumbled off my horse and dashed, half fainting, into Peliti's for a glass of cherry-brandy. There two or three couples were gathered round the coffee-tables discussing the gossip of the day. Their trivialities were more comforting to me just then than the consolations of religion could have been. I plunged into the midst of the conversation at once; chatted, laughed, and jested with a face (when I caught a glimpse of it in a mirror) as white and drawn as that of a corpse. Three or four men noticed my condition; and, evidently setting it down to the results of over-many pegs, charitably endeavoured to draw me apart from the rest of the loungers. But I refused to be led away. I wanted the company of my kind – as a child rushes into the midst of the dinner-party after a fright in the dark. I must have talked for about ten minutes or so, though it seemed an eternity to me, when I heard Kitty's clear voice outside inquiring for me. In another minute she had entered the shop, prepared to roundly upbraid me for failing so signally in my duties. Something in my face stopped her.

'Why, Jack,' she cried, 'what have you been doing? What has happened? Are you ill?' Thus driven into a direct lie, I said that the sun had been a little too much for me. It was close upon five o'clock of a cloudy April afternoon, and the sun had been hidden all day. I saw my mistake as soon as the words were out of my mouth: attempted to recover it; blundered hopelessly and followed Kitty in a regal rage, out of doors, amid the smiles of my acquaintances. I made some excuse (I have forgotten what) on the score of my feeling faint; and cantered away to my hotel, leaving Kitty to finish the ride by herself.

In my room I sat down and tried calmly to reason out the matter. Here was I, Theobald Jack Pansay, a well-educated Bengal Civilian in the year of grace, 1885, presumably sane, certainly healthy, driven in terror from my sweetheart's side by the apparition of a woman who had been dead and buried eight months ago. These were facts that I could not blink. Nothing was further from my thought than any memory of Mrs. Wessington when Kitty and I left Hamilton's shop. Nothing was more utterly commonplace than the stretch of wall opposite Peliti's. It was broad daylight. The road was full of people; and yet here, look you, in defiance of every law of probability, in direct outrage of Nature's ordinance, there had appeared to me a face from the grave.

Kitty's Arab had gone through the 'rickshaw: so that my first hope that some woman marvelously like Mrs. Wessington had hired the carriage and the coolies with their old livery was lost. Again and again I went round this treadmill of thought; and again and again gave up baffled and in despair. The voice was as inexplicable as the apparition. I had originally some wild notion of confiding it all to Kitty; of begging her to marry me at once; and in her arms defying the ghostly occupant of the 'rickshaw. 'After all,' I argued, 'the presence of the 'rickshaw is in itself enough to prove the existence of a spectral illusion. One may see ghosts of men and women, but surely never of coolies and carriages. The whole thing is absurd. Fancy the ghost of a hillman!'

Next morning I sent a penitent note to Kitty, imploring her to overlook my strange conduct of the previous afternoon. My Divinity was still very wroth, and a personal apology was necessary. I explained, with a fluency born of night-long pondering over a falsehood, that I had been attacked with sudden palpitation of the heart – the result of indigestion. This eminently practical solution had its effect; and Kitty and I rode out that afternoon with the shadow of my first lie dividing us.

Nothing would please her save a canter round Jakko.

With my nerves still unstrung from the previous night I feebly protested against the notion, suggesting Observatory Hill, Jutogh, the Boileaugunge road – anything rather than the Jakko round. Kitty was angry and a little hurt: so I yielded from fear of provoking further misunderstanding, and we set out together toward Chota Simla. We walked a greater part of the way, and, according to our custom, cantered from a mile or so below the Convent to the stretch of level road by the Sanjowlie Reservoir. The wretched horses appeared to fly, and my heart beat quicker and quicker as we neared the crest of the ascent. My mind had been full of Mrs. Wessington all the afternoon; and every inch of the Jakko road bore witness to our oldtime walks and talks. The bowlders were full of it; the pines sang it aloud overhead; the rain-fed torrents giggled and chuckled unseen over the shameful story; and the wind in my ears chanted the iniquity aloud.

As a fitting climax, in the middle of the level men call the Ladies' Mile the Horror was awaiting me. No other 'rickshaw was in sight – only the four black and white jhampanies, the yellow-paneled carriage, and the golden head of the woman within – all apparently just as I had left them eight months and one fortnight ago! For an instant I fancied that Kitty must see what I saw – we were so marvelously sympathetic in all things. Her next words undeceived me – 'Not a soul in sight! Come along, Jack, and I'll race you to the Reservoir buildings!' Her wiry little Arab was off like a bird, my Waler following close behind, and in this order we dashed under the cliffs. Half a minute brought us within fifty yards of the 'rickshaw. I pulled my Waler and fell back a little. The 'rickshaw was directly in the middle of the road; and once more the Arab passed through it, my horse following. 'Jack! Jack dear! Please forgive me,' rang with a wail in my ears, and, after an interval: – 'It's a mistake, a hideous mistake!'

I spurred my horse like a man possessed. When I turned my head at the Reservoir works, the black and white liveries were still waiting – patiently waiting – under the grey hillside, and the wind brought me a mocking echo of the words I had just heard. Kitty bantered me a good deal on my silence throughout the remainder of the ride. I had been talking up till then wildly and at random. To save my life I could not speak afterward naturally, and from Sanjowlie to the Church wisely held my tongue.

I was to dine with the Mannerings that night, and had barely time to canter home to dress. On the road to Elysium Hill I overheard two men talking together in the dusk. – 'It's a curious thing,' said one, 'how completely all trace of it disappeared. You know my wife was insanely fond of the woman ('never could see anything in her myself), and wanted me to pick up her old 'rickshaw and coolies if they were to be got for love or money. Morbid sort of fancy I call it; but I've got to do what the Memsahib tells me. Would you believe that the man she hired it from tells me that all four of the men – they were brothers – died of cholera on the way to Hardwar, poor devils, and the 'rickshaw has been broken up by the man himself. 'Told me he never used a dead Memsahib's 'rickshaw. 'Spoiled his luck. Queer notion, wasn't it? Fancy poor little Mrs. Wessington spoiling any one's luck except her own!' I laughed aloud at this point; and my laugh jarred on me as I uttered it. So there were ghosts of 'rickshaws after all, and ghostly employments in the other world! How much did Mrs. Wessington give her men? What were their hours? Where did they go?

And for visible answer to my last question I saw the infernal Thing blocking my path in the twilight. The dead travel fast, and by short cuts unknown to ordinary coolies. I laughed aloud a second time and checked my laughter suddenly, for I was afraid I was going mad. Mad to a certain extent I must have been, for I recollect that I reined in my horse at the head of the 'rickshaw, and politely wished Mrs. Wessington 'Good-evening.' Her answer was one I knew only too well. I listened to the end; and replied that I had heard it all before, but should be delighted if she had anything further to say. Some malignant devil stronger than I must have entered into me that evening, for I have a dim recollection of talking the commonplaces of the day for five minutes to the Thing in front of me.

'Mad as a hatter, poor devil – or drunk. Max, try and get him to come home.'

Surely that was not Mrs. Wessington's voice! The two men had overheard me speaking to the empty air, and had returned to look after me. They were very kind and considerate, and from their words evidently gathered that I was extremely drunk. I thanked them confusedly and cantered away to my hotel, there changed, and arrived at the Mannerings' ten minutes late. I pleaded the darkness of the night as an excuse; was rebuked by Kitty for my unlover-like tardiness; and sat down.

The conversation had already become general; and under cover of it, I was addressing some tender small talk to my sweetheart when I was aware that at the further end of the table a short red-whiskered man was describing, with much broidery, his encounter with a mad unknown that evening.

A few sentences convinced me that he was repeating the incident of half an hour ago. In the middle of the story he looked round for applause, as professional story-tellers do, caught my eye, and straightway collapsed. There was a moment's awkward silence, and the red-whiskered man muttered something to the effect that he had 'forgotten the rest,' thereby sacrificing a reputation as a good story-teller which he had built up for six seasons past. I blessed him from the bottom of my heart, and – went on with my fish.

In the fulness of time that dinner came to an end; and with genuine regret I tore myself away from Kitty – as certain as I was of my own existence that It would be waiting for me outside the door. The red-whiskered man, who had been introduced to me as Doctor Heatherlegh, of Simla, volunteered to bear me company as far as our roads lay together. I accepted his offer with gratitude.

My instinct had not deceived me. It lay in readiness in the Mall, and, in what seemed devilish mockery of our ways, with a lighted head-lamp. The red-whiskered man went to the point at once, in a manner that showed he had been thinking over it all dinner time.

'I say, Pansay, what the deuce was the matter with you this evening on the Elysium road?' The suddenness of the question wrenched an answer from me before I was aware.

'That!' said I, pointing to It.

'That may be either D. T. or Eyes for aught I know.

Now you don't liquor. I saw as much at dinner, so it can't be D. T. There's nothing whatever where you're pointing, though you're sweating and trembling with fright like a scared pony. Therefore, I conclude that it's Eyes. And I ought to understand all about them. Come along home with me. I'm on the Blessington lower road.'

To my intense delight the 'rickshaw instead of waiting for us kept about twenty yards ahead – and this, too whether we walked, trotted, or cantered. In the course of that long night ride I had told my companion almost as much as I have told you here.

'Well, you've spoiled one of the best tales I've ever laid tongue to,' said he, 'but I'll forgive you for the sake of what you've gone through. Now come home and do what I tell you; and when I've cured you, young man, let this be a lesson to you to steer clear of women and indigestible food till the day of your death.'

The 'rickshaw kept steady in front; and my red-whiskered friend seemed to derive great pleasure from my account of its exact whereabouts.

'Eyes, Pansay – all Eyes, Brain, and Stomach. And the greatest of these three is Stomach. You've too much conceited Brain, too little Stomach, and thoroughly unhealthy Eyes. Get your Stomach straight and the rest follows. And all that's French for a liver pill. I'll take sole medical charge of you from this hour! for you're too interesting a phenomenon to be passed over.'

By this time we were deep in the shadow of the Blessington lower road and the 'rickshaw came to a dead stop under a pine-clad, over-hanging shale cliff. Instinctively

I halted too, giving my reason. Heatherlegh rapped out an oath.

'Now, if you think I'm going to spend a cold night on the hillside for the sake of a stomach-cum-Brain-cum-Eye illusion.... Lord, ha' mercy! What's that?'

There was a muffled report, a blinding smother of dust just in front of us, a crack, the noise of rent boughs, and about ten yards of the cliff-side − pines, undergrowth, and all − slid down into the road below, completely blocking it up. The uprooted trees swayed and tottered for a moment like drunken giants in the gloom, and then fell prone among their fellows with a thunderous crash. Our two horses stood motionless and sweating with fear. As soon as the rattle of falling earth and stone had subsided, my companion muttered: − 'Man, if we'd gone forward we should have been ten feet deep in our graves by now. 'There are more things in heaven and earth.'... Come home, Pansay, and thank God. I want a peg badly.'

We retraced our way over the Church Ridge, and I arrived at Dr. Heatherlegh's house shortly after midnight.

His attempts toward my cure commenced almost immediately, and for a week I never left his sight. Many a time in the course of that week did I bless the good-fortune which had thrown me in contact with Simla's best and kindest doctor. Day by day my spirits grew lighter and more equable. Day by day, too, I became more and more inclined to fall in with Heatherlegh's 'spectral illusion' theory, implicating eyes, brain, and stomach. I wrote to Kitty, telling her that a slight sprain caused by a fall from my horse kept me indoors for a few days; and that I should be recovered before she had time to regret my absence.

Heatherlegh's treatment was simple to a degree. It consisted of liver pills, cold-water baths, and strong exercise, taken in the dusk or at early dawn – for, as he sagely observed: 'A man with a sprained ankle doesn't walk a dozen miles a day, and your young woman might be wondering if she saw you.'

At the end of the week, after much examination of pupil and pulse, and strict injunctions as to diet and pedestrianism, Heatherlegh dismissed me as brusquely as he had taken charge of me. Here is his parting benediction: 'Man, I can certify to your mental cure, and that's as much as to say I've cured most of your bodily ailments. Now, get your traps out of this as soon as you can; and be off to make love to Miss Kitty.'

I was endeavoring to express my thanks for his kindness. He cut me short.

'Don't think I did this because I like you. I gather that you've behaved like a blackguard all through. But, all the same, you're a phenomenon, and as queer a phenomenon as you are a blackguard. No!' – checking me a second time – 'not a rupee, please. Go out and see if you can find the eyes-brain-and-stomach business again. I'll give you a lakh for each time you see it.'

Half an hour later I was in the Mannerings' drawing-room with Kitty – drunk with the intoxication of present happiness and the fore-knowledge that I should never more be troubled with Its hideous presence. Strong in the sense of my new-found security, I proposed a ride at once; and, by preference, a canter round Jakko.

Never had I felt so well, so overladen with vitality and mere animal spirits, as I did on the afternoon of the 30th of April. Kitty was delighted at the change in my appearance, and complimented me on it in her delightfully frank and outspoken manner. We left the Mannerings' house together, laughing and talking, and cantered along the Chota Simla road as of old.

I was in haste to reach the Sanjowlie Reservoir and there make my assurance doubly sure. The horses did their best, but seemed all too slow to my impatient mind. Kitty was astonished at my boisterousness. 'Why, Jack!' she cried at last, 'you are behaving like a child. What are you doing?'

We were just below the Convent, and from sheer wantonness I was making my Waler plunge and curvet across the road as I tickled it with the loop of my riding-whip.

'Doing?' I answered; 'nothing, dear. That's just it. If you'd been doing nothing for a week except lie up, you'd be as riotous as I.'

'Singing and murmuring in your feastful mirth,
    Joying to feel yourself alive;
Lord over Nature, Lord of the visible Earth,
    Lord of the senses five.'

My quotation was hardly out of my lips before we had rounded the corner above the Convent; and a few yards further on could see across to Sanjowlie. In the centre of the level road stood the black and white liveries, the yellow-paneled 'rickshaw, and Mrs. Keith-Wessington. I pulled up, looked, rubbed my eyes, and, I believe must have said something. The next thing I knew was that I was lying face downward on the road with Kitty kneeling above me in tears.

'Has it gone, child!' I gasped. Kitty only wept more bitterly.

'Has what gone, Jack dear? what does it all mean? There must be a mistake somewhere, Jack. A hideous mistake.' Her last words brought me to my feet – mad – raving for the time being.

'Yes, there is a mistake somewhere,' I repeated, 'a hideous mistake. Come and look at It.'

I have an indistinct idea that I dragged Kitty by the wrist along the road up to where It stood, and implored her for pity's sake to speak to It; to tell It that we were betrothed; that neither Death nor Hell could break the tie between us; and Kitty only knows how much more to the same effect. Now and again I appealed passionately to the Terror in the 'rickshaw to bear witness to all I had said, and to release me from a torture that was killing me. As I talked I suppose I must have told Kitty of my old relations with Mrs. Wessington, for I saw her listen intently with white face and blazing eyes.

'Thank you, Mr. Pansay,' she said, 'that's quite enough. Syce ghora láo.'

The syces, impassive as Orientals always are, had come up with the recaptured horses; and as Kitty sprang into her saddle I caught hold of the bridle, entreating her to hear me out and forgive. My answer was the cut of her riding-whip across my face from mouth to eye, and a word or two of farewell that even now I cannot write down. So I judged, and judged rightly, that Kitty knew all; and I staggered back to the side of the 'rickshaw. My face was cut and bleeding, and the blow of the riding-whip had raised a livid blue wheal on it. I had no self-respect. Just then, Heatherlegh, who must have been following Kitty and me at a distance, cantered up.

'Doctor,' I said, pointing to my face, 'here's Miss Mannering's signature to my order of dismissal and... I'll thank you for that lakh as soon as convenient.'

Heatherlegh's face, even in my abject misery, moved me to laughter.

'I'll stake my professional reputation' – he began.

'Don't be a fool,' I whispered. 'I've lost my life's happiness and you'd better take me home.'

As I spoke the 'rickshaw was gone. Then I lost all knowledge of what was passing. The crest of Jakko seemed to heave and roll like the crest of a cloud and fall in upon me.

Seven days later (on the 7th of May, that is to say) I was aware that I was lying in Heatherlegh's room as weak as a little child. Heatherlegh was watching me intently from behind the papers on his writing-table. His first words were not encouraging; but I was too far spent to be much moved by them.

'Here, Miss Kitty has sent back your letters. You corresponded a good deal, you young people. Here's a packet that looks like a ring, and a cheerful sort of a note from Mannering Papa, which I've taken the liberty of reading and burning. The old gentleman's not pleased with you.'

'And Kitty?' I asked, dully.

'Rather more drawn than her father from what she says. By the same token you must have been letting out any number of queer reminiscences just before I met you.

'Says that a man who would have behaved to a woman as you did to Mrs. Wessington ought to kill himself out of sheer pity for his kind. She's a hot-headed little virago, your mash. 'Will have it too that you were suffering from D. T. when that row on the Jakko road turned up. 'Says she'll die before she ever speaks to you again.'

I groaned and turned over to the other side.

'Now you've got your choice, my friend. This engagement has to be broken off; and the Mannerings don't want to be too hard on you. Was it broken through D. T. or epileptic fits? Sorry I can't offer you a better exchange unless you'd prefer hereditary insanity. Say the word and I'll tell 'em it's fits. All Simla knows about that scene on the Ladies' Mile. Come! I'll give you five minutes to think over it.'

During those five minutes I believe that I explored thoroughly the lowest circles of the Inferno which it is permitted man to tread on earth. And at the same time I myself was watching myself faltering through the dark labyrinths of doubt, misery, and utter despair. I wondered, as Heatherlegh in his chair might have wondered, which dreadful alternative I should adopt. Presently I heard myself answering in a voice that I hardly recognised, –

'They're confoundedly particular about morality in these parts. Give 'em fits, Heatherlegh, and my love. Now let me sleep a bit longer.'

Then my two selves joined, and it was only I (half crazed, devil-driven I) that tossed in my bed, tracing step by step the history of the past month.

'But I am in Simla,' I kept repeating to myself. 'I, Jack Pansay, am in Simla and there are no ghosts here. It's unreasonable of that woman to pretend there are. Why couldn't Agnes have left me alone? I never did her any harm. It might just as well have been me as Agnes. Only I'd never have come back on purpose to kill her. Why can't I be left alone – left alone and happy?'

It was high noon when I first awoke: and the sun was low in the sky before I slept – slept as the tortured criminal sleeps on his rack, too worn to feel further pain.

Next day I could not leave my bed. Heatherlegh told me in the morning that he had received an answer from Mr. Mannering, and that, thanks to his (Heatherlegh's) friendly offices, the story of my affliction had traveled through the length and breadth of Simla, where I was on all sides much pitied.

'And that's rather more than you deserve,' he concluded, pleasantly, 'though the Lord knows you've been going through a pretty severe mill. Never mind; we'll cure you yet, you perverse phenomenon.'

I declined firmly to be cured. 'You've been much too good to me already, old man,' said I; 'but I don't think I need trouble you further.'

In my heart I knew that nothing Heatherlegh could do would lighten the burden that had been laid upon me.

With that knowledge came also a sense of hopeless, impotent rebellion against the unreasonableness of it all. There were scores of men no better than I whose punishments had at least been reserved for another world; and I felt that it was bitterly, cruelly unfair that I alone should have been singled out for so hideous a fate. This mood would in time give place to another where it seemed that the 'rickshaw and I were the only realities in a world of shadows; that Kitty was a ghost; that Mannering, Heatherlegh, and all the other men and women I knew were all ghosts; and the great, grey hills themselves but vain shadows devised to torture me. From mood to mood I tossed backward and forward for seven weary days; my body growing daily stronger and stronger, until the bedroom looking-glass told me that I had returned to everyday life, and was as other men once more. Curiously enough my face showed no signs of the struggle I had gone through. It was pale indeed, but as expression-less and commonplace as ever. I had expected some permanent alteration – visible evidence of the disease that was eating me away. I found nothing.

On the 15th of May, I left Heatherlegh's house at eleven o'clock in the morning; and the instinct of the bachelor drove me to the Club. There I found that every man knew my story as told by Heatherlegh, and was, in clumsy fashion, abnormally kind and attentive. Nevertheless I recognized that for the rest of my natural life I should be among but not of my fellows; and I envied very bitterly indeed the laughing coolies on the Mall below. I lunched at the Club, and at four o'clock wandered aimlessly down the Mall in the vague hope of meeting Kitty. Close to the Band-stand the black and white liveries joined me; and I heard Mrs. Wessington's old appeal at my side. I had been expecting this ever since I came out; and was only surprised at her delay. The phantom 'rickshaw and I went side by side along the Chota Simla road in silence. Close to the bazar, Kitty and a man on horseback over-took and passed us. For any sign she gave I might have been a dog in the road. She did not even pay me the compliment of quickening her pace; though the rainy afternoon had served for an excuse.

So Kitty and her companion, and I and my ghostly Light-o'-Love, crept round Jakko in couples. The road was streaming with water; the pines dripped like roof-pipes on the rocks below, and the air was full of fine, driving rain. Two or three times I found myself saying to myself almost aloud: 'I'm Jack Pansay on leave at Simla – at Simla! Everyday, ordinary Simla. I mustn't forget that – I mustn't forget that.' Then I would try to recollect some of the gossip I had heard at the Club: the prices of So-and-So's horses – anything, in fact, that related to the workaday Anglo-Indian world I knew so well. I even repeated the multiplication-table rapidly to myself, to make quite sure that I was not taking leave of my senses. It gave me much comfort; and must have prevented my hearing Mrs. Wessington for a time.

Once more I wearily climbed the Convent slope and entered the level road. Here Kitty and the man started off at a canter, and I was left alone with Mrs. Wessington. 'Agnes,' said I, 'will you put back your hood and tell me what it all means?' The hood dropped noiselessly, and I was face to face with my dead and buried mistress. She was wearing the dress in which I had last seen her alive; carried the same tiny handkerchief in her right hand; and the same cardcase in her left. (A woman eight months dead with a cardcase!) I had to pin myself down to the multiplication-table, and to set both hands on the stone parapet of the road, to assure myself that that at least was real.

'Agnes,' I repeated, 'for pity's sake tell me what it all

means.' Mrs. Wessington leaned forward, with that odd, quick turn of the head I used to know so well, and spoke.

If my story had not already so madly overleaped the bounds of all human belief I should apologize to you now. As I know that no one – no, not even Kitty, for whom it is written as some sort of justification of my conduct – will believe me, I will go on. Mrs. Wessington spoke and I walked with her from the Sanjowlie road to the turning below the Commander-in-Chief's house as I might walk by the side of any living woman's 'rickshaw, deep in conversation. The second and most tormenting of my moods of sickness had suddenly laid hold upon me, and like the Prince in Tennyson's poem, 'I seemed to move amid a world of ghosts.' There had been a garden-party at the Commander-in-Chief's, and we two joined the crowd of homeward-bound folk. As I saw them then it seemed that they were the shadows – impalpable, fantastic shadows – that divided for Mrs. Wessington's 'rickshaw to pass through. What we said during the course of that weird interview I cannot – indeed, I dare not – tell. Heatherlegh's comment would have been a short laugh and a remark that I had been 'mashing a brain-eye-and-stomach chimera.' It was a ghastly and yet in some indefinable way a marvelously dear experience. Could it be possible, I wondered, that I was in this life to woo a second time the woman I had killed by my own neglect and cruelty?

I met Kitty on the homeward road – a shadow among shadows.

If I were to describe all the incidents of the next fort-night in their order, my story would never come to an end; and your patience would be exhausted. Morning after morning and evening after evening the ghostly 'rickshaw and I used to wander through Simla together. Wherever I went there the four black and white liveries followed me and bore me company to and from my hotel. At the Theatre I found them amid the crowd or yelling jhampanies; outside the Club veranda, after a long evening of whist; at the Birthday Ball, waiting patiently for my reappearance; and in broad daylight when I went calling. Save that it cast no shadow, the 'rickshaw was in every respect as real to look upon as one of wood and iron. More than once, indeed, I have had to check myself from warning some hard-riding friend against cantering over it. More than once I have walked down the Mall deep in conversation with Mrs. Wessington to the unspeakable amazement of the passers-by.

Before I had been out and about a week I learned that the 'fit' theory had been discarded in favour of insanity. However, I made no change in my mode of life. I called, rode, and dined out as freely as ever. I had a passion for the society of my kind which I had never felt before; I hungered to be among the realities of life; and at the same time I felt vaguely unhappy when I had been separated too long from my ghostly companion. It would be almost impossible to describe my varying moods from the 15th of May up to today.

The presence of the 'rickshaw filled me by turns with horror, blind fear, a dim sort of pleasure, and utter despair. I dared not leave Simla; and I knew that my stay there was killing me. I knew, moreover, that it was my destiny to die slowly and a little every day. My only anxiety was to get the penance over as quietly as might be. Alternately I hungered for a sight of Kitty and watched her outrageous flirtations with my successor – to speak more accurately, my successors – with amused interest. She was as much out of my life as I was out of hers. By day I wandered with Mrs. Wessington almost content. By night I implored Heaven to let me return to the world as I used to know it. Above all these varying moods lay the sensation of dull, numbing wonder that the Seen and the Unseen should mingle so strangely on this earth to hound one poor soul to its grave.

August 27. – Heatherlegh has been indefatigable in his attendance on me; and only yesterday told me that I ought to send in an application for sick leave. An application to escape the company of a phantom! A request that the Government would graciously permit me to get rid of five ghosts and an airy 'rickshaw by going to England. Heatherlegh's proposition moved me to almost hysterical laughter. I told him that I should await the end quietly at Simla; and I am sure that the end is not far off. Believe me that I dread its advent more than any word can say; and I torture myself nightly with a thousand speculations as to the manner of my death.

Shall I die in my bed decently and as an English gentleman should die; or, in one last walk on the Mall, will my soul be wrenched from me to take its place forever and ever by the side of that ghastly phantasm? Shall I return to my old lost allegiance in the next world, or shall I meet Agnes loathing her and bound to her side through all eternity? Shall we two hover over the scene of our lives till the end of Time? As the day of my death draws nearer, the intense horror that all living flesh feels toward escaped spirits from beyond the grave grows more and more powerful. It is an awful thing to go down quick among the dead with scarcely one-half of your life completed. It is a thousand times more awful to wait as I do in your midst, for I know not what unimaginable terror. Pity me, at least on the score of my 'delusion,' for I know you will never believe what I have written here. Yet as surely as ever a man was done to death by the Powers of Darkness I am that man.

In justice, too, pity her. For as surely as ever woman was killed by man, I killed Mrs. Wessington. And the last portion of my punishment is ever now upon me.

THE
MALTESE
CAT

THEY HAD GOOD REASON TO BE PROUD, and better reason to be afraid, all twelve of them; for though they had fought their way, game by game, up the teams entered for the polo tournament, they were meeting the Archangels that afternoon in the final match; and the Archangels men were playing with half a dozen ponies apiece. As the game was divided into six quarters of eight minutes each, that meant a fresh pony after every halt. The Skidars' team, even supposing there were no accidents, could only supply one pony for every other change; and two to one is heavy odds. Again, as Shiraz, the grey Syrian, pointed out, they were meeting the pink and pick of the polo-ponies of Upper India, ponies that had cost from a thousand rupees each, while they themselves were a cheap lot gathered, often from country-carts, by their masters, who belonged to a poor but honest native infantry regiment.

'Money means pace and weight,' said Shiraz, rubbing his black-silk nose dolefully along his neat-fitting boot, 'and by the maxims of the game as I know it – '

'Ah, but we aren't playing the maxims,' said The Maltese Cat. 'We're playing the game; and we've the great advantage of knowing the game. Just think a stride, Shiraz! We've pulled up from bottom to second place in two weeks against all those fellows on the ground here. That's because we play with our heads as well as our feet.'

'It makes me feel undersized and unhappy all the same,' said Kittiwynk, a mouse-coloured mare with a red browband and the cleanest pair of legs that ever an aged pony owned. 'They've twice our style, these others.'

Kittiwynk looked at the gathering and sighed. The hard, dusty polo-ground was lined with thousands of soldiers, black and white, not counting hundreds and hundreds of carriages and drags and dog-carts, and ladies with brilliant-coloured parasols, and officers in uniform and out of it, and crowds of natives behind them; and orderlies on camels, who had halted to watch the game, instead of carrying letters up and down the station; and native horse-dealers running about on thin-eared Biluchi mares, looking for a chance to sell a few first-class polo-ponies. Then there were the ponies of thirty teams that had entered for the Upper India Free-for-All Cup – nearly every pony of worth and dignity, from Mhow to Peshawar, from Allahabad to Multan; prize ponies, Arabs, Syrian, Barb, country-bred, Deccanee, Waziri, and Kabul ponies of every colour and shape and temper that you could imagine. Some of them were in mat-roofed stables, close to the polo-ground, but most were under saddle, while their masters, who had been defeated in the earlier games, trotted in and out and told the world exactly how the game should be played.

It was a glorious sight, and the come and go of the little, quick hooves, and the incessant salutations of ponies that had met before on other polo-grounds or race-courses were enough to drive a four-footed thing wild.

But the Skidars' team were careful not to know their neighbours, though half the ponies on the ground were anxious to scrape acquaintance with the little fellows that had come from the North, and, so far, had swept the board.

'Let's see,' said a soft gold-coloured Arab, who had been playing very badly the day before, to The Maltese Cat; 'didn't we meet in Abdul Rahman's stable in Bombay, four seasons ago? I won the Paikpattan Cup next season, you may remember?'

'Not me,' said The Maltese Cat, politely. 'I was at Malta then, pulling a vegetable-cart. I don't race. I play the game.'

'Oh!' said the Arab, cocking his tail and swaggering off.

'Keep yourselves to yourselves,' said The Maltese Cat to his companions. 'We don't want to rub noses with all those goose-rumped half-breeds of Upper India. When we've won this Cup they'll give their shoes to know *us*.'

'We sha'n't win the Cup,' said Shiraz. 'How do you feel?'

'Stale as last night's feed when a muskrat has run over it,' said Polaris, a rather heavy-shouldered grey; and the rest of the team agreed with him.

'The sooner you forget that the better,' said The Maltese Cat, cheerfully. 'They've finished tiffin in the big tent. We shall be wanted now. If your saddles are not comfy, kick. If your bits aren't easy, rear, and let the *saises* know whether your boots are tight.'

Each pony had his *sais*, his groom, who lived and ate and slept with the animal, and had betted a good deal more than he could afford on the result of the game. There was no chance of anything going wrong, but to make sure, each *sais* was shampooing the legs of his pony to the last minute. Behind the *saises* sat as many of the Skidars' regiment as had leave to attend the match – about half the native officers, and a hundred or two dark, black-bearded men with the regimental pipers nervously fingering the big, beribboned bagpipes. The Skidars were what they call a Pioneer regiment, and the bagpipes made the national music of half their men. The native officers held bundles of polo-sticks, long cane-handled mallets, and as the grand stand filled after lunch they arranged themselves by ones and twos at different points round the ground, so that if a stick were broken the player would not have far to ride for a new one. An impatient British Cavalry Band struck up 'If you want to know the time, ask a p'leeceman!' and the two umpires in light dust-coats danced out on two little excited ponies. The four players of the Archangels' team followed, and the sight of their beautiful mounts made Shiraz groan again.

'Wait till we know,' said The Maltese Cat. 'Two of 'em

are playing in blinkers, and that means they can't see to get out of the way of their own side, or they *may* shy at the umpires' ponies. They've *all* got white web-reins that are sure to stretch or slip!'

'And,' said Kittiwynk, dancing to take the stiffness out of her, 'they carry their whips in their hands instead of on their wrists. Hah!'

'True enough, No man can manage his stick and his reins and his whip that way,' said The Maltese Cat. 'I've fallen over every square yard of the Malta ground, and I ought to know.'

He quivered his little, flea-bitten withers just to show how satisfied he felt; but his heart was not so light. Ever since he had drifted into India on a troop-ship, taken, with an old rifle, as part payment for a racing debt, The Maltese Cat had played and preached polo to the Skidars' team on the Skidans' stony polo-ground. Now a polo-pony is like a poet. If he is born with a love for the game, he can be made. The Maltese Cat knew that bamboos grew solely in order that polo-balls might be turned from their roots, that grain was given to ponies to keep them in hard condition, and that ponies were shod to prevent them slipping on a turn. But, besides all these things, he knew every trick and device of the finest game in the world, and for two seasons had been teaching the others all he knew or guessed.

'Remember,' he said for the hundredth time, as the riders came up, 'you *must* play together, and you *must* play with your heads. Whatever happens, follow the ball. Who goes out first?'

Kittiwynk, Shiraz, Polaris, and a short high little bay fellow with tremendous hocks and no withers worth speaking of (he was called Corks) were being girthed up, and the soldiers in the background stared with all their eyes.

'I want you men to keep quiet,' said Lutyens, the captain of the team, 'and especially not to blow your pipes.'

'Not if we win, Captain Sahib?' asked the piper.

'If we win you can do what you please,' said Lutyens, with a smile, as he slipped the loop of his stick over his wrist, and wheeled to canter to his place. The Archangels' ponies were a little bit above themselves on account of the many-coloured crowd so close to the ground. Their riders were excellent players, but they were a team of crack players instead of a crack team; and that made all the difference in the world. They honestly meant to play together, but it is very hard for four men, each the best of the team he is picked from, to remember that in polo no brilliancy in hitting or riding makes up for playing alone. Their captain shouted his orders to them by name, and it is a curious thing that if you call his name aloud in public after an Englishman you make him hot and fretty. Lutyens said nothing to his men, because it had all been said before. He pulled up Shiraz, for he was playing 'back,' to guard the goal. Powell on Polaris was half-back, and Macnamara and Hughes on Corks and Kittiwynk were forwards. The tough, bamboo ball was set in the middle of the ground, one hundred and fifty yards from the ends, and Hughes crossed sticks, heads up, with the Captain of the Archangels, who saw fit to play forward; that is a place from which you cannot easily control your team. The little click as the cane-shafts met was heard all over the ground, and then

Hughes made some sort of quick wrist-stroke that just dribbled the ball a few yards. Kittiwynk knew that stroke of old, and followed as a cat follows a mouse. While the Captain of the Archangels was wrenching his pony round, Hughes struck with all his strength, and next instant Kittiwynk was away, Corks following close behind her, their little feet pattering like raindrops on glass.

'Pull out to the left,' said Kittiwynk between her teeth; 'it's coming your way, Corks!'

The back and half-back of the Archangels were tearing down on her just as she was within reach of the ball. Hughes leaned forward with a loose rein, and cut it away to the left almost under Kittiwynk 's foot, and it hopped and skipped off to Corks, who saw that, if he was not quick it would run beyond the boundaries. That long bouncing drive gave the Archangels time to wheel and send three men across the ground to head off Corks. Kittiwynk stayed where she was; for she knew the game. Corks was on the ball half a fraction of a second before the others came up, and Macnamara, with a backhanded stroke, sent it back across the ground to Hughes, who saw the way clear to the Archangels' goal, and smacked the ball in before any one quite knew what had happened.

'That's luck,' said Corks, as they changed ends. 'A goal in three minutes for three hits, and no riding to speak of.'

'Don't know,' said Polaris. 'We've made 'em angry too soon. Shouldn't wonder if they tried to rush us off our feet next time.'

'Keep the ball hanging, then,' said Shiraz. 'That wears out every pony that is not used to it.'

Next time there was no easy galloping across the ground. All the Archangels closed up as one man, but there they stayed, for Corks, Kittiwynk, and Polaris were somewhere on the top of the ball, marking time among the rattling sticks, while Shiraz circled about outside, waiting for a chance.

'We can do *this* all day,' said Polaris, ramming his quarters into the side of another pony. 'Where do you think you're shoving to?'

'I'll – I'll be driven in an *ekka* if I know,' was the gasping reply, 'and I'd give a week's feed to get my blinkers off. I can't see anything.'

'The dust is rather bad. Whew! That was one for my off-hock. Where's the ball, Corks?'

'Under my tail. At least, the man's looking for it there! This is beautiful. They can't use their sticks, and it's driving 'em wild. Give old Blinkers a push and then he'll go over.'

'Here, don't touch me! I can't see. I'll – I'll back out, I think,' said the pony in blinkers, who knew that if you can't see all round your head, you cannot prop yourself against the shock.

Corks was watching the ball where it lay in the dust, close to his near fore-leg, with Macnamara's shortened stick tap-tapping it from time to time. Kittiwynk was edging her way out of the scrimmage, whisking her stump of a tail with nervous excitement.

'Ho! They've got it,' she snorted. 'Let me out!' and she galloped like a rifle-bullet just behind a tall lanky pony of the Archangels, whose rider was swinging up his stick for a stroke.

'Not today, thank you,' said Hughes, as the blow slid off his raised stick, and Kittiwynk laid her shoulder to the tall pony's quarters, and shoved him aside just as Lutyens on Shiraz sent the ball where it had come from, and the tall pony went skating and slipping away to the left. Kittiwynk, seeing that Polaris had joined Corks in the chase for the ball up the ground, dropped into Polaris' place, and then 'time' was called.

The Skidars' ponies wasted no time in kicking or fuming. They knew that each minute's rest meant so much gain, and trotted off to the rails, and their *saises* began to scrape and blanket and rub them at once.

'Whew!' said Corks, stiffening up to get all the tickle of the big vulcanite scraper. 'If we were playing pony for pony, we would bend those Archangels double in half an hour. But they'll bring up fresh ones and fresh ones and fresh ones after that – you see.'

'Who cares?' said Polaris. 'We've drawn first blood. Is my hock swelling?'

'Looks puffy,' said Corks. 'You must have had rather a wipe. Don't let it stiffen. You'll be wanted again in half an hour.'

'What's the game like?' said The Maltese Cat.

'Ground's like your shoe, except where they put too much water on it,' said Kittiwynk. 'Then it's slippery. Don't play in the centre. There's a bog there. I don't know how their next four are going to behave, but we kept the ball hanging, and made 'em lather for nothing. Who goes out? Two Arabs and a couple of country-breds! That's bad. What a comfort it is to wash your mouth out!'

Kitty was talking with a neck of a lather-covered

soda-water bottle between her teeth, and trying to look over her withers at the same time. This gave her a very coquettish air.

'What's bad?' said Grey Dawn, giving to the girth and admiring his well-set shoulders.

'You Arabs can't gallop fast enough to keep yourselves warm – that's what Kitty means,' said Polaris, limping to show that his hock needed attention. 'Are you playing back, Grey Dawn?'

"Looks like it,' said Grey Dawn, as Lutyens swung himself up. Powell mounted The Rabbit, a plain bay country-bred much like Corks, but with mulish ears. Macnamara took Faiz-Ullah, a handy, short-backed little red Arab with a long tail, and Hughes mounted Benami, an old and sullen brown beast, who stood over in front more than a polo-pony should.

'Benami looks like business,' said Shiraz. 'How's your temper, Ben?' The old campaigner hobbled off without answering, and The Maltese Cat looked at the new Archangel ponies prancing about on the ground. They were four beautiful blacks, and they saddled big enough and strong enough to eat the Skidars' team and gallop away with the meal inside them.

'Blinkers again,' said The Maltese Cat. 'Good enough!'

'They're chargers – cavalry chargers!' said Kittiwynk, indignantly. '*They*'ll never see thirteen-three again.'

'They've all been fairly measured, and they 've all got their certificates,' said The Maltese Cat, 'or they wouldn't be here. We must take things as they come along, and keep your eyes on the ball.'

The game began, but this time the Skidars were penned

to their own end of the ground, and the watching ponies did not approve of that.

'Faiz-Ullah is shirking – as usual,' said Polaris, with a scornful grunt.

'Faiz-Ullah is eating whip,' said Corks. They could hear the leather-thonged polo quirt lacing the little fellow's well-rounded barrel. Then The Rabbit's shrill neigh came across the ground.

'I can't do all the work,' he cried, desperately.

'Play the game – don't talk,' The Maltese Cat whickered; and all the ponies wriggled with excitement, and the soldiers and the grooms gripped the railings and shouted. A black pony with blinkers had singled out old Benami, and was interfering with him in every possible way. They could see Benami shaking his head up and down, and napping his under lip.

'There'll be a fall in a minute,' said Polaris. 'Benami is getting stuffy.'

The game flickered up and down between goal-post and goal-post, and the black ponies were getting more confident as they felt they had the legs of the others. The ball was hit out of a little scrimmage, and Benami and The Rabbit followed it, Faiz-Ullah only too glad to be quiet for an instant.

The blinkered black pony came up like a hawk, with two of his own side behind him, and Benami's eye glittered as he raced. The question was which pony should make way for the other, for each rider was perfectly willing to risk a fall in a good cause. The black, who had been driven nearly crazy by his blinkers, trusted to his weight and his temper; but Benami knew how to apply his weight and how to keep his temper. They met, and there was a cloud of dust. The black was lying on his side, all the breath knocked out of his body. The Rabbit was a hundred yards up the ground with the ball, and Benami was sitting down. He had slid nearly ten yards on his tail, but he had had his revenge, and sat cracking his nostrils till the black pony rose.

'That's what you get for interfering. Do you want any more?' said Benami, and he plunged into the game. Nothing was done that quarter, because Faiz-Ullah would not gallop, though Macnamara beat him whenever he could spare a second. The fall of the black pony had impressed his companions tremendously, and so the Archangels could not profit by Faiz-Ullah's bad behaviour.

But as The Maltese Cat said when 'time' was called, and the four came back blowing and dripping, Faiz-Ullah ought to have been kicked all round Umballa. If he did not behave better next time The Maltese Cat promised to pull out his Arab tail by the roots and − eat it.

There was no time to talk, for the third four were ordered out.

The third quarter of a game is generally the hottest, for each side thinks that the others must be pumped; and most of the winning play in a game is made about that time.

Lutyens took over The Maltese Cat with a pat and a hug, for Lutyens valued him more than anything else in the world; Powell had Shikast, a little grey rat with no pedigree and no manners outside polo; Macnamara mounted Bamboo, the largest of the team; and Hughes Who's Who, alias The Animal. He was supposed to have

Australian blood in his veins, but he looked like a clothes-horse, and you could whack his legs with an iron crow-bar without hurting him.

They went out to meet the very flower of the Archangels' team; and when Who's Who saw their elegantly booted legs and their beautiful satin skins, he grinned a grin through his light, well-worn bridle.

'My word!' said Who's Who. 'We must give 'em a little football. These gentlemen need a rubbing down.'

'No biting,' said The Maltese Cat, warningly; for once or twice in his career Who's Who had been known to forget himself in that way.

'Who said anything about biting? I'm not playing tiddly-winks. I'm playing the game.'

The Archangels came down like a wolf on the fold, for they were tired of football, and they wanted polo. They got it more and more. Just after the game began, Lutyens hit a ball that was coming towards him rapidly, and it rolled in the air, as a ball sometimes will, with the whirl of a frightened partridge. Shikast heard, but could not see it for the minute, though he looked everywhere and up into the air as The Maltese Cat had taught him. When he saw it ahead and overhead he went forward with Powell as fast as he could put foot to ground. It was then that Powell, a quiet and level-headed man, as a rule, became inspired, and played a stroke that sometimes comes off successfully after long practice. He took his stick in both hands, and, standing up in his stirrups, swiped at the ball in the air, Munipore fashion. There was one second of paralysed astonishment, and then all four sides of the ground went up in a yell of applause and delight as the ball flew true (you could see the amazed Archangels ducking in their saddles to dodge the line of flight, and looking at it with open mouths), and the regimental pipes of the Skidars squealed from the railings as long as the pipers had breath.

Shikast heard the stroke; but he heard the head of the stick fly off at the same time. Nine hundred and ninety-nine ponies out of a thousand would have gone tearing on after the ball with a useless player pulling at their heads; but Powell knew him, and he knew Powell; and the instant he felt Powell's right leg shift a trifle on the saddle-flap, he headed to the boundary, where a native officer was frantically waving a new stick. Before the shouts had ended, Powell was armed again.

Once before in his life The Maltese Cat had heard that very same stroke played off his own back, and had prof-ited by the confusion it wrought. This time he acted on experience, and leaving Bamboo to guard the goal in case of accidents, came through the others like a flash, head and tail low – Lutyens standing up to ease him – swept on and on before the other side knew what was the matter, and nearly pitched on his head between the Archangels' goal-post as Lutyens kicked the ball in after a straight scurry of a hundred and fifty yards. If there was one thing more than another upon which The Maltese Cat prided himself, it was on this quick, streaking kind of run half across the ground. He did not believe in taking balls round the field unless you were clearly overmatched. After this they gave the Archangels five-minuted football; and an expensive fast pony hates football because it rumples his temper.

Who's Who showed himself even better than Polaris in this game. He did not permit any wriggling away, but bored joyfully into the scrimmage as if he had his nose in a feed-box and was looking for something nice. Little Shikast jumped on the ball the minute it got clear, and every time an Archangel pony followed it, he found Shikast standing over it, asking what was the matter.

'If we can live through this quarter,' said The Maltese Cat, 'I sha'n't care. Don't take it out of yourselves. Let them do the lathering.'

So the ponies, as their riders explained afterwards, 'shut-up.' The Archangels kept them tied fast in front of their goal, but it cost the Archangels' ponies all that was left of their tempers; and ponies began to kick, and men began to repeat compliments, and they chopped at the legs of Who's Who, and he set his teeth and stayed where he was, and the dust stood up like a tree over the scrimmage until that hot quarter ended.

They found the ponies very excited and confident when they went to their *saises*; and The Maltese Cat had to warn them that the worst of the game was coming.

'Now *we* are all going in for the second time,' said he, 'and *they* are trotting out fresh ponies. You think you can gallop, but you 'll find you can't; and then you'll be sorry.'

'But two goals to nothing is a halter-long lead,' said Kittiwynk, prancing.

'How long does it take to get a goal?' The Maltese Cat answered. 'For pity's sake, don't run away with a notion that the game is half-won just because we happen to be in luck *now!* They'll ride you into the grand stand, if they can; you must not give 'em a chance. Follow the ball.'

'Football, as usual?' said Polaris. 'My hock's half as big as a nose-bag.'

'Don't let them have a look at the ball, if you can help it. Now leave me alone. I must get all the rest I can before the last quarter.'

He hung down his head and let all his muscles go slack, Shikast, Bamboo, and Who's Who copying his example.

'Better not watch the game,' he said. 'We aren't playing, and we shall only take it out of ourselves if we grow anxious. Look at the ground and pretend it's fly-time.'

They did their best, but it was hard advice to follow. The hooves were drumming and the sticks were rattling all up and down the ground, and yells of applause from the English troops told that the Archangels were pressing the Skidars hard. The native soldiers behind the ponies groaned and grunted, and said things in undertones, and presently they heard a long-drawn shout and a clatter of hurrahs!

'One to the Archangels,' said Shikast, without raising his head. 'Time's nearly up. Oh, my sire – and *dam!*'

'Faiz-Ullah,' said The Maltese Cat, 'if you don't play to the last nail in your shoes this time, I'll kick you on the ground before all the other ponies.'

'I'll do my best when my time comes,' said the little Arab, sturdily.

The *saises* looked at each other gravely as they rubbed their ponies' legs. This was the time when long purses began to tell, and everybody knew it. Kittiwynk and the others came back, the sweat dripping over their hooves and their tails telling sad stories.

'They're better than we are,' said Shiraz. 'I knew how it would be.'

'Shut your big head,' said The Maltese Cat; 'we've one goal to the good yet.'

'Yes; but it's two Arabs and two country-breds to play now,' said Corks. 'Faiz-Ullah, remember!' He spoke in a biting voice.

As Lutyens mounted Grey Dawn he looked at his men, and they did not look pretty. They were covered with dust and sweat in streaks. Their yellow boots were almost black, their wrists were red and lumpy, and their eyes seemed two inches deep in their heads; but the expression in the eyes was satisfactory.

'Did you take anything at tiffin?' said Lutyens; and the team shook their heads. They were too dry to talk.

'All right. The Archangels did. They are worse pumped than we are.'

'They've got the better ponies,' said Powell. 'I sha'n't be sorry when this business is over.'

That fifth quarter was a painful one in every way. Faiz-Ullah played like a little red demon, and The Rabbit seemed to be everywhere at once, and Benami rode straight at anything and everything that came in his way; while the umpires on their ponies wheeled like gulls outside the shifting game. But the Archangels had the better mounts, – they had kept their racers till late in the game, – and never allowed the Skidars to play football. They hit the ball up and down the width of the ground till Benami and the rest were outpaced. Then they went forward, and time and again Lutyens and Grey Dawn were just, and only just, able to send the ball away with a long, spitting back-hander. Grey Dawn forgot that he was an Arab; and turned from grey to blue as he galloped. Indeed, he forgot too well, for he did not keep his eyes on the ground as an Arab should, but stuck out his nose and scuttled for the dear honour of the game. They had watered the ground once or twice between the quarters, and a careless waterman had emptied the last of his skinful all in one place near the Skidars' goal. It was close to the end of the play, and for the tenth time Grey Dawn was bolting after the ball, when his near hind-foot slipped on the greasy mud, and he rolled over and over, pitching Lutyens just clear of the goal-post; and the triumphant Archangels made their goal. Then 'time' was called – two goals all; but Lutyens had to be helped up, and Grey Dawn rose with his near hind-leg strained somewhere.

'What's the damage?' said Powell, his arm around Lutyens.

'Collar-bone, *of* course,' said Lutyens, between his teeth. It was the third time he had broken it in two years, and it hurt him. Powell and the others whistled.

'Game's up,' said Hughes.

'Hold on. We've five good minutes yet, and it isn't my right hand. We'll stick it out.'

'I say,' said the Captain of the Archangels, trotting up, 'are you hurt, Lutyens? We'll wait if you care to put in a substitute. I wish – I mean – the fact is, you fellows deserve this game if any team does. 'Wish we could give you a man, or some of our ponies – or something.'

'You're awfully good, but we'll play it to a finish, I think.'

The Captain of the Archangels stared for a little. 'That's

not half bad,' he said, and went back to his own side, while Lutyens borrowed a scarf from one of his native officers and made a sling of it. Then an Archangel galloped up with a big bath-sponge, and advised Lutyens to put it under his armpit to ease his shoulder, and between them they tied up his left arm scientifically; and one of the native officers leaped forward with four long glasses that fizzed and bubbled.

The team looked at Lutyens piteously, and he nodded. It was the last quarter, and nothing would matter after that. They drank out the dark golden drink, and wiped their moustaches, and things looked more hopeful.

The Maltese Cat had put his nose into the front of Lutyens' shirt and was trying to say how sorry he was.

'He knows,' said Lutyens, proudly. 'The beggar knows. I've played him without a bridle before now – for fun.'

'It's no fun now,' said Powell. 'But we haven't a decent substitute.'

'No,' said Lutyens. 'It's the last quarter, and we've got to make our goal and win. I'll trust The Cat.'

'If you fall this time, you'll suffer a little,' said Macnamara.

'I'll trust The Cat,' said Lutyens.

'You hear that?' said The Maltese Cat, proudly, to the others. 'It's worth while playing polo for ten years to have that said of you. Now then, my sons, come along. We'll kick up a little bit, just to show the Archangels this team haven't suffered.'

And, sure enough, as they went on to the ground, The Maltese Cat, after satisfying himself that Lutyens was home in the saddle, kicked out three or four times, and Lutyens laughed. The reins were caught up anyhow in the tips of his strapped left hand, and he never pretended to rely on them. He knew The Cat would answer to the least pressure of the leg, and by way of showing off – for his shoulder hurt him very much – he bent the little fellow in a close figure-of-eight in and out between the goal-posts. There was a roar from the native officers and men, who dearly loved a piece of *dugabashi* (horse-trick work), as they called it, and the pipes very quietly and scornfully droned out the first bars of a common bazaar tune called 'Freshly Fresh and Newly New,' just as a warning to the other regiments that the Skidars were fit. All the natives laughed.

'And now,' said The Maltese Cat, as they took their place, 'remember that this is the last quarter, and follow the ball!'

'Don't need to be told,' said Who's Who.

'Let me go on. All those people on all four sides will begin to crowd in – just as they did at Malta. You'll hear people calling out, and moving forward and being pushed back; and that is going to make the Archangel ponies very unhappy. But if a ball is struck to the boundary, you go after it, and let the people get out of your way. I went over the pole of a four-in-hand once, and picked a game out of the dust by it. Back me up when I run, and follow the ball.'

There was a sort of an all-round sound of sympathy and wonder as the last quarter opened, and then there began exactly what The Maltese Cat had foreseen. People crowded in close to the boundaries, and the Archangels' ponies kept looking sideways at the narrowing space. If you know how a man feels to be cramped at tennis – not because he wants to run out of the court, but because he likes to know that he can at a pinch – you will guess how ponies must feel when they are playing in a box of human beings.

'I'll bend some of those men if I can get away,' said Who's Who, as he rocketed behind the ball; and Bamboo nodded without speaking. They were playing the last ounce in them, and The Maltese Cat had left the goal undefended to join them. Lutyens gave him every order that he could to bring him back, but this was the first time in his career that the little wise grey had ever played polo on his own responsibility, and he was going to make the most of it.

'What are you doing here?' said Hughes, as The Cat crossed in front of him and rode off an Archangel.

'The Cat's in charge – mind the goal!' shouted Lutyens, and bowing forward hit the ball full, and followed on, forcing the Archangels towards their own goal.

'No football,' said The Maltese Cat. 'Keep the ball by the boundaries and cramp 'em. Play open order, and drive 'em to the boundaries.'

Across and across the ground in big diagonals flew the ball, and whenever it came to a flying rush and a stroke close to the boundaries the Archangel ponies moved stiffly. They did not care to go headlong at a wall of men and carriages, though if the ground had been open they could have turned on a sixpence.

'Wriggle her up the sides,' said The Cat. 'Keep her close to the crowd. They hate the carriages. Shikast, keep her up this side.'

Shikast and Powell lay left and right behind the uneasy

scuffle of an open scrimmage, and every time the ball was hit away Shikast galloped on it at such an angle that Powell was forced to hit it towards the boundary; and when the crowd had been driven away from that side, Lutyens would send the ball over to the other, and Shikast would slide desperately after it till his friends came down to help. It was billiards, and no football, this time – billiards in a corner pocket; and the cues were not well chalked.

'If they get us out in the middle of the ground they'll walk away from us. Dribble her along the sides,' cried The Maltese Cat.

So they dribbled all along the boundary, where a pony could not come on their right-hand side; and the Archangels were furious, and the umpires had to neglect the game to shout at the people to get back, and several blundering mounted policemen tried to restore order, all close to the scrimmage, and the nerves of the Archangels' ponies stretched and broke like cob-webs.

Five or six times an Archangel hit the ball up into the middle of the ground, and each time the watchful Shikast gave Powell his chance to send it back, and after each return, when the dust had settled, men could see that the Skidars had gained a few yards.

Every now and again there were shouts of 'Side! Off side!' from the spectators; but the teams were too busy to care, and the umpires had all they could do to keep their maddened ponies clear of the scuffle.

At last Lutyens missed a short easy stroke, and the Skidars had to fly back helter-skelter to protect their own goal, Shikast leading. Powell stopped the ball with a backhander when it was not fifty yards from the goal-posts, and Shikast spun round with a wrench that nearly hoisted Powell out of his saddle.

'Now's our last chance,' said The Cat, wheeling like a cockchafer on a pin. 'We've got to ride it out. Come along.'

Lutyens felt the little chap take a deep breath, and, as it were, crouch under his rider. The ball was hopping towards the right-hand boundary, an Archangel riding for it with both spurs and a whip; but neither spur nor whip would make his pony stretch himself as he neared the crowd. The Maltese Cat glided under his very nose, picking up his hind legs sharp, for there was not a foot to spare between his quarters and the other pony's bit. It was as neat an exhibition as fancy figure-skating. Lutyens hit with all the strength he had left, but the stick slipped a little in his hand, and the ball flew off to the left instead of keeping close to the boundary. Who's Who was far across the ground, thinking hard as he galloped. He repeated stride for stride The Cat's manoeuvres with another Archangel pony, nipping the ball away from under his bridle, and clearing his opponent by half a fraction of an inch, for Who's Who was clumsy behind. Then he drove away towards the right as The Maltese Cat came up from the left; and Bamboo held a middle course exactly between them. The three were making a sort of Government-broad-arrow-shaped attack; and there was only the Archangels' back to guard the goal; but immediately behind them were three Archangels racing all they knew, and mixed up with them was Powell sending Shikast along on what he felt was their last hope. It takes a very good man to stand up to the rush of seven crazy ponies in the last quarters of a Cup game, when men are riding with their necks for sale, and the ponies are delirious. The Archangels' back missed his stroke and pulled aside just in time to let the rush go by. Bamboo and Who's Who shortened stride to give The Cat room, and Lutyens got the goal with a clean, smooth, smacking stroke that was heard all over the field. But there was no stopping the ponies. They poured through the goal-posts in one mixed mob, winners and losers together, for the pace had been terrific. The Maltese Cat knew by experience what would happen, and, to save Lutyens, turned to the right with one last effort, that strained a back-sinew beyond hope of repair. As he did so he heard the right-hand goal-post crack as a pony cannoned into it – crack, splinter and fall like a mast. It had been sawed three parts through in case of accidents, but it upset the pony nevertheless, and he blundered into another, who blundered into the left-hand post, and then there was confusion and dust and wood. Bamboo was lying on the ground, seeing stars; an Archangel pony rolled beside him, breathless and angry; Shikast had sat down dog-fashion to avoid falling over the others, and was sliding along on his little bobtail in a cloud of dust; and Powell was sitting on the ground, hammering with his stick and trying to cheer. All the others were shouting at the top of what was left of their voices, and the men who had been spilt were shouting too. As soon as the people saw no one was hurt, ten thousand native and English shouted and clapped and yelled, and before any one could stop them the pipers of the Skidars broke on to the ground, with all the native officers and men behind them, and marched up and down, playing a wild Northern tune called 'Zakhme Bagán,' and through the insolent blaring of the pipes and the high-pitched native yells you could hear the Archangels' band hammering, 'For they are all jolly good fellows,' and then reproachfully to the losing team, 'Ooh, Kafoozalum! Kafoozalum! Kafoozalum!'

Besides all these things and many more, there was a Commander-in-chief, and an Inspector-General of Cavalry, and the principal veterinary officer of all India standing on the top of a regimental coach, yelling like school-boys; and brigadiers and colonels and commissioners, and hundreds of pretty ladies joined the chorus. But The Maltese Cat stood with his head down, wondering how many legs were left to him; and Lutyens watched the men and ponies pick themselves out of the wreck of the two goal-posts, and he patted The Maltese Cat very tenderly.

'I say,' said the Captain of the Archangels, spitting a pebble out of his mouth, 'will you take three thousand for that pony – as he stands?'

'No thank you. I've an idea he's saved my life,' said Lutyens, getting off and lying down at full length. Both teams were on the ground too, waving their boots in the air, and coughing and drawing deep breaths, as the *saises* ran up to take away the ponies, and an officious water-carrier sprinkled the players with dirty water till they sat up.

'My aunt!' said Powell, rubbing his back, and looking at the stumps of the goal-posts, 'That was a game!'

They played it over again, every stroke of it, that night at the big dinner, when the Free-for-All Cup was filled and passed down the table, and emptied and filled again, and everybody made most eloquent speeches. About two in the morning, when there might have been some singing, a wise little, plain little, grey little head looked in through the open door.

'Hurrah! Bring him in,' said the Archangels; and his *sais*, who was very happy indeed, patted The Maltese Cat on the flank, and he limped in to the blaze of light and the glittering uniforms, looking for Lutyens. He was used to messes, and men's bedrooms, and places where ponies are not usually encouraged, and in his youth had jumped on and off a mess-table for a bet. So he behaved himself very politely, and ate bread dipped in salt, and was petted all round the table, moving gingerly; and they drank his health, because he had done more to win the Cup than any man or horse on the ground.

That was glory and honour enough for the rest of his days, and The Maltese Cat did not complain much when the veterinary surgeon said that he would be no good for polo any more. When Lutyens married, his wife did not allow him to play, so he was forced to be an umpire; and his pony on these occasions was a flea-bitten grey with a neat polo-tail, lame all round, but desperately quick on his feet, and, as everybody knew, Past Pluperfect Prestissimo Player of the Game.

THE STRANGE RIDE OF MORROWBIE JUKES

Alive or dead – there is no other way.
– Native Proverb.

THERE IS, AS THE CONJURERS SAY, NO deception about this tale. Jukes by accident stumbled upon a village that is well known to exist, though he is the only Englishman who has been there. A somewhat similar institution used to flourish on the outskirts of Calcutta, and there is a story that if you go into the heart of Bikanir, which is in the heart of the Great Indian Desert, you shall come across not a village but a town where the Dead who did not die but may not live have established their headquarters. And, since it is perfectly true that in the same Desert is a wonderful city where all the rich money lenders retreat after they have made their fortunes (fortunes so vast that the owners cannot trust even the strong hand of the Government to protect them, but take refuge in the waterless sands), and drive sumptuous C-spring barouches, and buy beautiful girls and decorate their palaces with gold and ivory and Minton tiles and mother-n'-pearl, I do not see why Jukes's tale should not be true. He is a Civil Engineer, with a head for plans and distances and things of that kind, and he certainly would not take the trouble to invent imaginary traps. He could earn more by doing his legitimate work. He never varies the tale in the telling, and grows very hot and indignant when he thinks of the disrespectful treatment he received. He wrote this quite straightforwardly at first, but he has since touched it up in places and introduced Moral Reflections, thus:

In the beginning it all arose from a slight attack of fever. My work necessitated my being in camp for some months between Pakpattan and Muharakpur – a desolate sandy stretch of country as every one who has had the misfortune to go there may know. My coolies were neither more nor less exasperating than other gangs, and my work demanded sufficient attention to keep me from moping, had I been inclined to so unmanly a weakness.

On the 23rd December, 1884, I felt a little feverish. There was a full moon at the time, and, in consequence, every dog near my tent was baying it. The brutes assembled in twos and threes and drove me frantic. A few days previously I had shot one loud-mouthed singer and suspended his carcass in terrorem about fifty yards from my tent-door. But his friends fell upon, fought for, and ultimately devoured the body; and, as it seemed to me, sang their hymns of thanksgiving afterward with renewed energy.

The light-heartedness which accompanies fever acts differently on different men. My irritation gave way, after a short time, to a fixed determination to slaughter one huge black and white beast who had been foremost in song and first in flight throughout the evening. Thanks to a shaking hand and a giddy head I had already missed him twice with both barrels of my shot-gun, when it struck me that my best plan would be to ride him down in the open and finish him off with a hog-spear. This, of course, was merely the semi-delirious notion of a fever patient; but I remember that it struck me at the time as being eminently practical and feasible.

I therefore ordered my groom to saddle Pornic and bring him round quietly to the rear of my tent. When the pony was ready, I stood at his head prepared to mount and dash out as soon as the dog should again lift up his voice. Pornic, by the way, had not been out of his pickets for a couple of days; the night air was crisp and chilly; and I was armed with a specially long and sharp pair of persuaders with which I had been rousing a sluggish cob that afternoon. You will easily believe, then, that when he was let go he went quickly. In one moment, for the brute bolted as straight as a die, the tent was left far behind, and we were flying over the smooth sandy soil at racing speed.

In another we had passed the wretched dog, and I had

almost forgotten why it was that I had taken the horse and hogspear.

The delirium of fever and the excitement of rapid motion through the air must have taken away the remnant of my senses. I have a faint recollection of standing upright in my stirrups, and of brandishing my hog-spear at the great white Moon that looked down so calmly on my mad gallop; and of shout-log challenges to the camel-thorn bushes as they whizzed past. Once or twice I believe, I swayed forward on Pornic's neck, and literally hung on by my spurs – as the marks next morning showed.

The wretched beast went forward like a thing possessed, over what seemed to be a limitless expanse of moonlit sand. Next, I remember, the ground rose suddenly in front of us, and as we topped the ascent I saw the waters of the Sutlej shining like a silver bar below. Then Pornic blundered heavily on his nose, and we rolled together down some unseen slope.

I must have lost consciousness, for when I recovered I was lying on my stomach in a heap of soft white sand, and the dawn was beginning to break dimly over the edge of the slope down which I had fallen. As the light grew stronger I saw that I was at the bottom of a horse-shoe-shaped crater of sand, opening on one side directly on to the shoals of the Sutlej. My fever had altogether left me, and, with the exception of a slight dizziness in the head, I felt no had effects from the fall over night.

Pornic, who was standing a few yards away, was naturally a good deal exhausted, but had not hurt himself in the least. His saddle, a favorite polo one was much knocked about, and had been twisted under his belly. It took me some time to put him to rights, and in the meantime I had ample opportunities of observing the spot into which I had so foolishly dropped.

At the risk of being considered tedious, I must describe it at length: inasmuch as an accurate mental picture of its peculiarities will be of material assistance in enabling the reader to understand what follows.

Imagine then, as I have said before, a horseshoe-shaped crater of sand with steeply graded sand walls about thirty-five feet high. (The slope, I fancy, must have been about 65 degrees.) This crater enclosed a level piece of ground about fifty yards long by thirty at its broadest part, with a crude well in the centre. Round the bottom of the crater, about three feet from the level of the ground proper, ran a series of eighty-three semi-circular ovoid, square, and multilateral holes, all about three feet at the mouth. Each hole on inspection showed that it was carefully shored internally with drift-wood and bamboos, and over the mouth a wooden drip-board projected, like the peak of a jockey's cap, for two feet. No sign of life was visible in these tunnels, but a most sickening stench pervaded the entire amphitheatre – a stench fouler than any which my wanderings in Indian villages have introduced me to.

Having remounted Pornic, who was as anxious as I to get back to camp, I rode round the base of the horseshoe to find some place whence an exit would be practicable. The inhabitants, whoever they might be, had not thought fit to put in an appearance, so I was left to my own devices. My first attempt to 'rush' Pornic up the steep sand-banks showed me that I had fallen into a trap exactly on the same model as that which the ant-lion sets for its prey. At each step the shifting sand poured down from above in tons, and rattled on the drip-boards of the holes like small shot. A couple of ineffectual charges sent us both rolling down to the bottom, half choked with the torrents of sand; and I was constrained to turn my attention to the river-bank.

Here everything seemed easy enough. The sand hills ran down to the river edge, it is true, but there were plenty of shoals and shallows across which I could gallop Pornic, and find my way back to terra firma by turning sharply to the right or left. As I led Pornic over the sands I was startled by the faint pop of a rifle across the river; and at the same moment a bullet dropped with a sharp 'whit' close to Pornic's head.

There was no mistaking the nature of the missile – a regulation Martini-Henry 'picket.' About five hundred yards away a country-boat was anchored in midstream; and a jet of smoke drifting away from its bows in the still morning air showed me whence the delicate attention had come. Was ever a respectable gentleman in such an impasse? The treacherous sand slope allowed no escape from a spot which I had visited most involuntarily, and a promenade on the river frontage was the signal for a bombardment from some insane native in a boat. I'm afraid that I lost my temper very much indeed.

Another bullet reminded me that I had better save my breath to cool my porridge; and I retreated hastily up the sands and back to the horseshoe, where I saw that the noise of the rifle had drawn sixty-five human beings from the badger-holes which I had up till that point supposed to be untenanted. I found myself in the midst of a crowd of spectators – about forty men, twenty women, and one child who could not have been more than five years old. They were all scantily clothed in that salmon-colored cloth which one associates with Hindu mendicants, and, at first sight, gave me the impression of a band of loathsome fakirs. The filth and repulsiveness of the assembly were beyond all description, and I shuddered to think what their life in the badger-holes must be.

Even in these days, when local self-government has destroyed the greater part of a native's respect for a Sahib, I have been accustomed to a certain amount of civility from my inferiors, and on approaching the crowd naturally expected that there would be some recognition of my presence. As a matter of fact there was; but it was by no means what I had looked for.

The ragged crew actually laughed at me – such laughter I hope I may never hear again. They cackled, yelled, whistled, and howled as I walked into their midst; some of them literally throwing themselves down on the ground in convulsions of unholy mirth. In a moment I had let go Pornic's head, and, irritated beyond expression at the morning's adventure, commenced cuffing those nearest to me with all the force I could. The wretches dropped under my blows like nine-pins, and the laughter gave place to wails for mercy; while those yet untouched clasped me round the knees, imploring me in all sorts of uncouth tongues to spare them.

In the tumult, and just when I was feeling very much ashamed of myself for having thus easily given way to my temper, a thin, high voice murmured in English from behind my shoulder: 'Sahib! Sahib! Do you not know me? Sahib, it is Gunga Dass, the telegraph-master.'

I spun round quickly and faced the speaker.

Gunga Dass, (I have, of course, no hesitation in mentioning the man's real name) I had known four years before as a Deccanee Brahmin loaned by the Punjab Government to one of the Khalsia States. He was in charge of a branch telegraph-office there, and when I had last met him was a jovial, full-stomached, portly Government servant with a marvelous capacity for making bad puns in English – a peculiarity which made me remember him long after I had forgotten his services to me in his official capacity. It is seldom that a Hindu makes English puns.

Now, however, the man was changed beyond all recognition. Caste-mark, stomach, slate-colored continuations, and unctuous speech were all gone. I looked at a withered skeleton, turban-less and almost naked, with long matted hair and deep-set codfish-eyes. But for a crescent-shaped scar on the left cheek – the result of an accident for which I was responsible I should never have known him. But it was indubitably Gunga Dass, and – for this I was thankful – an English-speaking native who might at least tell me the meaning of all that I had gone through that day.

The crowd retreated to some distance as I turned toward the miserable figure, and ordered him to show me some method of escaping from the crater. He held a freshly plucked crow in his hand, and in reply to my question climbed slowly on a platform of sand which ran in front of the holes, and commenced lighting a fire there in silence. Dried bents, sand-poppies, and driftwood burn quickly; and I derived much consolation from the fact that he lit them with an ordinary sulphur-match. When they were in a bright glow, and the crow was nearly spitted in front thereof, Gunga Dass began without a word of preamble:

'There are only two kinds of men, Sar. The alive and the dead. When you are dead you are dead, but when you are alive you live.' (Here the crow demanded his attention for an instant as it twirled before the fire in danger of being burned to a cinder.) 'If you die at home and do not die when you come to the ghât to be burned you come here.'

The nature of the reeking village was made plain now, and all that I had known or read of the grotesque and the horrible paled before the fact just communicated by the ex-Brahmin. Sixteen years ago, when I first landed in Bombay, I had been told by a wandering Armenian of the existence, somewhere in India, of a place to which such Hindus as had the misfortune to recover from trance or catalepsy were conveyed and kept, and I recollect laughing heartily at what I was then pleased to consider a traveler's tale.

Sitting at the bottom of the sand-trap, the memory of Watson's Hotel, with its swinging punkahs, white-robed attendants, and the sallow-faced Armenian, rose up in my mind as vividly as a photograph, and I burst into a loud fit of laughter. The contrast was too absurd!

Gunga Dass, as he bent over the unclean bird, watched me curiously. Hindus seldom laugh, and his surroundings were not such as to move Gunga Dass to any undue excess of hilarity. He removed the crow solemnly from the wooden spit and as solemnly devoured it. Then he continued his story, which I give in his own words:

'In epidemics of the cholera you are carried to be burned almost before you are dead. When you come to the riverside the cold air, perhaps, makes you alive, and then, if you are only little alive, mud is put on your nose and mouth and you die conclusively. If you are rather more alive, more mud is put; but if you are too lively they let you go and take you away. I was too lively, and made protestation with anger against the indignities that they endeavored to press upon me. In those days I was Brahmin and proud man. Now I am dead man and eat' – here he eyed the well-gnawed breast bone with the first sign of emotion that I had seen in him since we met – 'crows, and other things. They took me from my sheets when they saw that I was too lively and gave me medicines for one week, and I survived successfully. Then they sent me by rail from my place to Okara Station, with a man to take care of me; and at Okara Station we met two other men, and they conducted we three on camels, in the night, from Okara Station to this place, and they propelled me from the top to the bottom, and the other two succeeded, and I have been here ever since two and a half years. Once I was Brahmin and proud man, and now I eat crows.'

'There is no way of getting out?'

'None of what kind at all. When I first came I made experiments frequently and all the others also, but we have always succumbed to the sand which is precipitated upon our heads.'

'But surely,' I broke in at this point, 'the river-front is open, and it is worth while dodging the bullets; while at night' – I had already matured a rough plan of escape which a natural instinct of selfishness forbade me sharing with Gunga Dass. He, however, divined my unspoken thought almost as soon as it was formed; and, to my intense astonishment, gave vent to a long low chuckle of derision – the laughter, be it understood, of a superior or at least of an equal.

'You will not' – he had dropped the Sir completely after his opening sentence – 'make any escape that way. But you can try. I have tried. Once only.'

The sensation of nameless terror and abject fear which I had in vain attempted to strive against overmastered me completely. My long fast – it was now close upon ten o'clock, and I had eaten nothing since tiffin on the previous day – combined with the violent and unnatural agitation of the ride had exhausted me, and I verily believe that, for a few minutes, I acted as one mad. I hurled myself against the pitiless sand–slope I ran round the base of the crater, blaspheming and praying by turns. I crawled out among the sedges of the river-front, only to be driven back each time in an agony of nervous dread by the rifle-bullets which cut up the sand round me – for I dared not face the death of a mad dog among that hideous crowd – and finally fell, spent and raving, at the curb of the well. No one had taken the slightest notion of an exhibition which makes me blush hotly even when I think of it now.

Two or three men trod on my panting body as they drew water, but they were evidently used to this sort of thing, and had no time to waste upon me. The situation was humiliating. Gunga Dass, indeed, when he had banked the embers of his fire with sand, was at some pains to throw half a cupful of fetid water over my head, an attention for which I could have fallen on my knees and thanked him, but he was laughing all the while in the same mirthless, wheezy key that greeted me on my first attempt to force the shoals. And so, in a semi-comatose condition, I lay till noon. Then, being only a man after all, I felt hungry, and intimated as much to Gunga Dass, whom I had begun to regard as my natural protector. Following the impulse of the outer world when dealing with natives, I put my hand into my pocket and drew out four annas. The absurdity of the gift struck me at once, and I was about to replace the money.

Gunga Dass, however, was of a different opinion. 'Give me the money,' said he; 'all you have, or I will get help, and we will kill you!' All this as if it were the most natural thing in the world!

A Briton's first impulse, I believe, is to guard the contents of his pockets; but a moment's reflection convinced me of the futility of differing with the one man who had it in his power to make me comfortable; and with whose help it was possible that I might eventually escape from the crater. I gave him all the money in my possession, Rs. 9-8-5 – nine rupees eight annas and five pie – for I always keep small change as bakshish when I am in camp. Gunga Dass clutched the coins, and hid them at once in his ragged loin cloth, his expression changing to something diabolical as he looked round to assure himself that no one had observed us.

'Now I will give you something to eat,' said he.

What pleasure the possession of my money could have afforded him I am unable to say; but inasmuch as it did give him evident delight I was not sorry that I had parted with it so readily, for I had no doubt that he would have had me killed if I had refused. One does not protest against the vagaries of a den of wild beasts; and my companions were lower than any beasts. While I devoured what Gunga Dass had provided, a coarse chapatti and a cupful of the foul well-water, the people showed not the faintest sign of curiosity – that curiosity which is so rampant, as a rule, in an Indian village.

I could even fancy that they despised me. At all events they treated me with the most chilling indif- ference, and Gunga Dass was nearly as bad. I plied him with questions about the terrible village, and received extremely unsatisfactory answers. So far as I could gather, it had been in existence from time immemorial – whence I concluded that it was at least a century old – and during that time no one had ever been known to escape from it. [I had to control myself here with both hands, lest the blind terror should lay hold of me a second time and drive me raving round the crater.] Gunga Dass took a malicious pleasure in empha- sizing this point and in watching me wince. Nothing that I could do would induce him to tell me who the mysterious 'They' were.

'It is so ordered,' he would reply, 'and I do not yet know any one who has disobeyed the orders.'

'Only wait till my servants find that I am missing,' I retorted, 'and I promise you that this place shall be cleared off the face of the earth, and I'll give you a lesson in civility, too, my friend.'

'Your servants would be torn in pieces before they came near this place; and, besides, you are dead, my dear friend. It is not your fault, of course, but none the less you are dead and buried.'

At irregular intervals supplies of food, I was told, were dropped down from the land side into the amphitheatre, and the inhabitants fought for them like wild beasts. When a man felt his death coming on he retreated to his lair and died there. The body was sometimes dragged out of the hole and thrown on to the sand, or allowed to rot where it lay.

The phrase 'thrown on to the sand' caught my attention, and I asked Gunga Dass whether this sort of thing was not likely to breed a pestilence.

'That,' said he with another of his wheezy chuckles, 'you may see for yourself subsequently. You will have much time to make observations.'

Whereat, to his great delight, I winced once more and hastily continued the conversation: 'And how do you live here from day to day? What do you do?' The question elicited exactly the same answer as before – coupled with the information that 'this place is like your European heaven; there is neither marrying nor giving in marriage.'

Gunga Dass had been educated at a Mission School, and, as he himself admitted, had he only changed his religion 'like a wise man,' might have avoided the living grave which was now his portion. But as long as I was with him I fancy he was happy.

Here was a Sahib, a representative of the dominant

race, helpless as a child and completely at the mercy of his native neighbors. In a deliberate lazy way he set himself to torture me as a schoolboy would devote a rapturous half-hour to watching the agonies of an impaled beetle, or as a ferret in a blind burrow might glue himself comfortably to the neck of a rabbit. The burden of his conversation was that there was no escape 'of no kind whatever,' and that I should stay here till I died and was 'thrown on to the sand.' If it were possible to forejudge the conversation of the Damned on the advent of a new soul in their abode, I should say that they would speak as Gunga Dass did to me throughout that long afternoon. I was powerless to protest or answer; all my energies being devoted to a struggle against the inexplicable terror that threatened to overwhelm me again and again. I can compare the feeling to nothing except the struggles of a man against the overpowering nausea of the Channel passage – only my agony was of the spirit and infinitely more terrible.

As the day wore on, the inhabitants began to appear in full strength to catch the rays of the afternoon sun, which were now sloping in at the mouth of the crater. They assembled in little knots, and talked among themselves without even throwing a glance in my direction. About four o'clock, as far as I could judge Gunga Dass rose and dived into his lair for a moment, emerging with a live crow in his hands. The wretched bird was in a most draggled and deplorable condition, but seemed to be in no way afraid of its master. Advancing cautiously to the river front, Gunga Dass stepped from tussock to tussock until he had reached a smooth patch of sand directly in the line of the boat's fire. The occupants of the boat took no notice. Here he stopped, and, with a couple of dexterous turns of the wrist, pegged the bird on its back with outstretched wings. As was only natural, the crow began to shriek at once and beat the air with its claws. In a few seconds the clamor had attracted the attention of a bevy of wild crows on a shoal a few hundred yards away, where they were discussing something that looked like a corpse. Half a dozen crows flew over at once to see what was going on, and also, as it proved, to attack the pinioned bird. Gunga Dass, who had lain down on a tussock, motioned to me to be quiet, though I fancy this was a needless precaution. In a moment, and before I could see how it happened, a wild crow, who had grappled with the shrieking and helpless bird, was entangled in the latter's claws, swiftly disengaged by Gunga Dass, and pegged down beside its companion in adversity. Curiosity, it seemed, overpowered the rest of the flock, and almost before Gunga Dass and I had time to withdraw to the tussock, two more captives were struggling in the upturned claws of the decoys. So the chase – if I can give it so dignified a name – continued until Gunga Dass had captured seven crows. Five of them he throttled at once, reserving two for further operations another day. I was a good deal impressed by this, to me, novel method of securing food, and complimented Gunga Dass on his skill.

'It is nothing to do,' said he. 'Tomorrow you must do it for me. You are stronger than I am.'

This calm assumption of superiority upset me not a little, and I answered peremptorily: 'Indeed, you old ruffian! What do you think I have given you money for?'

'Very well,' was the unmoved reply. 'Perhaps not tomorrow, nor the day after, nor subsequently; but in the end, and for many years, you will catch crows and eat crows, and you will thank your European God that you have crows to catch and eat.'

I could have cheerfully strangled him for this; but judged it best under the circumstances to smother my resentment. An hour later I was eating one of the crows; and, as Gunga Dass had said, thanking my God that I had a crow to eat. Never as long as I live shall I forget that evening meal. The whole population were squatting on the hard sand platform opposite their dens, huddled over tiny fires of refuse and dried rushes. Death, having once laid his hand upon these men and forborne to strike, seemed to stand aloof from them now; for most of our company were old men, bent and worn and twisted with years, and women aged to all appearance as the Fates themselves. They sat together in knots and talked – God only knows what they found to discuss – in low equable tones, curiously in contrast to the strident babble with which natives are accustomed to make day hideous. Now and then an access of that sudden fury which had possessed me in the morning would lay hold on a man or woman; and with yells and imprecations the sufferer would attack the steep slope until, baffled and bleeding, he fell back on the platform incapable of moving a limb. The others would never even raise their eyes when this happened, as men too well aware of the futility of their fellows' attempts and wearied with their useless repetition. I saw four such outbursts in the course of the evening.

Gunga Dass took an eminently business-like view of

my situation, and while we were dining – I can afford to laugh at the recollection now, but it was painful enough at the time – propounded the terms on which he would consent to 'do' for me. My nine rupees eight annas, he argued, at the rate of three annas a day, would provide me with food for fifty-one days, or about seven weeks; that is to say, he would be willing to cater for me for that length of time. At the end of it I was to look after myself. For a further consideration – videlicet my boots – he would be willing to allow me to occupy the den next to his own, and would supply me with as much dried grass for bedding as he could spare.

'Very well, Gunga Dass,' I replied; 'to the first terms I cheerfully agree, but, as there is nothing on earth to prevent my killing you as you sit here and taking everything that you have' (I thought of the two invaluable crows at the time), 'I flatly refuse to give you my boots and shall take whichever den I please.'

The stroke was a bold one, and I was glad when I saw that it had succeeded. Gunga Dass changed his tone immediately, and disavowed all intention of asking for my boots. At the time it did not strike me as at all strange that I, a Civil Engineer, a man of thirteen years' standing in the Service, and, I trust, an average Englishman, should thus calmly threaten murder and violence against the man who had, for a consideration it is true, taken me under his wing. I had left the world, it seemed, for centuries. I was as certain then as I am now of my own existence, that in the accursed settlement there was no law save that of the strongest; that the living dead men had thrown behind them every canon of the world which had cast them out; and that I had to depend for my own life on my strength and vigilance alone. The crew of the ill-fated Mignonette are the only men who would understand my frame of mind. 'At present,' I argued to myself, 'I am strong and a match for six of these wretches. It is imperatively necessary that I should, for my own sake, keep both health and strength until the hour of my release comes – if it ever does.'

Fortified with these resolutions, I ate and drank as much as I could, and made Gunga Dass understand that I intended to be his master, and that the least sign of insubordination on his part would be visited with the only punishment I had it in my power to inflict – sudden and violent death. Shortly after this I went to bed. That is to say, Gunga Dass gave me a double armful of dried bents which I thrust down the mouth of the lair to the right of his, and followed myself, feet foremost; the hole running about nine feet into the sand with a slight downward inclination, and being neatly shored with timbers. From my den, which faced the river-front, I was able to watch the waters of the Sutlej flowing past under the light of a young moon and compose myself to sleep as best I might.

The horrors of that night I shall never forget. My den was nearly as narrow as a coffin, and the sides had been worn smooth and greasy by the contact of innumerable naked bodies, added to which it smelled abominably. Sleep was altogether out of the question to one in my excited frame of mind. As the night wore on, it seemed that the entire amphitheatre was filled with legions of unclean devils that, trooping up from the shoals below, mocked the unfortunates in their lairs.

Personally I am not of an imaginative temperament, – very few Engineers are, – but on that occasion I was as completely prostrated with nervous terror as any woman. After half an hour or so, however, I was able once more to calmly review my chances of escape. Any exit by the steep sand walls was, of course, impracticable. I had been thoroughly convinced of this some time before. It was possible, just possible, that I might, in the uncertain moonlight, safely run the gauntlet of the rifle shots. The place was so full of terror for me that I was prepared to undergo any risk in leaving it. Imagine my delight, then, when after creeping stealthily to the river-front I found that the infernal boat was not there. My freedom lay before me in the next few steps!

By walking out to the first shallow pool that lay at the foot of the projecting left horn of the horseshoe, I could wade across, turn the flank of the crater, and make my way inland. Without a moment's hesitation I marched briskly past the tussocks where Gunga Dass had snared the crows, and out in the direction of the smooth white sand beyond. My first step from the tufts of dried grass showed me how utterly futile was any hope of escape; for, as I put my foot down, I felt an indescribable drawing, sucking motion of the sand below. Another moment and my leg was swallowed up nearly to the knee. In the moonlight the whole surface of the sand seemed to be shaken with devilish delight at my disappointment. I struggled clear, sweating with terror and exertion, back to the tussocks behind me and fell on my face.

My only means of escape from the semicircle was protected with a quicksand!

How long I lay I have not the faintest idea; but I was roused at last by the malevolent chuckle of Gunga Dass at my ear 'I would advise you, Protector of the Poor' (the ruffian was speaking English) 'to return to your house. It is unhealthy to lie down here. Moreover, when the boat returns, you will most certainly be rifled at.' He stood over me in the dim light of the dawn, chuckling and laughing to himself. Suppressing my first impulse to catch the man by the neck and throw him on to the quicksand, I rose sullenly and followed him to the platform below the burrows.

Suddenly, and futilely as I thought while I spoke, I asked: 'Gunga Dass, what is the good of the boat if I can't get out anyhow?' I recollect that even in my deepest trouble I had been speculating vaguely on the waste of ammunition in guarding an already well protected fore-shore.

Gunga Dass laughed again and made answer: 'They have the boat only in daytime. It is for the reason that there is a way. I hope we shall have the pleasure of your company for much longer time. It is a pleasant spot when you have been here some years and eaten roast crow long enough.'

I staggered, numbed and helpless, toward the fetid burrow allotted to me, and fell asleep. An hour or so later I was awakened by a piercing scream – the shrill, high-pitched scream of a horse in pain. Those who have once heard that will never forget the sound. I found some little difficulty in scrambling out of the burrow. When I was in the open, I saw Pornic, my poor old Pornic, lying dead on the sandy soil. How they had killed him I cannot guess. Gunga Dass explained that horse was better than crow, and 'greatest good of greatest number is political maxim. We are now Republic, Mister Jukes, and you are entitled to a fair share of the beast. If you like, we will pass a vote of thanks. Shall I propose?'

Yes, we were a Republic indeed! A Republic of wild beasts penned at the bottom of a pit, to eat and fight and sleep till we died. I attempted no protest of any kind, but sat down and stared at the hideous sight in front of me. In less time almost than it takes me to write this, Pornic's body was divided, in some unclear way or other; the men and women had dragged the fragments on to the platform and were preparing their normal meal. Gunga Dass cooked mine. The almost irresistible impulse to fly at the sand walls until I was wearied laid hold of me afresh, and I had to struggle against it with all my might. Gunga Dass was offensively jocular till I told him that if he addressed another remark of any kind whatever to me I should strangle him where he sat. This silenced him till silence became insupportable, and I bade him say something.

'You will live here till you die like the other Feringhi,' he said, coolly, watching me over the fragment of gristle that he was gnawing.

'What other Sahib, you swine? Speak at once, and don't stop to tell me a lie.'

'He is over there,' answered Gunga Dass, pointing to a burrow-mouth about four doors to the left of my own. 'You can see for yourself. He died in the burrow as you will die, and I will die, and as all these men and women and the one child will also die.'

'For pity's sake tell me all you know about him. Who was he? When did he come, and when did he die?'

This appeal was a weak step on my part. Gunga Dass only leered and replied: 'I will not – unless you give me something first.'

Then I recollected where I was, and struck the man between the eyes, partially stunning him. He stepped down from the platform at once, and, cringing and fawning and weeping and attempting to embrace my feet, led me round to the burrow which he had indicated.

'I know nothing whatever about the gentleman. Your God be my witness that I do not. He was as anxious to escape as you were, and he was shot from the boat, though we all did all things to prevent him from attempting. He was shot here.' Gunga Dass laid his hand on his lean stomach and bowed to the earth.

'Well, and what then? Go on!'

'And then – and then, Your Honour, we carried him in to his house and gave him water, and put wet cloths on the wound, and he laid down in his house and gave up the ghost.'

'In how long? In how long?'

'About half an hour, after he received his wound. I call Vishnu to witness,' yelled the wretched man, 'that I did everything for him. Everything which was possible, that I did!'

He threw himself down on the ground and clasped my ankles. But I had my doubts about Gunga Dass's benevolence, and kicked him off as he lay protesting.

'I believe you robbed him of everything he had. But I can find out in a minute or two. How long was the Sahib here?'

'Nearly a year and a half. I think he must have gone

mad. But hear me swear Protector of the Poor! Won't Your Honour hear me swear that I never touched an article that belonged to him? What is Your Worship going to do?'

I had taken Gunga Dass by the waist and had hauled him on to the platform opposite the deserted burrow. As I did so I thought of my wretched fellow-prisoner's unspeakable misery among all these horrors for eighteen months, and the final agony of dying like a rat in a hole, with a bullet-wound in the stomach. Gunga Dass fancied I was going to kill him and howled pitifully. The rest of the population, in the plethora that follows a full flesh meal, watched us without stirring.

'Go inside, Gunga Dass,' said I, 'and fetch it out.'

I was feeling sick and faint with horror now. Gunga Dass nearly rolled off the platform and howled aloud.

'But I am Brahmin, Sahib — a high-caste Brahmin. By your soul, by your father's soul, do not make me do this thing!'

'Brahmin or no Brahmin, by my soul and my father's soul, in you go!' I said, and, seizing him by the shoulders, I crammed his head into the mouth of the burrow, kicked the rest of him in, and, sitting down, covered my face with my hands.

At the end of a few minutes I heard a rustle and a creak; then Gunga Dass in a sobbing, choking whisper speaking to himself; then a soft thud — and I uncovered my eyes.

The dry sand had turned the corpse entrusted to its keeping into a yellow-brown mummy. I told Gunga Dass to stand off while I examined it. The body — clad in an olive-green hunting-suit much stained and worn, with leather pads on the shoulders — was that of a man between thirty and forty, above middle height, with light, sandy hair, long mustache, and a rough unkempt beard. The left canine of the upper jaw was missing, and a portion of the lobe of the right ear was gone. On the second finger of the left hand was a ring – a shield-shaped bloodstone set in gold, with a monogram that might have been either 'B.K.' or 'B.L.' On the third finger of the right hand was a silver ring in the shape of a coiled cobra, much worn and tarnished. Gunga Dass deposited a handful of trifles he had picked out of the burrow at my feet, and, covering the face of the body with my handkerchief, I turned to examine these. I give the full list in the hope that it may lead to the identification of the unfortunate man:

1. Bowl of a briarwood pipe, serrated at the edge; much worn and blackened; bound with string at the crew.
2. Two patent-lever keys; wards of both broken.
3. Tortoise-shell-handled penknife, silver or nickel, name-plate, marked with monogram 'B.K.'
4. Envelope, postmark undecipherable, bearing a Victorian stamp, addressed to 'Miss Mon – ' (rest illegible) – 'ham' – 'nt.'
5. Imitation crocodile-skin notebook with pencil. First forty-five pages blank; four and a half illegible; fifteen others filled with private memoranda relating chiefly to three persons – a Mrs. L. Singleton, abbreviated several times to 'Lot Single,' 'Mrs. S. May,' and 'Garmison,' referred to in places as 'Jerry' or 'Jack.'
6. Handle of small-sized hunting-knife. Blade snapped short. Buck's horn, diamond cut, with swivel and ring on the butt; fragment of cotton cord attached.

It must not be supposed that I inventoried all these things on the spot as fully as I have here written them down. The notebook first attracted my attention, and I put it in my pocket with a view of studying it later on.

The rest of the articles I conveyed to my burrow for safety's sake, and there being a methodical man, I inventoried them. I then returned to the corpse and ordered Gunga Dass to help me to carry it out to the river-front. While we were engaged in this, the exploded shell of an old brown cartridge dropped out of one of the pockets and rolled at my feet. Gunga Dass had not seen it; and I fell to thinking that a man does not carry exploded cartridge-cases, especially 'browns,' which will not bear loading twice, about with him when shooting. In other words, that cartridge-case had been fired inside the crater. Consequently there must be a gun somewhere. I was on the verge of asking Gunga Dass, but checked myself, knowing that he would lie. We laid the body down on the edge of the quicksand by the tussocks. It was my intention to push it out and let it be swallowed up – the only possible mode of burial that I could think of. I ordered Gunga Dass to go away.

Then I gingerly put the corpse out on the quicksand. In doing so, it was lying face downward, I tore the frail and rotten khaki shooting-coat open, disclosing a hideous cavity in the back. I have already told you that the dry sand had, as it were, mummified the body. A moment's glance showed that the gaping hole had been caused by a gun-shot wound; the gun must have been fired with the muzzle almost touching the back. The shooting-coat, being intact, had been drawn over the body after death, which must have been instantaneous. The secret of the poor wretch's death was plain to me in a flash. Someone of the crater, presumably Gunga Dass, must have shot him with his own gun – the gun that fitted the brown cartridges. He had never attempted to escape in the face of the rifle-fire from the boat.

I pushed the corpse out hastily, and saw it sink from sight literally in a few seconds. I shuddered as I watched. In a dazed, half-conscious way I turned to peruse the notebook. A stained and discolored slip of paper had been inserted between the binding and the back, and dropped out as I opened the pages. This is what it contained: 'Four out from crow-clump: three left; nine out; two right; three back; two left; fourteen out; two left; seven out; one left; nine back; two right; six back; four right; seven back.' The paper had been burned and charred at the edges. What it meant I could not understand. I sat down on the dried bents turning it over and over between my fingers, until I was aware of Gunga Dass standing immediately behind me with glowing eyes and outstretched hands.

'Have you got it?' he panted. 'Will you not let me look at it also? I swear that I will return it.'

'Got what? Return what?' asked.

'That which you have in your hands. It will help us both.' He stretched out his long, bird-like talons, trembling with eagerness.

'I could never find it,' he continued. 'He had secreted it about his person. Therefore I shot him, but nevertheless I was unable to obtain it.'

Gunga Dass had quite forgotten his little fiction about the rifle-bullet. I received the information perfectly calmly.

Morality is blunted by consorting with the Dead who are alive.

'What on earth are you raving about? What is it you want me to give you?'

'The piece of paper in the notebook. It will help us both. Oh, you fool! You fool! Can you not see what it will do for us? We shall escape!'

His voice rose almost to a scream, and he danced with excitement before me. I own I was moved at the chance of my getting away.

'Don't skip! Explain yourself. Do you mean to say that this slip of paper will help us? What does it mean?'

'Read it aloud! Read it aloud! I beg and I pray you to read it aloud.'

I did so. Gunga Dass listened delightedly, and drew an irregular line in the sand with his fingers.

'See now! It was the length of his gun-barrels without the stock. I have those barrels. Four gun-barrels out from the place where I caught crows. Straight out; do you follow me? Then three left. Ah! how well I remember when that man worked it out night after night. Then nine out, and so on. Out is always straight before you across the quicksand. He told me so before I killed him.'

'But if you knew all this why didn't you get out before?'

'I did not know it. He told me that he was working it out a year and a half ago, and how he was working it out night after night when the boat had gone away, and he could get out near the quicksand safely. Then he said that we would get away together. But I was afraid that he would leave me behind one night when he had worked it all out, and so I shot him. Besides, it is not advisable that the men who once get in here should escape. Only I, and I am a Brahmin.'

The prospect of escape had brought Gunga Dass's caste back to him. He stood up, walked about and gesticulated violently. Eventually I managed to make him talk soberly, and he told me how this Englishman had spent six months night after night in exploring, inch by inch, the passage across the quicksand; how he had declared it to be simplicity itself up to within about twenty yards of the river bank after turning the flank of the left horn of the horseshoe. This much he had evidently not completed when Gunga Dass shot him with his own gun.

In my frenzy of delight at the possibilities of escape I recollect shaking hands effusively with Gunga Dass, after we had decided that we were to make an attempt to get away that very night. It was weary work waiting throughout the afternoon.

About ten o'clock, as far as I could judge, when the Moon had just risen above the lip of the crater, Gunga Dass made a move for his burrow to bring out the gun-barrels whereby to measure our path. All the other wretched inhabitants had retired to their lairs long ago. The guardian boat drifted downstream some hours before, and we were utterly alone by the crow-clump. Gunga Dass, while carrying the gun-barrels, let slip the piece of paper which was to be our guide. I stooped down hastily to recover it, and, as I did so, I was aware that the diabolical Brahmin was aiming a violent blow at the back of my head with the gun-barrels. It was too late to turn round. I must have received the blow somewhere on the nape of my neck. A hundred thousand fiery stars danced before my eyes, and I fell forwards senseless at the edge of, the quicksand.

When I recovered consciousness, the Moon was going down, and I was sensible of intolerable pain in the back of my head. Gunga Dass had disappeared and my mouth was full of blood. I lay down again and prayed that I might die without more ado. Then the unreasoning fury which I had before mentioned, laid hold upon me, and I staggered inland toward the walls of the crater. It seemed that some one was calling to me in a whisper – 'Sahib! Sahib! Sahib!' exactly as my bearer used to call me in the morning I fancied that I was delirious until a handful of sand fell at my feet. Then I looked up and saw a head peering down into the amphitheatre – the head of Dunnoo, my dog-boy, who attended to my collies. As soon as he had attracted my attention, he held up his hand and showed a rope. I motioned, staggering to and fro for the while, that he should throw it down. It was a couple of leather punkah-ropes knotted together, with a loop at one end. I slipped the loop over my head and under my arms; heard Dunnoo urge something forward; was conscious that I was being dragged, face downward, up the steep sand slope, and the next instant found myself choked and half fainting on the sand hills overlooking the crater. Dunnoo, with his face ashy grey in the moon-light, implored me not to stay but to get back to my tent at once.

It seems that he had tracked Pornic's footprints fourteen miles across the sands to the crater; had returned and told my servants, who flatly refused to meddle with any one, white or black, once fallen into the hideous Village of the Dead; whereupon Dunnoo had taken one of my ponies and a couple of punkah-ropes, returned to the crater, and hauled me out as I have described.

To cut a long story short, Dunnoo is now my personal servant on a gold mohur a month – a sum which I still think far too little for the services he has rendered. Nothing on earth will induce me to go near that devilish spot again, or to reveal its whereabouts more clearly than I have done. Of Gunga Dass I have never found a trace, nor do I wish to do. My sole motive in giving this to be published is the hope that someone may possibly identify, from the details and the inventory which I have given above, the corpse of the man in the olive-green hunting-suit.

AT THE
END OF THE
PASSAGE

The sky is lead and our faces are red,
And the gates of Hell are opened and riven,
And the winds of Hell are loosened and driven,
And the dust flies up in the face of Heaven,
And the clouds come down in a fiery sheet,
Heavy to raise and hard to be borne.
And the soul of man is turned from his meat,
Turned from the trifles for which he has striven
Sick in his body, and heavy hearted,
And his soul flies up like the dust in the sheet
Breaks from his flesh and is gone and departed,
As the blasts they blow on the cholera-horn.

                                        HIMALAYAN.

FOUR MEN, EACH ENTITLED TO 'LIFE, liberty, and the pursuit of happiness,' sat at a table playing whist. The thermometer marked – for them – one hundred and one degrees of heat. The room was darkened till it was only just possible to distinguish the pips of the cards and the very white faces of the players. A tattered, rotten punkah of whitewashed calico was puddling the hot air and whining dolefully at each stroke. Outside lay gloom of a November day in London. There was neither sky, sun, nor horizon, – nothing but a brown purple haze of heat. It was as though the earth were dying of apoplexy.

From time to time clouds of tawny dust rose from the ground without wind or warning, flung themselves tablecloth-wise among the tops of the parched trees, and came down again. Then a whirling dust-devil would scutter across the plain for a couple of miles, break, and fall outward, though there was nothing to check its flight save a long low line of piled railway-sleepers white with the dust, a cluster of huts made of mud, condemned rails, and canvas, and the one squat four-roomed bungalow that belonged to the assistant engineer in charge of a section of the Gaudhari State line then under construction.

The four, stripped to the thinnest of sleeping-suits, played whist crossly, with wranglings as to leads and returns. It was not the best kind of whist, but they had taken some trouble to arrive at it. Mottram of the Indian Survey had ridden thirty and railed one hundred miles from his lonely post in the desert since the night before; Lowndes of the Civil Service, on special duty in the political department, had come as far to escape for an instant the miserable intrigues of an impoverished native State whose king alternately fawned and blustered for more money from the pitiful revenues contributed by hard-wrung peasants and despairing camel-breeders; Spurstow, the doctor of the line, had left a cholera-stricken camp of coolies to look after itself for forty-eight hours while he associated with white men once more. Hummil, the assistant engineer, was the host. He stood fast and received his friends thus every Sunday if they could come in. When one of them failed to appear, he would send a telegram to his last address, in order that he might know whether the defaulter were dead or alive. There are very many places in the East where it is not good or kind to let your acquaintances drop out of sight even for one short week.

The players were not conscious of any special regard for each other. They squabbled whenever they met; but they ardently desired to meet, as men without water desire to drink. They were lonely folk who understood the dread meaning of loneliness. They were all under thirty years of age, – which is too soon for any man to possess that knowledge.

'Pilsener?' said Spurstow, after the second rubber, mopping his forehead.

'Beer's out, I'm sorry to say, and there's hardly enough soda-water for to-night,' said Hummil.

'What filthy bad management!' Spurstow snarled.

'Can't help it. I've written and wired; but the trains don't come through regularly yet. Last week the ice ran out, – as Lowndes knows.'

'Glad I didn't come. I could ha' sent you some if I had

known, though. Phew! it's too hot to go on playing bumblepuppy.' This with a savage scowl at Lowndes, who only laughed. He was a hardened offender.

Mottram rose from the table and looked out of a chink in the shutters.

'What a sweet day!' said he.

The company yawned all together and betook themselves to an aimless investigation of all Hummil's possessions, – guns, tattered novels, saddlery, spurs, and the like. They had fingered them a score of times before, but there was really nothing else to do.

'Got anything fresh?' said Lowndes.

'Last week's Gazette of India, and a cutting from a home paper. My father sent it out. It's rather amusing.'

'One of those vestrymen that call 'emselves M.P.'s again, is it?' said Spurstow, who read his newspapers when he could get them.

'Yes. Listen to this. It's to your address, Lowndes. The man was making a speech to his constituents, and he piled it on. Here's a sample: 'And I assert unhesitatingly that the Civil Service in India is the preserve – the pet preserve – of the aristocracy of England. What does the democracy – what do the masses – get from that country, which we have step by step fraudulently annexed? I answer, nothing whatever. It is farmed with a single eye to their own interests by the scions of the aristocracy. They take good care to maintain their lavish scale of incomes, to avoid or stifle any inquiries into the nature and conduct of their administration, while they themselves force the unhappy peasant to pay with the sweat of his brow for all the luxuries in which they are lapped." Hummil waved the cutting above his head. "Ear! 'ear!' said his audience.

Then Lowndes, meditatively: 'I'd give – I'd give three months' pay to have that gentleman spend one month with me and see how the free and independent native prince works things. Old Timbersides' – this was his flippant title for an honoured and decorated feudatory prince – 'has been wearing my life out this week past for money. By Jove, his latest performance was to send me one of his women as a bribe!'

'Good for you! Did you accept it?' said Mottram.

'No. I rather wish I had, now. She was a pretty little person, and she yarned away to me about the horrible destitution among the king's women-folk. The darlings haven't had any new clothes for nearly a month, and the old man wants to buy a new drag from Calcutta, – solid silver railings and silver lamps, and trifles of that kind. I've tried to make him understand that he has played the deuce with the revenues for the last twenty years and must go slow. He can't see it.'

'But he has the ancestral treasure-vaults to draw on. There must be three millions at least in jewels and coin under his palace,' said Hummil.

'Catch a native king disturbing the family treasure! The priests forbid it except as the last resort. Old Timbersides has added something like a quarter of a million to the deposit in his reign.'

'Where the mischief does it all come from?' said Mottram.

'The country. The state of the people is enough to make you sick. I've known the tax-men wait by a milch-camel till the foal was born and then hurry off the mother for arrears. And what can I do? I can't get the court clerks to give me any accounts; I can't raise anything more than a fat smile from the commander-in-chief when I find out the troops are three months in arrears; and old Timbersides begins to weep when I speak to him. He has taken to the King's Peg heavily, – liqueur brandy for whisky, and Heidsieck for soda-water.'

'That's what the Rao of Jubela took to. Even a native can't last long at that,' said Spurstow. 'He'll go out.'

'And a good thing, too. Then I suppose we'll have a council of regency, and a tutor for the young prince, and hand him back his kingdom with ten years' accumulations.'

'Whereupon that young prince, having been taught all the vices of the English, will play ducks and drakes with the money and undo ten years' work in eighteen months. I've seen that business before,' said Spurstow. 'I should tackle the king with a light hand, if I were you, Lowndes. They'll hate you quite enough under any circumstances.'

'That's all very well. The man who looks on can talk about the light hand; but you can't clean a pig-stye with a pen dipped in rose-water. I know my risks; but nothing has happened yet. My servant's an old Pathan, and he cooks for me. They are hardly likely to bribe him, and I don't accept food from my true friends, as they call themselves. Oh, but it's weary work! I'd sooner be with you, Spurstow. There's shooting near your camp.'

'Would you? I don't think it. About fifteen deaths a day don't incite a man to shoot anything but himself. And the worst of it is that the poor devils look at you as though you ought to save them. Lord knows, I've tried everything. My last attempt was empirical, but it pulled an old man through. He was brought to me apparently past hope, and I gave him gin and Worcester sauce with cayenne. It cured him; but I don't recommend it.'

'How do the cases run generally?' said Hummil.

'Very simply indeed. Chlorodyne, opium pill, chlorodyne, collapse, nitre, bricks to the feet, and then – the burning-ghat. The last seems to be the only thing that stops the trouble. It's black cholera, you know. Poor devils! But, I will say, little Bunsee Lal, my apothecary, works like a demon. I've recommended him for promotion if he comes through it all alive.'

'And what are your chances, old man?' said Mottram.

'Don't know; don't care much; but I've sent the letter in. What are you doing with yourself generally?'

'Sitting under a table in the tent and spitting on the sextant to keep it cool,' said the man of the survey. 'Washing my eyes to avoid ophthalmia, which I shall certainly get, and trying to make a sub-surveyor understand that an error of five degrees in an angle isn't quite so small as it looks. I'm altogether alone, y' know, and shall be till the end of the hot weather.'

'Hummil's the lucky man,' said Lowndes, flinging himself into a long chair. 'He has an actual roof – torn as to the ceiling-cloth, but still a roof – over his head. He sees one train daily. He can get beer and soda-water and ice 'em when God is good. He has books, pictures, – they were torn from the Graphic, – 'and the society of the excellent sub-contractor Jevins, besides the pleasure of receiving us weekly.'

Hummil smiled grimly. 'Yes, I'm the lucky man, I suppose. Jevins is luckier.'

'How? Not – '

'Yes. Went out. Last Monday.'

'By his own hand?' said Spurstow quickly, hinting the suspicion that was in everybody's mind. There was no cholera near Hummil's section. Even fever gives a man at least a week's grace, and sudden death generally implied self-slaughter.

'I judge no man this weather,' said Hummil. 'He had a touch of the sun, I fancy; for last week, after you fellows had left, he came into the verandah and told me that he was going home to see his wife, in Market Street, Liverpool, that evening.

'I got the apothecary in to look at him, and we tried to make him lie down. After an hour or two he rubbed his eyes and said he believed he had had a fit, – hoped he hadn't said anything rude. Jevins had a great idea of bettering himself socially. He was very like Chucks in his language.'

'Well?'

'Then he went to his own bungalow and began cleaning a rifle. He told the servant that he was going to shoot buck in the morning. Naturally he fumbled with the trigger, and shot himself through the head – accidentally. The apothecary sent in a report to my chief, and Jevins is buried somewhere out there. I'd have wired to you, Spurstow, if you could have done anything.'

'You're a queer chap,' said Mottram. 'If you'd killed the man yourself you couldn't have been more quiet about the business.'

'Good Lord! what does it matter?' said Hummil calmly. 'I've got to do a lot of his overseeing work in addition to my own. I'm the only person that suffers. Jevins is out of it, – by pure accident, of course, but out of it. The apothecary was going to write a long screed on suicide. Trust a babu to drivel when he gets the chance.'

'Why didn't you let it go in as suicide?' said Lowndes.

'No direct proof. A man hasn't many privileges in this country, but he might at least be allowed to mishandle his own rifle. Besides, some day I may need a man to smother up an accident to myself. Live and let live. Die and let die.'

'You take a pill,' said Spurstow, who had been watching Hummil's white face narrowly. 'Take a pill, and don't be an ass. That sort of talk is skittles. Anyhow, suicide is shirking your work. If I were Job ten times over, I should be so interested in what was going to happen next that I'd stay on and watch.'

'Ah! I've lost that curiosity,' said Hummil.

'Liver out of order?' said Lowndes feelingly.

'No. Can't sleep. That's worse.'

'By Jove, it is!' said Mottram. 'I'm that way every now and then, and the fit has to wear itself out. What do you take for it?'

'Nothing. What's the use? I haven't had ten minutes' sleep since Friday morning.'

'Poor chap! Spurstow, you ought to attend to this,' said Mottram. 'Now you mention it, your eyes are rather gummy and swollen.'

Spurstow, still watching Hummil, laughed lightly. 'I'll patch him up, later on. Is it too hot, do you think, to go for a ride?'

'Where to?' said Lowndes wearily. 'We shall have to go

away at eight, and there'll be riding enough for us then. I hate a horse, when I have to use him as a necessity. Oh, heavens! what is there to do?'

'Begin whist again, at chick points ['a chick' is supposed to be eight shillings] and a gold mohur on the rub,' said Spurstow promptly.

'Poker. A month's pay all round for the pool, – no limit, – and fifty-rupee raises. Somebody would be broken before we got up,' said Lowndes.

'Can't say that it would give me any pleasure to break any man in this company,' said Mottram. 'There isn't enough excitement in it, and it's foolish.' He crossed over to the worn and battered little camp-piano, – wreckage of a married household that had once held the bungalow, – and opened the case.

'It's used up long ago,' said Hummil. 'The servants have picked it to pieces.'

The piano was indeed hopelessly out of order, but Mottram managed to bring the rebellious notes into a sort of agreement, and there rose from the ragged keyboard something that might once have been the ghost of a popular music-hall song. The men in the long chairs turned with evident interest as Mottram banged the more lustily.

'That's good!' said Lowndes. 'By Jove! the last time I heard that song was in '79, or thereabouts, just before I came out.'

'Ah!' said Spurstow with pride,' I was home in '80.' And he mentioned a song of the streets popular at that date.

Mottram executed it roughly. Lowndes criticised and

volunteered emendations. Mottram dashed into another ditty, not of the music-hall character, and made as if to rise.

'Sit down,' said Hummil. 'I didn't know that you had any music in your composition. Go on playing until you can't think of anything more. I'll have that piano tuned up before you come again. Play something festive.'

Very simple indeed were the tunes to which Mottram's art and the limitations of the piano could give effect, but the men listened with pleasure, and in the pauses talked all together of what they had seen or heard when they were last at home. A dense dust-storm sprung up outside, and swept roaring over the house, enveloping it in the choking darkness of midnight, but Mottram continued unheeding, and the crazy tinkle reached the ears of the listeners above the flapping of the tattered ceiling-cloth.

In the silence after the storm he glided from the more directly personal songs of Scotland, half humming them as he played, into the Evening Hymn.

'Sunday,' said he, nodding his head.

'Go on. Don't apologise for it,' said Spurstow.

Hummil laughed long and riotously. 'Play it, by all means. You're full of surprises to-day. I didn't know you had such a gift of finished sarcasm. How does that thing go?'

Mottram took up the tune.

'Too slow by half. You miss the note of gratitude,' said Hummil. 'It ought to go to the 'Grasshopper's Polka,' – this way.' And he chanted, prestissimo, –

'Glory to thee, my God, this night. For all the blessings of the light.

That shows we really feel our blessings. How does it go on? –

'If in the night I sleepless lie, My soul with sacred thoughts supply; May no ill dreams disturb my rest.' –

Quicker, Mottram! –

'Or powers of darkness me molest!'

'Bah! what an old hypocrite you are!'

'Don't be an ass,' said Lowndes. 'You are at full liberty to make fun of anything else you like, but leave that hymn alone. It's associated in my mind with the most sacred recollections –'

'Summer evenings in the country, – stained-glass window, – light going out, and you and she jamming your heads together over one hymn-book,' said Mottram.

'Yes, and a fat old cockchafer hitting you in the eye when you walked home. Smell of hay, and a moon as big as a bandbox sitting on the top of a haycock; bats, – roses, – milk and midges,' said Lowndes.

'Also mothers. I can just recollect my mother singing me to sleep with that when I was a little chap,' said Spurstow.

The darkness had fallen on the room. They could hear Hummil squirming in his chair.

'Consequently,' said he testily, 'you sing it when you are seven fathom deep in Hell! It's an insult to the intelligence of the Deity to pretend we're anything but tortured rebels.'

'Take *two* pills,' said Spurstow; 'that's tortured liver.'

'The usually placid Hummil is in a vile bad temper. I'm sorry for his coolies to-morrow,' said Lowndes, as the servants brought in the lights and prepared the table for dinner.

As they were settling into their places about the miserable goat-chops, and the smoked tapioca pudding, Spurstow took occasion to whisper to Mottram, 'Well done, David!'

'Look after Saul, then,' was the reply.

'What are you two whispering about?' said Hummil suspiciously.

'Only saying that you are a damned poor host. This fowl can't be cut,' returned Spurstow with a sweet smile. 'Call this a dinner?'

'I can't help it. You don't expect a banquet, do you?'

Throughout that meal Hummil contrived laboriously to insult directly and pointedly all his guests in succession, and at each insult Spurstow kicked the aggrieved persons under the table; but he dared not exchange a glance of intelligence with either of them. Hummil's face was white and pinched, while his eyes were unnaturally large. No man dreamed for a moment of resenting his savage personalities, but as soon as the meal was over they made haste to get away. 'Don't go. You're just getting amusing, you fellows. I hope I haven't said anything that annoyed you. You're such touchy devils.' Then, changing the note into one of almost abject entreaty, Hummil added, 'I say, you surely aren't going?'

'In the language of the blessed Jorrocks, where I dines I sleeps,' said Spurstow. 'I want to have a look at your coolies to-morrow, if you don't mind. You can give me a place to lie down in, I suppose?'

The others pleaded the urgency of their several duties next day, and, saddling up, departed together, Hummil begging them to come next Sunday. As they jogged off, Lowndes unbosomed himself to Mottram –

'... And I never felt so like kicking a man at his own table in my life. He said I cheated at whist, and reminded me I was in debt! 'Told you you were as good as a liar to your face! You aren't half indignant enough over it.'

'Not I,' said Mottram. 'Poor devil! Did you ever know old Hummy behave like that before or within a hundred miles of it?'

'That's no excuse. Spurstow was hacking my shin all the time, so I kept a hand on myself. Else I should have – '

'No, you wouldn't. You'd have done as Hummy did about Jevins; judge no man this weather. By Jove! the buckle of my bridle is hot in my hand! Trot out a bit, and 'ware rat-holes.'

Ten minutes' trotting jerked out of Lowndes one very sage remark when he pulled up, sweating from every pore –

"Good thing Spurstow's with him to-night.'

'Ye-es. Good man, Spurstow. Our roads turn here. See you again next Sunday, if the sun doesn't bowl me over.'

'S'pose so, unless old Timbersides' finance minister manages to dress some of my food. Good-night, and – God bless you!'

'What's wrong now?'

'Oh, nothing.' Lowndes gathered up his whip, and, as he flicked Mottram's mare on the flank, added, 'You're not a bad little chap, – that's all.' And the mare bolted half a mile across the sand, on the word.

In the assistant engineer's bungalow Spurstow and Hummil smoked the pipe of silence together, each narrowly watching the other. The capacity of a bachelor's establishment is as elastic as its arrangements are simple. A servant cleared away the dining-room table, brought in a couple of rude native bedsteads made of tape strung on a light wood frame, flung a square of cool Calcutta matting over each, set them side by side, pinned two towels to the punkah so that their fringes should just sweep clear of the sleepers' nose and mouth, and announced that the couches were ready.

The men flung themselves down, ordering the punkah-coolies by all the powers of Hell to pull. Every door and window was shut, for the outside air was that of an oven. The atmosphere within was only 104 degrees, as the thermometer bore witness, and heavy with the foul smell of badly-trimmed kerosene lamps; and this stench, combined with that of native tobacco, baked brick, and dried earth, sends the heart of many a strong man down to his boots, for it is the smell of the Great Indian Empire when she turns herself for six months into a house of torment. Spurstow packed his pillows craftily so that he reclined rather than lay, his head at a safe elevation above his feet. It is not good to sleep on a low pillow in the hot weather if you happen to be of thick-necked build, for you may pass with lively snores and gugglings from natural sleep into the deep slumber of heat-apoplexy.

'Pack your pillows,' said the doctor sharply, as he saw Hummil preparing to lie down at full length.

The night-light was trimmed; the shadow of the punkah wavered across the room, and the 'flick' of the punkah-towel and the soft whine of the rope through the wall-hole followed it. Then the punkah flagged, almost ceased. The sweat poured from Spurstow's brow. Should he go out and harangue the coolie? It started forward again with a savage jerk, and a pin came out of the towels. When this was replaced, a tomtom in the coolie-lines began to beat with the steady throb of a swollen artery inside some brain-fevered skull. Spurstow turned on his side and swore gently. There was no movement on Hummil's part. The man had composed himself as rigidly as a corpse, his hands clinched at his sides. The respiration was too hurried for any suspicion of sleep. Spurstow looked at the set face. The jaws were clinched, and there was a pucker round the quivering eyelids.

'He's holding himself as tightly as ever he can,' thought Spurstow. 'What in the world is the matter with him? – Hummil!'

'Yes,' in a thick constrained voice.

'Can't you get to sleep?'

'No.'

'Head hot? 'Throat feeling bulgy? or how?'

'Neither, thanks. I don't sleep much, you know.'

'Feel pretty bad?'

'Pretty bad, thanks. There is a tomtom outside, isn't there? I thought it was my head at first.... Oh, Spurstow, for pity's sake give me something that will put me asleep, – sound asleep, – if it's only for six hours!' He sprang up, trembling from head to foot. 'I haven't been able to sleep naturally for days, and I can't stand it! – I can't stand it!'

'Poor old chap!'

'That's no use. Give me something to make me sleep. I tell you I'm nearly mad. I don't know what I say half my time. For three weeks I've had to think and spell out every word that has come through my lips before I dared say it. Isn't that enough to drive a man mad? I can't see things correctly now, and I've lost my sense of touch. My skin aches – my skin aches! Make me sleep. Oh, Spurstow, for the love of God make me sleep sound. It isn't enough merely to let me dream. Let me sleep!'

'All right, old man, all right. Go slow; you aren't half as bad as you think.'

The flood-gates of reserve once broken, Hummil was clinging to him like a frightened child. 'You're pinching my arm to pieces.'

'I'll break your neck if you don't do something for me. No, I didn't mean that. Don't be angry, old fellow.' He wiped the sweat off himself as he fought to regain composure. 'I'm a bit restless and off my oats, and perhaps you could recommend some sort of sleeping mixture, – bromide of potassium.'

'Bromide of skittles! Why didn't you tell me this before? Let go of my arm, and I'll see if there's anything in my cigarette-case to suit your complaint.' Spurstow hunted among his day-clothes, turned up the lamp, opened a little silver cigarette-case, and advanced on the expectant Hummil with the daintiest of fairy squirts.

'The last appeal of civilisation,' said he, 'and a thing I hate to use. Hold out your arm. Well, your sleeplessness hasn't ruined your muscle; and what a thick hide it is! Might as well inject a buffalo subcutaneously. Now in a few minutes the morphia will begin working. Lie down and wait.'

A smile of unalloyed and idiotic delight began to creep over Hummil's face. 'I think,' he whispered, – 'I think I'm going off now. Gad! it's positively heavenly! Spurstow, you must give me that case to keep; you – ' The voice ceased as the head fell back.

'Not for a good deal,' said Spurstow to the unconscious form. 'And now, my friend, sleeplessness of your kind being very apt to relax the moral fibre in little matters of life and death, I'll just take the liberty of spiking your guns.'

He paddled into Hummil's saddle-room in his bare feet and uncased a twelve-bore rifle, an express, and a revolver. Of the first he unscrewed the nipples and hid them in the bottom of a saddlery-case; of the second he abstracted the lever, kicking it behind a big wardrobe. The third he merely opened, and knocked the doll-head bolt of the grip up with the heel of a riding-boot.

'That's settled,' he said, as he shook the sweat off his hands. 'These little precautions will at least give you time to turn. You have too much sympathy with gun-room accidents.'

And as he rose from his knees, the thick muffled voice of Hummil cried in the doorway, 'You fool!'

Such tones they use who speak in the lucid intervals of delirium to their friends a little before they die.

Spurstow started, dropping the pistol. Hummil stood in the doorway, rocking with helpless laughter.

'That was awf'ly good of you, I'm sure,' he said, very slowly, feeling for his words. 'I don't intend to go out by my own hand at present. I say, Spurstow, that stuff won't work. What shall I do? What shall I do?' And panic terror stood in his eyes.

'Lie down and give it a chance. Lie down at once.'

'I daren't. It will only take me half-way again, and I

shan't be able to get away this time. Do you know it was all I could do to come out just now? Generally I am as quick as lightning; but you had clogged my feet. I was nearly caught.'

'Oh yes, I understand. Go and lie down.'

'No, it isn't delirium; but it was an awfully mean trick to play on me. Do you know I might have died?'

As a sponge rubs a slate clean, so some power unknown to Spurstow had wiped out of Hummil's face all that stamped it for the face of a man, and he stood at the doorway in the expression of his lost innocence. He had slept back into terrified childhood.

'Is he going to die on the spot?' thought Spurstow. Then, aloud, 'All right, my son. Come back to bed, and tell me all about it. You couldn't sleep; but what was all the rest of the nonsense?'

'A place, – a place down there,' said Hummil, with simple sincerity. The drug was acting on him by waves, and he was flung from the fear of a strong man to the fright of a child as his nerves gathered sense or were dulled.

'Good God! I've been afraid of it for months past, Spurstow. It has made every night hell to me; and yet I'm not conscious of having done anything wrong.'

'Be still, and I'll give you another dose. We'll stop your nightmares, you unutterable idiot!'

'Yes, but you must give me so much that I can't get away. You must make me quite sleepy, – not just a little sleepy. It's so hard to run then.'

'I know it; I know it. I've felt it myself. The symptoms are exactly as you describe.'

'Oh, don't laugh at me, confound you! Before this awful sleeplessness came to me I've tried to rest on my elbow and put a spur in the bed to sting me when I fell back. Look!'

'By Jove! the man has been rowelled like a horse! Ridden by the nightmare with a vengeance! And we all thought him sensible enough. Heaven send us understanding! You like to talk, don't you?'

'Yes, sometimes. Not when I'm frightened. *Then* I want to run. Don't you?'

'Always. Before I give you your second dose try to tell me exactly what your trouble is.'

Hummil spoke in broken whispers for nearly ten minutes, whilst Spurstow looked into the pupils of his eyes and passed his hand before them once or twice.

At the end of the narrative the silver cigarette-case was produced, and the last words that Hummil said as he fell back for the second time were, 'Put me quite to sleep; for if I'm caught I die, – I die!'

'Yes, yes; we all do that sooner or later, – thank Heaven who has set a term to our miseries,' said Spurstow, settling the cushions under the head. 'It occurs to me that unless I drink something I shall go out before my time. I've stopped sweating, and – I wear a seventeen-inch collar.' He brewed himself scalding hot tea, which is an excellent remedy against heat-apoplexy if you take three or four cups of it in time. Then he watched the sleeper.

'A blind face that cries and can't wipe its eyes, a blind face that chases him down corridors! H'm! Decidedly, Hummil ought to go on leave as soon as possible; and, sane or otherwise, he undoubtedly did rowel himself most cruelly. Well, Heaven send us understanding!'

At mid-day Hummil rose, with an evil taste in his mouth, but an unclouded eye and a joyful heart.

'I was pretty bad last night, wasn't I?' said he.

'I have seen healthier men. You must have had a touch of the sun. Look here: if I write you a swingeing medical certificate, will you apply for leave on the spot?'

'No.'

'Why not? You want it.'

'Yes, but I can hold on till the weather's a little cooler.'

'Why should you, if you can get relieved on the spot?'

'Burkett is the only man who could be sent; and he's a born fool.'

'Oh, never mind about the line. You aren't so important as all that. Wire for leave, if necessary.'

Hummil looked very uncomfortable.

'I can hold on till the Rains,' he said evasively.

'You can't. Wire to headquarters for Burkett.'

'I won't. If you want to know why, particularly, Burkett is married, and his wife's just had a kid, and she's up at Simla, in the cool, and Burkett has a very nice billet that takes him into Simla from Saturday to Monday. That little woman isn't at all well. If Burkett was transferred she'd try to follow him. If she left the baby behind she'd fret herself to death. If she came, – and Burkett's one of those selfish little beasts who are always talking about a wife's place being with her husband, – she'd die. It's murder to bring a woman here just now. Burkett hasn't the physique of a rat. If he came here he'd go out; and I know she hasn't any money, and I'm pretty sure she'd go out too.

I'm salted in a sort of way, and I'm not married. Wait till the Rains, and then Burkett can get thin down here. It'll do him heaps of good.'

'Do you mean to say that you intend to face – what you have faced, till the Rains break?'

'Oh, it won't be so bad, now you've shown me a way out of it. I can always wire to you. Besides, now I've once got into the way of sleeping, it'll be all right. Anyhow, I shan't put in for leave. That's the long and the short of it.'

'My great Scott! I thought all that sort of thing was dead and done with.'

'Bosh! You'd do the same yourself. I feel a new man, thanks to that cigarette-case. You're going over to camp now, aren't you?'

'Yes; but I'll try to look you up every other day, if I can.'

'I'm not bad enough for that. I don't want you to bother. Give the coolies gin and ketchup.'

'Then you feel all right?'

'Fit to fight for my life, but not to stand out in the sun talking to you. Go along, old man, and bless you!'

Hummil turned on his heel to face the echoing desolation of his bungalow, and the first thing he saw standing in the verandah was the figure of himself. He had met a similar apparition once before, when he was suffering from overwork and the strain of the hot weather.

'This is bad, – already,' he said, rubbing his eyes. 'If the thing slides away from me all in one piece, like a ghost, I shall know it is only my eyes and stomach that are out of order. If it walks – my head is going.'

He approached the figure, which naturally kept at an

unvarying distance from him, as is the use of all spectres that are born of overwork. It slid through the house and dissolved into swimming specks within the eyeball as soon as it reached the burning light of the garden. Hummil went about his business till even. When he came in to dinner he found himself sitting at the table. The vision rose and walked out hastily. Except that it cast no shadow it was in all respects real.

No living man knows what that week held for Hummil. An increase of the epidemic kept Spurstow in camp among the coolies, and all he could do was to telegraph to Mottram, bidding him go to the bungalow and sleep there. But Mottram was forty miles away from the nearest telegraph, and knew nothing of anything save the needs of the survey till he met, early on Sunday morning, Lowndes and Spurstow heading towards Hummil's for the weekly gathering.

'Hope the poor chap's in a better temper,' said the former, swinging himself off his horse at the door. 'I suppose he isn't up yet.'

'I'll just have a look at him,' said the doctor. 'If he's asleep there's no need to wake him.'

And an instant later, by the tone of Spurstow's voice calling upon them to enter, the men knew what had happened. There was no need to wake him.

The punkah was still being pulled over the bed, but Hummil had departed this life at least three hours.

The body lay on its back, hands clinched by the side, as Spurstow had seen it lying seven nights previously. In the staring eyes was written terror beyond the expression of any pen.

Mottram, who had entered behind Lowndes, bent over the dead and touched the forehead lightly with his lips. 'Oh, you lucky, lucky devil!' he whispered.

But Lowndes had seen the eyes, and withdrew shuddering to the other side of the room.

'Poor chap! poor old chap! And the last time I met him I was angry. Spurstow, we should have watched him. Has he – ?'

Deftly Spurstow continued his investigations, ending by a search round the room.

'No, he hasn't,' he snapped. 'There's no trace of anything. Call the servants.'

They came, eight or ten of them, whispering and peering over each other's shoulders.

'When did your Sahib go to bed?' said Spurstow.

'At eleven or ten, we think,' said Hummil's personal servant.

'He was well then? But how should you know?'

'He was not ill, as far as our comprehension extended. But he had slept very little for three nights. This I know, because I saw him walking much, and specially in the heart of the night.'

As Spurstow was arranging the sheet, a big straight-necked hunting-spur tumbled on the ground. The doctor groaned. The personal servant peeped at the body.

'What do you think, Chuma?' said Spurstow, catching the look on the dark face.

'Heaven-born, in my poor opinion, this that was my master has descended into the Dark Places, and there has been caught because he was not able to escape with sufficient speed. We have the spur for evidence that he fought with Fear. Thus have I seen men of my race do with thorns when a spell was laid upon them to overtake them in their sleeping hours and they dared not sleep.'

'Chuma, you're a mud-head. Go out and prepare seals to be set on the Sahib's property.'

'God has made the Heaven-born. God has made me. Who are we, to inquire into the dispensations of God? I will bid the other servants hold aloof while you are reckoning the tale of the Sahib's property. They are all thieves, and would steal.'

'As far as I can make out, he died from – oh, anything; stoppage of the heart's action, heat-apoplexy, or some other visitation,' said Spurstow to his companions. 'We must make an inventory of his effects, and so on.'

'He was scared to death,' insisted Lowndes. 'Look at those eyes! For pity's sake don't let him be buried with them open!'

'Whatever it was, he's clear of all the trouble now,' said Mottram softly.

Spurstow was peering into the open eyes.

'Come here,' said he. 'Can you see anything there?'

'I can't face it!' whimpered Lowndes. 'Cover up the face! Is there any fear on earth that can turn a man into that likeness? It's ghastly. Oh, Spurstow, cover it up!'

'No fear – on earth,' said Spurstow. Mottram leaned over his shoulder and looked intently.

'I see nothing except some gray blurs in the pupil. There can be nothing there, you know.'

'Even so. Well, let's think. It'll take half a day to knock up any sort of coffin; and he must have died at midnight. Lowndes, old man, go out and tell the coolies to break ground next to Jevins's grave. Mottram, go round the house with Chuma and see that the seals are put on things. Send a couple of men to me here, and I'll arrange.'

The strong-armed servants when they returned to their own kind told a strange story of the doctor Sahib vainly trying to call their master back to life by magic arts, – to wit, the holding of a little green box that clicked to each of the dead man's eyes, and of a bewildered muttering on the part of the doctor Sahib, who took the little green box away with him.

The resonant hammering of a coffin-lid is no pleasant thing to hear, but those who have experience maintain that much more terrible is the soft swish of the bed-linen, the reeving and unreeving of the bed-tapes, when he who has fallen by the roadside is apparelled for burial, sinking gradually as the tapes are tied over, till the swad-dled shape touches the floor and there is no protest against the indignity of hasty disposal.

At the last moment Lowndes was seized with scruples of conscience. 'Ought you to read the service, – from beginning to end?' said he to Spurstow.

'I intend to. You're my senior as a civilian. You can take it if you like.'

'I didn't mean that for a moment. I only thought if we could get a chaplain from somewhere, – I'm willing to ride anywhere, – and give poor Hummil a better chance. That's all.'

'Bosh!' said Spurstow, as he framed his lips to the tremendous words that stand at the head of the burial service.

After breakfast they smoked a pipe in silence to the memory of the dead. Then Spurstow said absently –

"Tisn't in medical science.'

'What?'

'Things in a dead man's eye.'

'For goodness' sake leave that horror alone!' said Lowndes. 'I've seen a native die of pure fright when a tiger chivied him. I know what killed Hummil.'

'The deuce you do! I'm going to try to see.' And the doctor retreated into the bath-room with a Kodak camera. After a few minutes there was the sound of something being hammered to pieces, and he emerged, very white indeed.

'Have you got a picture?' said Mottram. 'What does the thing look like?'

'It was impossible, of course. You needn't look, Mottram. I've torn up the films. There was nothing there. It was impossible.'

'That,' said Lowndes, very distinctly, watching the shaking hand striving to relight the pipe, 'is a damned lie.'

Mottram laughed uneasily. 'Spurstow's right,' he said. 'We're all in such a state now that we'd believe anything. For pity's sake let's try to be rational.'

There was no further speech for a long time. The hot wind whistled without, and the dry trees sobbed. Presently the daily train, winking brass, burnished steel, and spouting steam, pulled up panting in the intense glare. 'We'd better go on on that,' said Spurstow. 'Go back to work. I've written my certificate. We can't do any more good here, and work'll keep our wits together. Come on.'

No one moved. It is not pleasant to face railway journeys at mid-day in June. Spurstow gathered up his hat and whip, and, turning in the doorway, said –

'There may be Heaven, – there must be Hell. Meantime, there is our life here. We-ell?'

Neither Mottram nor Lowndes had any answer to the question.

THE EDUCATION OF OTIS YEERE

I

In the pleasant orchard-closes
'God bless all our gains,' say we;
But 'May God bless all our losses,'
Better suits with our degree.
The Lost Bower.

THIS IS THE HISTORY OF A FAILURE; BUT the woman who failed said that it might be an instructive tale to put into print for the benefit of the younger generation. The younger generation does not want instruction, being perfectly willing to instruct if any one will listen to it. None the less, here begins the story where every right-minded story should begin, that is to say at Simla, where all things begin and many come to an evil end.

The mistake was due to a very clever woman making a blunder and not retrieving it. Men are licensed to stumble, but a clever woman's mistake is outside the regular course of Nature and Providence; since all good people know that a woman is the only infallible thing in this world, except Government Paper of the '79 issue, bearing interest at four and a half per cent. Yet, we have to remember that six consecutive days of rehearsing the leading part of The Fallen Angel, at the New Gaiety Theatre where the plaster is not yet properly dry, might have brought about an unhingement of spirits which, again, might have led to eccentricities.

Mrs. Hauksbee came to 'The Foundry' to tiffin with Mrs. Mallowe, her one bosom friend, for she was in no sense 'a woman's woman.' And it was a woman's tiffin, the door shut to all the world; and they both talked chiffons, which is French for Mysteries.

'I've enjoyed an interval of sanity,' Mrs. Hauksbee announced, after tiffin was over and the two were comfortably settled in the little writing-room that opened out of Mrs. Mallowe's bedroom.

'My dear girl, what has he done?' said Mrs. Mallowe sweetly. It is noticeable that ladies of a certain age call each other 'dear girl,' just as commissioners of twenty-eight years' standing address their equals in the Civil List as 'my boy.'

'There's no he in the case. Who am I that an imaginary man should be always credited to me? Am I an Apache?'

'No, dear, but somebody's scalp is generally drying at your wigwam-door. Soaking rather.'

This was an allusion to the Hawley Boy, who was in the habit of riding all across Simla in the Rains, to call on Mrs. Hauksbee. That lady laughed.

'For my sins, the Aide at Tyrconnel last night told me off to The Mussuck. Hsh! Don't laugh. One of my most devoted admirers. When the duff came someone really ought to teach them to make puddings at Tyrconnel The Mussuck was at liberty to attend to me.'

'Sweet soul! I know his appetite,' said Mrs. Mallowe. 'Did he, oh did he, begin his wooing?'

'By a special mercy of Providence, no. He explained his importance as a Pillar of the Empire. I didn't laugh.'

'Lucy, I don't believe you.'

'Ask Captain Sangar; he was on the other side. Well, as I was saying, The Mussuck dilated.'

'I think I can see him doing it,' said Mrs. Mallowe pensively, scratching her fox-terrier's ears.

'I was properly impressed. Most properly. I yawned openly. 'Strict supervision, and play them off one against the other,' said The Mussuck, shovelling down his ice by tureenfuls, I assure you. 'That, Mrs. Hauksbee, is the secret of our Government.'

Mrs. Mallowe laughed long and merrily. 'And what did you say?'

'Did you ever know me at loss for an answer yet? I said: 'So I have observed in my dealings with you.' The

Mussuck swelled with pride. He is coming to call on me tomorrow. The Hawley Boy is coming too.'

"Strict supervision and play them off one against the other. That, Mrs. Hauksbee, is the secret of our Government.' And I daresay if we could get to The Mussuck's heart, we should find that he considers himself a man of the world.'

'As he is of the other two things. I like The Mussuck, and I won't have you call him names. He amuses me.'

'He has reformed you, too, by what appears. Explain the interval of sanity, and hit Tim on the nose with the paper-cutter, please. That dog is too fond of sugar. Do you take milk in yours?'

'No, thanks. Polly, I'm wearied of this life. It's hollow.'

'Turn religious, then. I always said that Rome would be your fate.'

'Only exchanging half-a-dozen attaches in red for one in black, and if I fasted, the wrinkles would come, and never, never go. Has it ever struck you, dear, that I'm getting old?'

'Thanks for your courtesy. I'll return it. Ye-es, we are both not exactly how shall I put it?'

'What we have been. 'I feel it in my bones,' as Mrs. Crossley says. Polly, I've wasted my life.'

'As how?'

'Never mind how. I feel it. I want to be a Power before I die.'

'Be a Power then. You've wits enough for anything and beauty!'

Mrs. Hauksbee pointed a teaspoon straight at her hostess. 'Polly, if you heap compliments on me like this,

I shall cease to believe that you're a woman. Tell me how I am to be a Power.'

'Inform The Mussuck that he is the most fascinating and slimmest man in Asia, and he'll tell you anything and everything you please.'

'Bother The Mussuck! I mean an intellectual Power not a gas-power. Polly, I'm going to start a salon.'

Mrs. Mallowe turned lazily on the sofa and rested her head on her hand. 'Hear the words of the Preacher, the son of Baruch,' she said.

'Will you talk sensibly?'

'I will, dear, for I see that you are going to make a mistake.'

'I never made a mistake in my life at least, never one that I couldn't explain away afterwards.'

'Going to make a mistake,' went on Mrs. Mallowe composedly. 'It is impossible to start a salon in Simla. A bar would be much more to the point.'

'Perhaps, but why? It seems so easy.'

'Just what makes it so difficult. How many clever women are there in Simla?'

'Myself and yourself,' said Mrs. Hauksbee, without a moment's hesitation.

'Modest woman! Mrs. Feardon would thank you for that. And how many clever men?'

'Oh er hundreds,' said Mrs. Hauksbee vaguely.

'What a fatal blunder! Not one. They are all bespoke by the Government. Take my husband, for instance. Jack was a clever man, though I say so who shouldn't. Government has eaten him up. All his ideas and powers of conversation he really used to be a good talker, even to his wife in the old days are taken from him by this this kitchen-sink of a Government. That's the case with every man up here who is at work. I don't suppose a Russian convict under the knout is able to amuse the rest of his gang; and all our men-folk here are gilded convicts.'

'But there are scores − '

'I know what you're going to say. Scores of idle men up on leave. I admit it, but they are all of two objection-able sets. The Civilian who'd be delightful if he had the military man's knowledge of the world and style, and the military man who'd be adorable if he had the Civilian's culture.'

'Detestable word! Have Civilians culchaw? I never studied the breed deeply.'

'Don't make fun of Jack's Service. Yes. They're like the teapoys in the Lakka Bazar good material but not polished. They can't help themselves, poor dears. A Civilian only begins to be tolerable after he has knocked about the world for fifteen years.'

'And a military man?'

'When he has had the same amount of service. The young of both species are horrible. You would have scores of them in your salon.'

'I would not!' said Mrs. Hauksbee fiercely.

'I would tell the bearer to darwaza band them. I'd put their own colonels and commissioners at the door to turn them away. I'd give them to the Topsham Girl to play with.'

'The Topsham Girl would be grateful for the gift. But to go back to the salon. Allowing that you had gathered all your men and women together, what would you do with them? Make them talk? They would all with one accord begin to flirt. Your salon would become a glorified Peliti's a 'Scandal Point' by lamplight.'

'There's a certain amount of wisdom in that view.'

'There's all the wisdom in the world in it. Surely, twelve Simla seasons ought to have taught you that you can't focus anything in India; and a salon, to be any good at all, must be permanent. In two seasons your roomful would be scattered all over Asia. We are only little bits of dirt on the hillsides here one day and blown down the road the next. We have lost the art of talking at least our men have. We have no cohesion.'

'George Eliot in the flesh,' interpolated Mrs. Hauksbee wickedly.

'And collectively, my dear scoffer, we, men and women alike, have no influence. Come into the verandah and look at the Mall!'

The two looked down on the now rapidly filling road, for all Simla was abroad to steal a stroll between a shower and a fog.

'How do you propose to fix that river? Look! There's The Mussuck head of goodness knows what. He is a power in the land, though he does eat like a costermonger. There's Colonel Blone, and General Grucher, and Sir Dugald Delane, and Sir Henry Haughton, and Mr. Jellalatty. All Heads of Departments, and all powerful.'

'And all my fervent admirers,' said Mrs. Hauksbee piously. 'Sir Henry Haughton raves about me. But go on.'

'One by one, these men are worth something. Collectively, they're just a mob of Anglo–Indians. Who cares for what

Anglo–Indians say? Your salon won't weld the Departments together and make you mistress of India, dear. And these creatures won't talk administrative 'shop' in a crowd in your salon because they are so afraid of the men in the lower ranks overhearing it. They have forgotten what of Literature and Art they ever knew, and the women – '

'Can't talk about anything except the last Gymkhana, or the sins of their last nurse. I was calling on Mrs. Derwills this morning.'

'You admit that? They can talk to the subalterns though, and the subalterns can talk to them. Your salon would suit their views admirably, if you respected the religious prejudices of the country and provided plenty of kala juggahs.'

'Plenty of kala juggahs. Oh my poor little idea! Kala juggahs in a salon! But who made you so awfully clever?'

'Perhaps I've tried myself; or perhaps I know a woman who has. I have preached and expounded the whole matter and the conclusion thereof.'

'You needn't go on. "Is Vanity." Polly, I thank you. These vermin' Mrs. Hauksbee waved her hand from the verandah to two men in the crowd below who had raised their hats to her 'these vermin shall not rejoice in a new Scandal Point or an extra Peliti's. I will abandon the notion of a salon. It did seem so tempting, though. But what shall I do? I must do something.'

'Why? Are not Abana and Pharpar.'

'Jack has made you nearly as bad as himself! I want to, of course. I'm tired of everything and everybody, from a moonlight picnic at Seepee to the blandishments of The Mussuck.'

'Yes that comes, too, sooner or later. Have you nerve enough to make your bow yet?'

Mrs. Hauksbee's mouth shut grimly. Then she laughed. 'I think I see myself doing it. Big pink placards on the Mall: 'Mrs. Hauksbee! Positively her last appearance on any stage! This is to give notice!' No more dances; no more rides; no more luncheons; no more theatricals with supper to follow; no more sparring with one's dearest, dearest friend; no more fencing with an inconvenient man who hasn't wit enough to clothe what he's pleased to call his sentiments in passable speech; no more parading of The Mussuck while Mrs. Tarkass calls all round Simla, spreading horrible stories about me! No more of anything that is thoroughly wearying, abominable, and detestable, but, all the same, makes life worth the having. Yes! I see it all! Don't interrupt, Polly, I'm inspired. A mauve and white striped 'cloud' round my excellent shoulders, a seat in the fifth row of the Gaiety, and both horses sold. Delightful vision! A comfortable arm-chair, situated in three different draughts, at every ball-room; and nice, large, sensible shoes for all the couples to stumble over as they go into the verandah! Then at supper. Can't you imagine the scene? The greedy mob gone away. Reluctant subaltern, pink all over like a newly-powdered baby, they really ought to tan subalterns before they are exported, Polly, sent back by the hostess to do his duty. Slouches up to me across the room, tugging at a glove two sizes too large for him I hate a man who wears gloves like overcoats and trying to look as if he'd thought of it from the first. 'May I ah-have the pleasure 'f takin' you 'nt' supper?' Then I get up with a hungry smile. Just like this.'

'Lucy, how can you be so absurd?'

'And sweep out on his arm. So! After supper I shall go away early, you know, because I shall be afraid of catching cold. No one will look for my 'rickshaw. Mine, so please you! I shall stand, always with that mauve and white 'cloud' over my head, while the wet soaks into my dear, old, venerable feet, and Tom swears and shouts for the mem-sahib's gharri. Then home to bed at half-past eleven! Truly excellent life helped out by the visits of the Padri, just fresh from burying somebody down below there.' She pointed through the pines toward the Cemetery, and continued with vigorous dramatic gesture,

'Listen! I see it all down, down even to the stays! Such stays! Six-eight a pair, Polly, with red flannel or list, is it? that they put into the tops of those fearful things. I can draw you a picture of them.'

'Lucy, for Heaven's sake, don't go waving your arms about in that idiotic manner! Recollect every one can see you from the Mall.'

'Let them see! They'll think I am rehearsing for The Fallen Angel. Look! There's The Mussuck. How badly he rides. There!'

She blew a kiss to the venerable Indian administrator with infinite grace.

'Now,' she continued, 'he'll be chaffed about that at the Club in the delicate manner those brutes of men affect, and the Hawley Boy will tell me all about it softening the details for fear of shocking me. That boy is too good to live, Polly. I've serious thoughts of recommending him to throw up his commission and go into the Church. In his present frame of mind he would obey me. Happy, happy child!'

'Never again,' said Mrs. Mallowe, with an affectation of indignation, 'shall you tiffin here! 'Lucindy your behaviour is scand'lus."

'All your fault,' retorted Mrs. Hauksbee, 'for suggesting such a thing as my abdication. No! jamais! nevaire! I will act, dance, ride, frivol, talk scandal, dine out, and appropriate the legitimate captives of any woman I choose, until I d-r-r-rop, or a better woman than I puts me to shame before all Simla, and it's dust and ashes in my mouth while I'm doing it!'

She swept into the drawing-room. Mrs. Mallowe followed and put an arm round her waist.

'I'm not!' said Mrs. Hauksbee defiantly, rummaging for her handkerchief. 'I've been dining out the last ten nights, and rehearsing in the afternoon. You'd be tired yourself. It's only because I'm tired.'

Mrs. Mallowe did not offer Mrs. Hauksbee any pity or ask her to lie down, but gave her another cup of tea, and went on with the talk.

'I've been through that too, dear,' she said.

'I remember,' said Mrs. Hauksbee, a gleam of fun on her face. 'In '84, wasn't it? You went out a great deal less next season.'

Mrs. Mallowe smiled in a superior and Sphinx-like fashion.

'I became an Influence,' said she.

'Good gracious, child, you didn't join the Theosophists

and kiss Buddha's big toe, did you? I tried to get into
their set once, but they cast me out for a sceptic without
a chance of improving my poor little mind, too.'

'No, I didn't Theosophilander. Jack says – '

'Never mind Jack. What a husband says is known before.
What did you do?'

'I made a lasting impression.'

'So have I for four months. But that didn't console me
in the least. I hated the man. Will you stop smiling in
that inscrutable way and tell me what you mean?'

Mrs. Mallowe told.

'And you mean to say that it is absolutely Platonic on
both sides?'

'Absolutely, or I should never have taken it up.'

'And his last promotion was due to you?'

Mrs. Mallowe nodded.

'And you warned him against the Topsham Girl?'

Another nod.

'And told him of Sir Dugald Delane's private memo
about him?'

A third nod.

'Why?'

'What a question to ask a woman! Because it amused
me at first. I am proud of my property now. If I live, he
shall continue to be successful. Yes, I will put him upon
the straight road to Knighthood, and everything else that
a man values. The rest depends upon himself.'

'Polly, you are a most extraordinary woman.'

'Not in the least. I'm concentrated, that's all. You diffuse
yourself, dear; and though all Simla knows your skill in
managing a team.'

'Can't you choose a prettier word?'

'Team, of half-a-dozen, from The Mussuck to the Hawley Boy, you gain nothing by it. Not even amusement.'

'And you?'

'Try my recipe. Take a man, not a boy, mind, but an almost mature, unattached man, and be his guide, philosopher, and friend. You'll find it the most interesting occupation that you ever embarked on. It can be done you needn't look like that because I've done it.'

'There's an element of risk about it that makes the notion attractive. I'll get such a man and say to him, 'Now, understand that there must be no flirtation. Do exactly what I tell you, profit by my instruction and counsels, and all will yet be well.' Is that the idea?'

'More or less,' said Mrs. Mallowe, with an unfathomable smile. 'But be sure he understands.'

II

Dribble-dribble trickle-trickle
What a lot of raw dust!
My dollie's had an accident
And out came all the sawdust!
Nursery Rhyme.

SO MRS. HAUKSBEE, IN 'THE FOUNDRY' which overlooks Simla Mall, sat at the feet of Mrs. Mallowe and gathered wisdom. The end of the Conference was the Great Idea upon which Mrs. Hauksbee so plumed herself.

'I warn you,' said Mrs. Mallowe, beginning to repent

of her suggestion, 'that the matter is not half so easy as it looks. Any woman even the Topsham Girl can catch a man, but very, very few know how to manage him when caught.'

'My child,' was the answer, 'I've been a female St. Simon Stylites looking down upon men for these these years past. Ask The Mussuck whether I can manage them.'

Mrs. Hauksbee departed humming, 'I'll go to him and say to him in manner most ironical.' Mrs. Mallowe laughed to herself. Then she grew suddenly sober. 'I wonder whether I've done well in advising that amusement? Lucy's a clever woman, but a thought too careless.'

A week later the two met at a Monday Pop. 'Well?' said Mrs. Mallowe.

'I've caught him!' said Mrs. Hauksbee: her eyes were dancing with merriment.

'Who is it, mad woman? I'm sorry I ever spoke to you about it.'

'Look between the pillars. In the third row; fourth from the end. You can see his face now. Look!'

'Otis Yeere! Of all the improbable and impossible people! I don't believe you.'

'Hsh! Wait till Mrs. Tarkass begins murdering Milton Wellings; and I'll tell you all about it. S-s-ss! That woman's voice always reminds me of an Underground train coming into Earl's Court with the brakes on. Now listen. It is really Otis Yeere.'

'So I see, but does it follow that he is your property!'

'He is! By right of trove. I found him, lonely and unbefriended, the very next night after our talk, at the Dugald Delanes' burra-khana. I liked his eyes, and I talked to him. Next day he called. Next day we went for a ride together, and today he's tied to my 'richshaw-wheels hand and foot. You'll see when the concert's over. He doesn't know I'm here yet.'

'Thank goodness you haven't chosen a boy. What are you going to do with him, assuming that you've got him?'

'Assuming, indeed! Does a woman do I ever make a mistake in that sort of thing? First,' Mrs. Hauksbee ticked off the items ostentatiously on her little gloved fingers 'First, my dear, I shall dress him properly. At present his raiment is a disgrace, and he wears a dress-shirt like a crumpled sheet of the Pioneer. Secondly, after I have made him presentable, I shall form his manners his morals are above reproach.'

'You seem to have discovered a great deal about him considering the shortness of your acquaintance.'

'Surely you ought to know that the first proof a man gives of his interest in a woman is by talking to her about his own sweet self. If the woman listens without yawning, he begins to like her. If she flatters the animal's vanity, he ends by adoring her.'

'In some cases.'

'Never mind the exceptions. I know which one you are thinking of. Thirdly, and lastly, after he is polished and made pretty, I shall, as you said, be his guide, philosopher, and friend, and he shall become a success as great a success as your friend. I always wondered how that man got on. Did The Mussuck come to you with the Civil List and, dropping on one knee no, two knees, a la Gibbon hand it to you and say, 'Adorable angel, choose your friend's appointment'?'

'Lucy, your long experiences of the Military Department have demoralised you. One doesn't do that sort of thing on the Civil Side.'

'No disrespect meant to Jack's Service, my dear. I only asked for information. Give me three months, and see what changes I shall work in my prey.'

'Go your own way since you must. But I'm sorry that I was weak enough to suggest the amusement.'

"I am all discretion, and may be trusted to an infinite extent," quoted Mrs. Hauksbee from The Fallen Angel; and the conversation ceased with Mrs. Tarkass's last, long-drawn war-whoop.

Her bitterest enemies and she had many could hardly accuse Mrs. Hauksbee of wasting her time. Otis Yeere was one of those wandering 'dumb' characters, foredoomed through life to be nobody's property. Ten years in Her Majesty's Bengal Civil Service, spent, for the most part, in undesirable Districts, had given him little to be proud of, and nothing to bring confidence. Old enough to have lost the first fine careless rapture that showers on the immature 'Stunt imaginary Commissionerships and Stars, and sends him into the collar with coltish earnestness and abandon; too young to be yet able to look back upon the progress he had made, and thank Providence that under the conditions of the day he had come even so far, he stood upon the dead-centre of his career. And when a man stands still he feels the slightest impulse from without. Fortune had ruled that Otis Yeere should be, for the first part of his service, one of the rank and file who are ground up in the wheels of the Administration; losing heart and soul, and mind and strength, in the process.

Until steam replaces manual power in the working of the Empire, there must always be this percentage must always be the men who are used up, expended, in the mere mechanical routine. For these promotion is far off and the mill-grind of every day very instant. The Secretariats know them only by name; they are not the picked men of the Districts with Divisions and Collectorates awaiting them. They are simply the rank and file the food for fever sharing with the ryot and the plough-bullock the honour of being the plinth on which the State rests. The older ones have lost their aspirations; the younger are putting theirs aside with a sigh. Both learn to endure patiently until the end of the day. Twelve years in the rank and file, men say, will sap the hearts of the bravest and dull the wits of the most keen.

Out of this life Otis Yeere had fled for a few months; drifting, in the hope of a little masculine society, into Simla. When his leave was over he would return to his swampy, sour-green, under-manned Bengal district; to the native Assistant, the native Doctor, the native Magistrate, the steaming, sweltering Station, the ill-kempt City, and the undisguised insolence of the Municipality that babbled away the lives of men. Life was cheap, however. The soil spawned humanity, as it bred frogs in the Rains, and the gap of the sickness of one season was filled to overflowing by the fecundity of the next. Otis was unfeignedly thankful to lay down his work for a little while and escape from the seething, whining, weakly hive, impotent to help itself, but strong in its power to cripple, thwart, and annoy the sunkeneyed man who, by official irony, was said to be 'in charge' of it.

'I knew there were women-dowdies in Bengal. They come up here sometimes. But I didn't know that there were men-dowds, too.'

Then, for the first time, it occurred to Otis Yeere that his clothes wore rather the mark of the ages. It will be seen that his friendship with Mrs. Hauksbee had made great strides.

As that lady truthfully says, a man is never so happy as when he is talking about himself. From Otis Yeere's lips Mrs. Hauksbee, before long, learned everything that she wished to know about the subject of her experiment: learned what manner of life he had led in what she vaguely called 'those awful cholera districts'; learned, too, but this knowledge came later, what manner of life he had purposed to lead and what dreams he had dreamed in the year of grace '77, before the reality had knocked the heart out of him. Very pleasant are the shady bridle-paths round Prospect Hill for the telling of such confidences.

'Not yet,' said Mrs. Hauksbee to Mrs. Maliowe. 'Not yet. I must wait until the man is properly dressed, at least. Great heavens, is it possible that he doesn't know what an honour it is to be taken up by Me!'

Mrs. Hauksbee did not reckon false modesty as one of her failings.

'Always with Mrs. Hauksbee!' murmured Mrs. Mallowe, with her sweetest smile, to Otis. 'Oh you men, you men! Here are our Punjabis growling because you've monop-olised the nicest woman in Simla. They'll tear you to pieces on the Mall, some day, Mr. Yeere.'

Mrs. Mallowe rattled downhill, having satisfied herself,

by a glance through the fringe of her sunshade, of the effect of her words.

The shot went home. Of a surety Otis Yeere was somebody in this bewildering whirl of Simla had monopolised the nicest woman in it, and the Punjabis were growling. The notion justified a mild glow of vanity. He had never looked upon his acquaintance with Mrs. Hauksbee as a matter for general interest.

The knowledge of envy was a pleasant feeling to the man of no account. It was intensified later in the day when a luncher at the Club said spitefully, 'Well, for a debilitated Ditcher, Yeere, you are going it. Hasn't any kind friend told you that she's the most dangerous woman in Simla?'

Yeere chuckled and passed out. When, oh, when would his new clothes be ready? He descended into the Mall to inquire; and Mrs. Hauksbee, coming over the Church Ridge in her 'rickshaw, looked down upon him approvingly. 'He's learning to carry himself as if he were a man, instead of a piece of furniture, and,' she screwed up her eyes to see the better through the sunlight 'he is a man when he holds himself like that. O blessed Conceit, what should we be without you?'

With the new clothes came a new stock of self-confidence. Otis Yeere discovered that he could enter a room without breaking into a gentle perspiration could cross one, even to talk to Mrs. Hauksbee, as though rooms were meant to be crossed. He was for the first time in nine years proud of himself, and contented with his life, satisfied with his new clothes, and rejoicing in the friendship of Mrs. Hauksbee.

'Conceit is what the poor fellow wants,' she said in confidence to Mrs. Mallowe. 'I believe they must use Civilians to plough the fields with in Lower Bengal. You see I have to begin from the very beginning haven't I? But you'll admit, won't you, dear, that he is immensely improved since I took him in hand. Only give me a little more time and he won't know himself.'

Indeed, Yeere was rapidly beginning to forget what he had been. One of his own rank and file put the matter brutally when he asked Yeere, in reference to nothing, 'And who has been making you a Member of Council, lately? You carry the side of half-a-dozen of 'em.'

'I I'm awf'ly sorry. I didn't mean it, you know,' said Yeere apologetically.

'There'll be no holding you,' continued the old stager grimly. 'Climb down, Otis climb down, and get all that beastly affectation knocked out of you with fever! Three thousand a month wouldn't support it.'

Yeere repeated the incident to Mrs. Hauksbee. He had come to look upon her as his Mother Confessor.

'And you apologised!' she said. 'Oh, shame! I hate a man who apologises. Never apologise for what your friend called 'side.' Never! It's a man's business to be insolent and overbearing until he meets with a stronger. Now, you bad boy, listen to me.'

Simply and straightforwardly, as the 'rickshaw loitered round Jakko, Mrs. Hauksbee preached to Otis Yeere the Great Gospel of Conceit, illustrating it with living pictures encountered during their Sunday afternoon stroll.

'Good gracious!' she ended with the personal argument, 'you'll apologise next for being my attaché – '

'Never!' said Otis Yeere. 'That's another thing altogether. I shall always be.'

'What's coming?' thought Mrs. Hauksbee.

'Proud of that,' said Otis.

'Safe for the present,' she said to herself.

'But I'm afraid I have grown conceited. Like Jeshurun, you know. When he waxed fat, then he kicked. It's the having no worry on one's mind and the Hill air, I suppose.'

'Hill air, indeed!' said Mrs. Hauksbee to herself. 'He'd have been hiding in the Club till the last day of his leave, if I hadn't discovered him.' And aloud,

'Why shouldn't you be? You have every right to.'

'I! Why?'

'Oh, hundreds of things. I'm not going to waste this lovely afternoon by explaining; but I know you have. What was that heap of manuscript you showed me about the grammar of the aboriginal what's their names?'

'Gullals. A piece of nonsense. I've far too much work to do to bother over Gullals now. You should see my District. Come down with your husband some day and I'll show you round. Such a lovely place in the Rains! A sheet of water with the railway-embankment and the snakes sticking out, and, in the summer, green flies and green squash. The people would die of fear if you shook a dogwhip at 'em. But they know you're forbidden to do that, so they conspire to make your life a burden to you. My District's worked by some man at Darjiling, on the strength of a native pleader's false reports. Oh, it's a heavenly place!'

Otis Yeere laughed bitterly.

'There's not the least necessity that you should stay in it. Why do you?'

'Because I must. How'm I to get out of it?'

'How! In a hundred and fifty ways. If there weren't so many people on the road I'd like to box your ears. Ask, my dear boy, ask! Look! There is young Hexarly with six years' service and half your talents. He asked for what he wanted, and he got it. See, down by the Convent! There's McArthurson, who has come to his present position by asking sheer, downright asking after he had pushed himself out of the rank and file. One man is as good as another in your service believe me. I've seen Simla for more seasons than I care to think about. Do you suppose men are chosen for appointments because of their special fitness beforehand? You have all passed a high test what do you call it? in the beginning, and, except for the few who have gone altogether to the bad, you can all work hard. Asking does the rest. Call it cheek, call it insolence, call it anything you like, but ask! Men argue yes, I know what men say that a man, by the mere audacity of his request, must have some good in him. A weak man doesn't say: 'Give me this and that.' He whines: 'Why haven't I been given this and that?' If you were in the Army, I should say learn to spin plates or play a tambourine with your toes. As it is ask! You belong to a Service that ought to be able to command the Channel Fleet, or set a leg at twenty minutes' notice, and yet you hesitate over asking to escape from a squashy green district where you admit you are not master. Drop the Bengal Government alto-gether. Even Darjiling is a little out-of-the-way hole. I was there once, and the rents were extortionate. Assert yourself. Get the Government of India to take you over. Try to get on the Frontier, where every man has a grand chance if he can trust himself. Go somewhere! Do something! You have twice the wits and three times the presence of the men up here, and, and' Mrs. Hauksbee paused for breath; then continued 'and in any way you look at it, you ought to. You who could go so far!'

'I don't know,' said Yeere, rather taken aback by the unexpected eloquence. 'I haven't such a good opinion of myself.'

It was not strictly Platonic, but it was Policy. Mrs. Hauksbee laid her hand lightly upon the ungloved paw that rested on the turned-back 'rickshaw hood, and, looking the man full in the face, said tenderly, almost too tenderly, 'I believe in you if you mistrust yourself. Is that enough, my friend?'

'It is enough,' answered Otis very solemnly.

He was silent for a long time, redreaming the dreams that he had dreamed eight years ago, but through them all ran, as sheet-lightning through golden cloud, the light of Mrs. Hauksbee's violet eyes.

Curious and impenetrable are the mazes of Simla life the only existence in this desolate land worth the living. Gradually it went abroad among men and women, in the pauses between dance, play, and Gymkhana, that Otis Yeere, the man with the newly-lit light of self-confidence in his eyes, had 'done something decent' in the wilds whence he came. He had brought an erring Municipality to reason, appropriated the funds on his own responsibility, and saved the lives of hundreds. He knew more about the Gullals than any living man. Had a vast knowledge of the aboriginal tribes; was, in spite of his juniority, the greatest authority on the aboriginal Gullals. No one quite knew who or what the Gullals were till The Mussuck, who had been calling on Mrs. Hauksbee, and prided himself upon picking people's brains, explained they were a tribe of ferocious hillmen, somewhere near Sikkim, whose friendship even the Great Indian Empire would find it worth her while to secure. Now we know that Otis Yeere had showed Mrs. Hauksbee his MS. notes of six years' standing on these same Gullals. He had told her, too, how, sick and shaken with the fever their negligence had bred, crippled by the loss of his pet clerk, and savagely angry at the desolation in his charge, he had once damned the collective eyes of his 'intelligent local board' for a set of haramzadas. Which act of 'brutal and tyrannous oppression' won him a Reprimand Royal from the Bengal Government; but in the anecdote as amended for Northern consumption we find no record of this. Hence we are forced to conclude that Mrs. Hauksbee edited his reminiscences before sowing them in idle ears, ready, as she well knew, to exaggerate good or evil. And Otis Yeere bore himself as befitted the hero of many tales.

'You can talk to me when you don't fall into a brown study. Talk now, and talk your brightest and best,' said Mrs. Hauksbee.

Otis needed no spur. Look to a man who has the counsel of a woman of or above the world to back him. So long as he keeps his head, he can meet both sexes on equal ground an advantage never intended by Providence, who fashioned Man on one day and Woman on another, in sign that neither should know more than a very little of the other's life. Such a man goes far, or, the counsel being withdrawn, collapses suddenly while his world seeks the reason.

Generalled by Mrs. Hauksbee, who, again, had all Mrs. Mallowe's wisdom at her disposal, proud of himself and, in the end, believing in himself because he was believed in, Otis Yeere stood ready for any fortune that might befall, certain that it would be good. He would fight for his own hand, and intended that this second struggle should lead to better issue than the first helpless surrender of the bewildered 'Stunt.

What might have happened it is impossible to say. This lamentable thing befell, bred directly by a statement of Mrs. Hauksbee that she would spend the next season in Darjiling.

'Are you certain of that?' said Otis Yeere.

'Quite. We're writing about a house now.'

Otis Yeere 'stopped dead,' as Mrs. Hauksbee put it in discussing the relapse with Mrs. Mallowe.

'He has behaved,' she said angrily, 'just like Captain Kerrington's pony only Otis is a donkey at the last Gymkhana. Planted his forefeet and refused to go on another step. Polly, my man's going to disappoint me. What shall I do?'

As a rule, Mrs. Mallowe does not approve of staring, but on this occasion she opened her eyes to the utmost.

'You have managed cleverly so far,'she said. 'Speak to him, and ask him what he means.'

'I will at tonight's dance.'

'No o, not at a dance,' said Mrs. Mallowe cautiously. 'Men are never themselves quite at dances. Better wait till tomorrow morning.'

'Nonsense. If he's going to 'vert in this insane way there isn't a day to lose. Are you going? No? Then sit up for me, there's a dear. I shan't stay longer than supper under any circumstances.'

Mrs. Mallowe waited through the evening, looking long and earnestly into the fire, and sometimes smiling to herself.

'Oh! oh! oh! The man's an idiot! A raving, positive idiot! I'm sorry I ever saw him!'

Mrs. Hauksbee burst into Mrs. Mallowe's house, at midnight, almost in tears.

'What in the world has happened?' said Mrs. Mallowe, but her eyes showed that she had guessed an answer.

'Happened! Everything has happened! He was there. I went to him and said, 'Now, what does this nonsense mean?' Don't laugh, dear, I can't bear it. But you know what I mean I said. Then it was a square, and I sat it out with him and wanted an explanation, and he said Oh! I haven't patience with such idiots! You know what I said about going to Darjiling next year? It doesn't matter to me where I go. I'd have changed the Station and lost the rent to have saved this. He said, in so many words, that he wasn't going to try to work up any more, because because he would be shifted into a province away from Darjiling, and his own District, where these creatures are, is within a day's journey.'

'Ah hh!' said Mrs. Mallowe, in a tone of one who has successfully tracked an obscure word through a large dictionary.

'Did you ever hear of anything so mad so absurd? And he had the ball at his feet. He had only to kick it! I would have made him anything! Anything in the wide world. He could have gone to the world's end. I would have helped him. I made him, didn't I, Polly? Didn't I create that man? Doesn't he owe everything to me? And to reward me, just when everything was nicely arranged, by this lunacy that spoilt everything!'

'Very few men understand your devotion thoroughly.'

'Oh, Polly, don't laugh at me! I give men up from this hour. I could have killed him then and there. What right had this man this Thing I had picked out of his filthy paddy – fields to make love to me?'

'He did that, did he?'

'He did. I don't remember half he said, I was so angry. Oh, but such a funny thing happened! I can't help laughing at it now, though I felt nearly ready to cry with rage. He raved and I stormed I'm afraid we must have made an awful noise in our kala juggah. Protect my character, dear, if it's all over Simla by tomorrow and then he bobbed forward in the middle of this insanity I firmly believe the man's demented and kissed me.'

'Morals above reproach,' purred Mrs. Mallowe.

'So they were so they are! It was the most absurd kiss. I don't believe he'd ever kissed a woman in his life before. I threw my head back, and it was a sort of slidy, pecking dab, just on the end of the chin here.' Mrs. Hauksbee tapped her masculine little chin with her fan. 'Then, of course, I was furiously angry, and told him that he was no gentleman, and I was sorry I'd ever met him, and so on. He was crushed so easily then I couldn't be very angry. Then I came away straight to you.'

'Was this before or after supper?'

'Oh! before oceans before. Isn't it perfectly disgusting?'

'Let me think. I withhold judgment till tomorrow. Morning brings counsel.'

But morning brought only a servant with a dainty bouquet of Annandale roses for Mrs. Hauksbee to wear at the dance at Viceregal Lodge that night.

'He doesn't seem to be very penitent,' said Mrs. Mallowe. 'What's the billet-doux in the centre?'

Mrs. Hauksbee opened the neatly-folded note, another accomplishment that she had taught Otis, read it, and groaned tragically.

'Last wreck of a feeble intellect! Poetry! Is it his own, do you think? Oh, that I ever built my hopes on such a maudlin idiot!'

'No. It's a quotation from Mrs. Browning, and in view of the facts of the case, as Jack says, uncommonly well chosen. Listen

Sweet, thou hast trod on a heart,
Pass! There's a world full of men;
And women as fair as thou art
Must do such things now and then.
Thou only hast stepped unaware
Malice not one can impute;
And why should a heart have been there,
In the way of a fair woman's foot?

'I didn't I didn't I didn't!' said Mrs. Hauksbee angrily, her eyes filling with tears; 'there was no malice at all. Oh, it's too vexatious!'

'You've misunderstood the compliment,' said Mrs.

Mallowe. 'He clears you completely and ahem I should think by this, that he has cleared completely too. My experience of men is that when they begin to quote poetry they are going to flit. Like swans singing before they die, you know.'

'Polly, you take my sorrows in a most unfeeling way.'

'Do I? Is it so terrible? If he's hurt your vanity, I should say that you've done a certain amount of damage to his heart.'

'Oh, you can never tell about a man!' said Mrs. Hauksbee.

AT THE PIT'S MOUTH

Men say it was a stolen tide –
The Lord that sent it He knows all,
But in mine ear will aye abide
The message that the bells let fall –
And awesome bells they were to me,
That in the dark rang, 'Enderby.'

ONCE UPON A TIME THERE WAS A MAN and his Wife and a Tertium Quid.

All three were unwise, but the Wife was the unwisest. The Man should have looked after his Wife, who should have avoided the Tertium Quid, who, again, should have married a wife of his own, after clean and open flirtations, to which nobody can possibly object, round Jakko or Observatory Hill. When you see a young man with his pony in a white lather and his hat on the back of his head, flying downhill at fifteen miles an hour to meet a girl who will be properly surprised to meet him, you naturally approve of that young man, and wish him Staff appointments, and take an interest in his welfare, and, as the proper time comes, give them sugar-tongs or side-saddles according to your means and generosity.

The Tertium Quid flew downhill on horseback, but it was to meet the Man's Wife; and when he flew uphill it was for the same end. The Man was in the Plains, earning money for his Wife to spend on dresses and four-hundred-rupee bracelets, and inexpensive luxuries of that kind. He worked very hard, and sent her a letter or a post-card daily. She also wrote to him daily, and said that she was longing for him to come up to Simla. The Tertium Quid used to lean over her shoulder and laugh as she wrote the notes. Then the two would ride to the Post-office together.

Now, Simla is a strange place and its customs are peculiar; nor is any man who has not spent at least ten seasons there qualified to pass judgment on circumstantial evidence, which is the most untrustworthy in the Courts. For these reasons, and for others which need not appear, I decline to state positively whether there was anything irretrievably wrong in the relations between the Man's Wife and the Tertium Quid. If there was, and hereon you must form your own opinion, it was the Man's Wife's fault. She was kittenish in her manners, wearing generally an air of soft and fluffy innocence. But she was deadlily learned and evil-instructed; and, now and again, when the mask dropped, men saw this, shuddered and – almost drew back. Men are occasionally particular, and the least particular men are always the most exacting.

Simla is eccentric in its fashion of treating friendships. Certain attachments which have set and crystallised through half-a-dozen seasons acquire almost the sanctity of the marriage bond, and are revered as such. Again, certain attachments equally old, and, to all appearance, equally venerable, never seem to win any recognised official status; while a chance-sprung acquaintance, not two months born, steps into the place which by right belongs to the senior. There is no law reducible to print which regulates these affairs.

Some people have a gift which secures them infinite toleration, and others have not. The Man's Wife had not. If she looked over the garden wall, for instance, women taxed her with stealing their husbands. She complained pathetically that she was not allowed to choose her own friends. When she put up her big white muff to her lips, and gazed over it and under her eyebrows at you as she said this thing, you felt that she had been infamously misjudged, and that all the other women's instincts were all wrong; which was absurd. She was not allowed to own the Tertium Quid in peace; and was so strangely constructed that she would not have enjoyed peace had she been so permitted. She preferred some semblance of intrigue to cloak even her most commonplace actions.

After two months of riding, first round Jakko, then

Elysium, then Summer Hill, then Observatory Hill, then under Jutogh, and lastly up and down the Cart Road as far as the Tara Devi gap in the dusk, she said to the Tertium Quid, 'Frank, people say we are too much together, and people are so horrid.'

The Tertium Quid pulled his moustache, and replied that horrid people were unworthy of the consideration of nice people.

'But they have done more than talk – they have written – written to my hubby – I'm sure of it,' said the Man's Wife, and she pulled a letter from her husband out of her saddle-pocket and gave it to the Tertium Quid.

It was an honest letter, written by an honest man, then stewing in the Plains on two hundred rupees a month (for he allowed his wife eight hundred and fifty), and in a silk banian and cotton trousers. It said that, perhaps, she had not thought of the unwisdom of allowing her name to be so generally coupled with the Tertium Quid's; that she was too much of a child to understand the dangers of that sort of thing; that he, her husband, was the last man in the world to interfere jealously with her little amusements and interests, but that it would be better were she to drop the Tertium Quid quietly and for her husband's sake. The letter was sweetened with many pretty little pet names, and it amused the Tertium Quid considerably. He and She laughed over it, so that you, fifty yards away, could see their shoulders shaking while the horses slouched along side by side.

Their conversation was not worth reporting. The upshot of it was that, next day, no one saw the Man's Wife and the Tertium Quid together. They had both gone down to the Cemetery, which, as a rule, is only visited officially by the inhabitants of Simla.

A Simla funeral with the clergyman riding, the mourners riding, and the coffin creaking as it swings between the bearers, is one of the most depressing things on this earth, particularly when the procession passes under the wet, dank dip beneath the Rockcliffe Hotel, where the sun is shut out, and all the hill streams are wailing and weeping together as they go down the valleys.

Occasionally folk tend the graves, but we in India shift and are transferred so often that, at the end of the second year, the Dead have no friends – only acquaintances who are far too busy amusing themselves up the hill to attend to old partners. The idea of using a Cemetery as a rendez-vous is distinctly a feminine one. A man would have said simply, 'Let people talk. We'll go down the Mall.' A woman is made differently, especially if she be such a woman as the Man's Wife. She and the Tertium Quid enjoyed each other's society among the graves of men and women whom they had known and danced with aforetime.

They used to take a big horse-blanket and sit on the grass a little to the left of the lower end, where there is a dip in the ground, and where the occupied graves stop short and the ready-made ones are not ready. Each well-regulated Indian Cemetery keeps half-a-dozen graves permanently open for contingencies and inci-dental wear and tear. In the Hills these are more usually baby's size, because children who come up weakened and sick from the Plains often succumb to the effects of the Rains in the Hills or get pneumonia from their *ayahs* taking them through damp pine-woods after the sun has set. In Cantonments, of course, the man's size is more in request; these arrangements varying with the climate and population.

One day when the Man's Wife and the Tertium Quid had just arrived in the Cemetery, they saw some coolies breaking ground. They had marked out a full-size grave, and the Tertium Quid asked them whether any Sahib was sick. They said that they did not know; but it was an order that they should dig a Sahib's grave.

'Work away,' said the Tertium Quid, 'and let's see how it's done.'

The coolies worked away, and the Man's Wife and the Tertium Quid watched and talked for a couple of hours while the grave was being deepened. Then a coolie, taking the earth in baskets as it was thrown up, jumped over the grave.

'That's queer,' said the Tertium Quid. 'Where's my ulster?'

'What's queer?' said the Man's Wife.

'I have got a chill down my back – just as if a goose had walked over my grave.'

'Why do you look at the thing, then?' said the Man's Wife. 'Let us go.'

The Tertium Quid stood at the head of the grave, and stared without answering for a space. Then he said, dropping a pebble down, 'It is nasty – and cold: horribly cold. I don't think I shall come to the Cemetery any more. I don't think grave-digging is cheerful.'

The two talked and agreed that the Cemetery was depressing. They also arranged for a ride next day out from the Cemetery through the Mashobra Tunnel up to

Fagoo and back, because all the world was going to a garden-party at Viceregal Lodge, and all the people of Mashobra would go too.

Coming up the Cemetery road, the Tertium Quid's horse tried to bolt uphill, being tired with standing so long, and managed to strain a back sinew.

'I shall have to take the mare tomorrow,' said the Tertium Quid, 'and she will stand nothing heavier than a snaffle.'

They made their arrangements to meet in the Cemetery, after allowing all the Mashobra people time to pass into Simla. That night it rained heavily, and, next day, when the Tertium Quid came to the trysting-place, he saw that the new grave had a foot of water in it, the ground being a tough and sour clay.

''Jove! That looks beastly,' said the Tertium Quid. 'Fancy being boarded up and dropped into that well!'

They then started off to Fagoo, the mare playing with the snaffle and picking her way as though she were shod with satin, and the sun shining divinely. The road below Mashobra to Fagoo is officially styled the Himalayan-Thibet road; but in spite of its name it is not much more than six feet wide in most places, and the drop into the valley below may be anything between one and two thousand feet.

'Now we're going to Thibet,' said the Man's Wife merrily, as the horses drew near to Fagoo. She was riding on the cliff-side.

'Into Thibet,' said the Tertium Quid, 'ever so far from people who say horrid things, and hubbies who write stupid letters. With you to the end of the world!'

A coolie carrying a log of wood came round a corner, and the mare went wide to avoid him – forefeet in and haunches out, as a sensible mare should go.

'To the world's end,' said the Man's Wife, and looked unspeakable things over her near shoulder at the Tertium Quid.

He was smiling, but, while she looked, the smile froze stiff as it were on his face, and changed to a nervous grin – the sort of grin men wear when they are not quite easy in their saddles. The mare seemed to be sinking by the stern, and her nostrils cracked while she was trying to realise what was happening. The rain of the night before had rotted the drop-side of the Himalayan-Thibet Road, and it was giving way under her. 'What are you doing?' said the Man's Wife. The Tertium Quid gave no answer. He grinned nervously and set his spurs into the mare, who rapped with her forefeet on the road, and the struggle began. The Man's Wife screamed, 'Oh, Frank, get off!'

But the Tertium Quid was glued to the saddle – his face blue and white – and he looked into the Man's Wife's eyes. Then the Man's Wife clutched at the mare's head and caught her by the nose instead of the bridle. The brute threw up her head and went down with a scream, the Tertium Quid upon her, and the nervous grin still set on his face.

The Man's Wife heard the tinkle-tinkle of little stones and loose earth falling off the roadway, and the sliding roar of the man and horse going down. Then everything was quiet, and she called on Frank to leave his mare and walk up. But Frank did not answer. He was underneath the mare, nine hundred feet below, spoiling a patch of Indian corn.

As the revellers came back from Viceregal Lodge in the mists of the evening, they met a temporarily insane woman, on a temporarily mad horse, swinging round the corners, with her eyes and her mouth open, and her head like the head of a Medusa. She was stopped by a man at the risk of his life, and taken out of the saddle, a limp heap, and put on the bank to explain herself. This wasted twenty minutes, and then she was sent home in a lady's 'rickshaw, still with her mouth open and her hands picking at her riding-gloves.

She was in bed through the following three days, which were rainy; so she missed attending the funeral of the Tertium Quid, who was lowered into eighteen inches of water, instead of the twelve to which he had first objected.

MARY
POSTGATE

OF MISS MARY POSTGATE, LADY McCausland wrote that she was 'thoroughly conscientious, tidy, companionable, and ladylike. I am very sorry to part with her, and shall always be interested in her welfare.' Miss Fowler engaged her on this recommendation, and to her surprise, for she had had experience of companions, found that it was true. Miss Fowler was nearer sixty than fifty at the time, but though she needed care she did not exhaust her attendant's vitality. On the contrary, she gave out, stimulatingly and with reminiscences. Her father had been a minor Court official in the days when the Great Exhibition of 1851 had just set its seal on Civilisation made perfect. Some of Miss Fowler's tales, none the less, were not always for the young. Mary was not young, and though her speech was as colourless as her eyes or her hair, she was never shocked. She listened unflinchingly to every one; said at the end, 'How interesting!' or 'How shocking!' as the case might be, and never again referred to it, for she prided herself on a trained mind, which 'did not dwell on these things.' She was, too, a treasure at domestic accounts, for which the village tradesmen, with their weekly books, loved her not. Otherwise she had no enemies; provoked no jealousy even among the plainest; neither gossip nor slander had ever been traced to her; she supplied the odd place at the Rector's or the Doctor's table at half an hour's notice; she was a sort of public aunt to very many small children of the village street, whose parents, while accepting everything would have been swift to resent what they called 'patronage'; she served on the Village Nursing Committee as Miss Fowler's nominee when Miss Fowler was crippled by rheumatoid arthritis, and came out of six months' fortnightly meetings equally respected by all the cliques.

And when Fate threw Miss Fowler's nephew, an unlovely orphan of eleven, on Miss Fowler's hands, Mary Postgate stood to her share of the business of education as practiced in private and public schools. She checked printed clothes-lists, and unitemised bills of extras; wrote to Head and House masters, matrons, nurses, and doctors, and grieved or rejoiced over half-term reports. Young Wyndham Fowler repaid her in his holidays by calling her 'Gatepost,' 'Posty,' or 'Packthread,' by thumping her between her narrow shoulders or by chasing her bleating, round the garden, her large mouth open, her large nose high in air at a stiff-necked shamble very like a camel's. Later on he filled the house with clamour, argument, and harangues as to his personal needs, likes and dislikes, and the limitations of 'you women,' reducing Mary to tears of physical fatigue, or, when he chose to be humorous, of helpless laughter. At crises, which multiplied as he grew older, she was his ambassadress and his interpretress to Miss Fowler, who had no large sympathy with the young; a vote in his interest at the councils on his future; his sewing-woman, strictly accountable for mislaid boots and garments; always his butt and his slave.

And when he decided to become a solicitor, and had entered an office in London; when his greeting had changed form 'Hullo, Postey, you old beast,' to 'Mornin, Packthread' there came a war which, unlike all wars that Mary could remember, did not stay decently outside England and in the newspapers, but intruded on the lives of people whom she knew. As she said to Miss Fowler, it was 'most vexatious.' It took the Rector's son who was going into business with his elder brother; it took the Colonel's nephew on the eve of fruit-farming in Canada; it took Mrs. Grant's son who, his mother said, was devoted to the ministry; and, very early indeed, it took Wynn Fowler, who announced on a postcard that he had joined the Flying Corps and wanted a cardigan waistcoat.

'He must go, and he must have the waistcoat,' said Miss Fowler. So Mary got the proper-sized needles and wool, while Miss Fowler told the men of her establishment – two gardeners and an old man, sixty – that those who could join the Army had better do so. The gardeners left. Cheape, the odd man, stayed on, and was promoted to the gardener's cottage. The cook, scorning to be limited in luxuries, also left, after a spirited scene with Miss Fowler, and took the house-maid with her. Miss Fowler gazetted Nellie, Cheape's seventeen-year-old daughter, to the vacant post; Mrs. Cheape to the rank of cook with occasional cleaning bouts; and the reduced establishment moved forward smoothly.

Wynn demanded an increase in his allowance. Miss Fowler, who always looked facts in the face, said, 'He must have it. The chances are he won't live long to draw it, and if three hundred makes him happy –'

Wynn was grateful, and came over, in his tight-buttoned uniform, to say so. His training centre was not thirty miles away, and his talk was so technical that it had to be explained by charts of the various types of machines. He gave Mary such a chart.

'And you'd better study it, Postey,' he said. 'You'll be seeing a lot of 'em soon.' So Mary studied the chart, but when Wynn next arrived to swell and exalt himself before his womenfolk, she failed badly in cross-examination, and he rated her as in the old days.

'You look more or less like a human being,' he said in his new Service voice. 'You must have had a brain at some time in your past. What have you done with it? Where'd you keep it? A sheep would know more than you do, Postey. You're lamentable. You are less use than an empty tin can, you dowey old cassowary.'

'I suppose that's how your superior officer talks to you?' said Miss Fowler from her chair.

'But Postey doesn't mind,' Wynn replied. 'Do you, Packthread?'

'Why? Was Wynn saying anything? I shall get this right next time you come,' she muttered, and knitted her pale brows again over the diagrams of Taubes, Farmans, and Zeppelins.

In a few weeks the mere land and sea battles which she read to Miss Fowler after breakfast passed her like idle breath. Her heart and her interest were high in the air with Wynn, who had finished 'rolling' (whatever that might be) and gone on from a 'taxi' to a machine more or less his own. One morning it circled over their very chimneys, alighted on Vegg's Heath, almost outside the garden gate, and Wynn came in, blue with cold, shouting for food. He and she drew Miss Fowler's bath-chair, as they had often done, along the Heath footpath to look at the biplane. Mary observed that 'it smelt very badly.'

'Postey, I believe you think with your nose,' said Wynn. 'I know you don't with your mind. Now, what type's that?'

'I'll go and get the chart,' said Mary.

'You're hopeless! You haven't the mental capacity of a white mouse,' he cried, and explained the dials and the sockets for bomb-dropping till it was time to mount and ride the wet clouds once more.

'Ah!' said Mary, as the stinking thing flared upward. 'Wait till our Flying Corps gets to work! Wynn says it's much safer than in the trenches.'

'I wonder,' said Miss Fowler. 'Tell Cheape to come and tow me home again.'

'It's all downhill. I can do it,' said Mary, 'if you put the brake on.' She laid her lean self against the pushing-bar and home they trundled.

'Now, be careful you aren't heated and catch a chill,' said overdressed Miss Fowler.

'Nothing makes me perspire,' said Mary. As she bumped the chair under the porch she straightened her long back. The exertion had given her a colour, and the wind had loosened a wisp of hair across her forehead. Miss Fowler glanced at her.

'What do you ever think of, Mary?' she demanded suddenly.

'Oh, Wynn says he wants another three pairs of stockings – as thick as we can make them.'

'Yes. But I mean the things that women think about Here you are, more than forty –'

'Forty-four,' said truthful Mary.

'Well?'

'Well?' Mary offered Miss Fowler her shoulder as usual.

'And you've been with me ten years now.'

'Let's see,' said Mary. 'Wynn was eleven when he came. He's twenty now, and I came two years before that. It must be eleven.'

'Eleven! And you've never told me anything that matters in all that while. Looking back, it seems to me that I've done all the talking.'

'I'm afraid I'm not much of a conversationalist. As Wynn says, I haven't the mind. Let me take your hat.'

Miss Fowler, moving stiffly from the hip, stamped her rubber-tipped stick on the tiled hall floor. 'Mary, aren't you anything except a companion? Would you ever have been anything except a companion?'

Mary hung up the garden hat on its proper peg. 'No,' she said after consideration. 'I don't imagine I ever should. But I've no imagination, I'm afraid.'

She fetched Miss Fowler her eleven o'clock glass of Contrexeville.

That was the wet December when it rained six inches to the month, and the women went abroad as little as might be. Wynn's flying chariot visited them several times, and for two mornings (he had warned her by postcard) Mary heard the thresh of his propellers at dawn. The second time she ran to the window, and stared at the whitening sky. A little blur passed overhead. She lifted her lean arms towards it.

That evening at six o'clock there came an announcement in an official envelope that Second Lieutenant W. Fowler had been killed during a trial flight. Death was instantaneous. She read it and carried it to Miss Fowler.

'I never expected anything else,' said Miss Fowler; 'but I'm sorry it happened before he had done anything.'

The room was whirling round Mary Postgate, but she found herself quite steady in the midst of it.

'Yes,' she said. 'It's a great pity he didn't die in action after he had killed somebody.'

'He was killed instantly. That's one comfort,' Miss Fowler went on.

'But Wynn says the shock of a fall kills a man at once – whatever happens to the tanks,' quoted Mary.

The room was coming to rest now. She heard Miss Fowler say impatiently, 'But why can't we cry, Mary?' and herself replying, 'There's nothing to cry for. He has done his duty as much as Mrs. Grant's son did.'

'And when he died, she came and cried all the morning,' said Miss Fowler. 'This only makes me feel tired – terribly tired. Will you help me to bed, please, Mary? – And I think I'd like the hot-water bottle.'

So Mary helped her and sat beside, talking of Wynn in his riotous youth.

'I believe,' said Miss Fowler suddenly, 'that old people and young people slip from under a stroke like this. The middle-aged feel it most.'

'I expect that's true,' said Mary, rising. 'I'm going to put away the things in his room now. Shall we wear mourning?'

'Certainly not,' said Miss Fowler. 'Except, of course, at the funeral. I can't go. You will. I want you to arrange about his being buried here. What a blessing it didn't happen at Salisbury!'

Every one, from the Authorities of the Flying Corps to the Rector, was most kind and sympathetic. Mary found herself for the moment in a world where bodies were in the habit of being despatched by all sorts of conveyances to all sorts of places. And at the funeral two young men in buttoned-up uniforms stood beside the grave and spoke to her afterwards.

'You're Miss Postgate, aren't you?' said one, 'Fowler told me about you. He was a good chap – a first-class fellow – a great loss.'

'Great loss!' growled his companion. 'We're all awfully sorry.'

'How high did he fall from?' Mary whispered.

'Pretty nearly four thousand feet, I should think, didn't he? You were up that day, Monkey?'

'All of that,' the other child replied. 'My bar made three thousand, and I wasn't as high as him by a lot.'

'Then that's all right,' said Mary. 'Thank you very much.'

They moved away as Mrs. Grant flung herself weeping on Mary's flat chest, under the lych-gate, and cried, 'I know how it feels! I know how it feels!'

'But both his parents are dead,' Mary returned, as she fended her off. 'Perhaps they've all met by now,' she added vaguely as she escaped towards the coach.

'I've thought of that too,' wailed Mrs. Grant; 'but then he'll be practically a stranger to them. Quite embarrassing!'

Mary faithfully reported every detail of the ceremony to Miss Fowler, who, when she described Mrs. Grant's outburst, laughed aloud.

'Oh, how Wynn would have enjoyed it! He was always utterly unreliable at funerals. D'you remember—' And they talked of him again, each piecing out the other's gaps. 'And now,' said Miss Fowler, 'we'll pull up the blinds and we'll have a general tidy. That always does us good. Have you seen to Wynn's things?'

'Everything – since he first came,' said Mary, 'He was never destructive – even with his toys.'

They faced that neat room.

'It can't be natural not to cry,' Mary said at last. 'I'm so afraid you'll have a reaction.'

'As I told you, we old people slip from under the stroke. It's you I'm afraid for. Have you cried yet?'

'I can't. It only makes me angry with the Germans.'

'That's sheer waste of vitality,' said Miss Fowler. 'We must live till the war's finished.' She opened a full wardrobe. 'Now, I've been thinking things over. This is my plan. All his civilian clothes can be given away – Belgian refugees, and so on.'

Mary nodded. 'Boots, collars, and gloves?'

'They came back yesterday with his Flying Corps clothes' – Mary pointed to a roll on the little iron bed.

'Ah, but keep his Service things. Some one may be glad of them later. Do you remember his sizes?'

'Five feet eight and a half; thirty-six inches round the chest. But he told me he's just put on an inch and a half. I'll mark it on a label and tie it on his sleeping-bag.'

'so that disposes of that,' said Miss Fowler, tapping the palm of one hand with the ringed third finger of the other. 'What a waste it all is! We'll get his old school trunk tomorrow and pack his civilian clothes.'

'And the rest?' said Mary. 'His books and pictures and the games and the toys – and – and the rest?'

'My plan is to burn every single thing,' said Miss Fowler. 'Then we shall know where they are and no one can handle them afterwards. What do you think?'

'I think that would be much the best,' said Mary. 'But there's such a lot of them.'

'We'll burn them in the destructor,' said Miss Fowler.

This was an open-air furnace for the consumption of refuse; a little circular four-foot tower of pierced brick over an iron grating. Miss Fowler had noticed the design in a gardening journal years ago, and had had it built at the bottom of the garden. It suited her tidy soul, for it saved unsightly rubbish-heaps and the ashes lightened the stiff clay soil.

Mary considered for a moment, saw her way clear, and nodded again. They spent the evening putting away well-remembered civilian suits, underclothes that Mary had marked, and the regiments of very gaudy socks and ties. A second trunk was needed, and, after that, a little packing case, and it was late next day when Cheape and the local carrier lifted them to the cart. The Rector luckily knew of a friend's son, about five feet eight and a half inches high, to whom a complete Flying Corps outfit would be most acceptable, and sent his gardener's son down with a barrow to take delivery of it. The cap was hung up in Miss Fowler's bedroom, the belt in Miss Postgate's; for, as Miss Fowler said, they had no desire to make tea-party talk of them.

'That disposes of that,' said Miss Fowler. 'I'll leave the rest to you, Mary. I can't run up and down in the garden. You'd better take the big clothes-basket and get Nellie to help you.'

'I shall take the wheel-barrow and do it myself,' said Mary, and for once in her life closed her mouth.

Miss Fowler, in moments of irritation, had called Mary deadly methodical. She put on her oldest water-proof and gardening-hat and her ever-slipping goloshes, for the weather was on the edge of more rain. She gathered firelighters from the kitchen, a half-scuttle of coals, and a faggot of brushwood. These she wheeled in the barrow down the mossed paths to the dank little laurel shrubbery where the destructor stood under the drip of three oaks. She climbed the wire fence into the Rector's glebe just behind, and from his tenant's rick pilled two large armfuls of good hay, which she spread neatly on the fire-bars. Next, journey by journey, passing Miss Fowler's white face at the morning-room window each time, she brought down in the towel-covered clothes-basket, on the wheel-barrow, thumbed and used Hentys, Marrayats, Levers, Stevensons, Baroness Orczys, Garvices, schoolbooks, and atlases, unrelated piles of the Motor Cyclist, the Light Car, and catalogues of Olympia Exhibitions; the remnants of a fleet of sailing-ships from nine-penney cutters to a three-guinea yacht; a prep-school dressing-gown; bats from three-and-sixpence to twenty-four shillings; cricket and tennis balls; disintegrated steam and clockwork loco-motives with their twisted rails; a grey and red tin model of a submarine; a dumb gramophone and cracked records; golf-clubs that had to be broken across the knee, like his walking-sticks, and an assegai; photographs of private and public school cricket and football elevens, and his O.T.C. on the line of march; kodaks, and film-rolls; some pewters, and one real silver cup, for boxing competitions and Junior Hurdles; sheaves of school photographs; Miss Fowler's photograph; her own which he had borne off in fun and (good care she take not to ask!) had never returned; a playbox with a secret drawer; a load of flannels, belts, and jerseys, and a pair of spiked shoes unearthed in the attic; a packet of all the letters that Miss Fowler and she had ever written to him, kept for some absurd reason through all these years; a five-day attempt at a diary; framed pictures of racing motors in full Brooklands career, and load upon load of undistinguishable wreckage of tool-boxes, rabbit-hutches, electric batteries, tin soldiers, fret-saw outfits, and jigsaw puzzles.

Miss Fowler at the window watched her come and go, and said to herself, 'Mary's an old woman. I never realised it before.'

After lunch she recommended her to rest.

'I'm not in the least tired,' said Mary. 'I've got it all arranged. I'm going to the village at two o'clock for some paraffin. Nellie hasn't enough, and the walk will do me good.'

She made one last quest round the house before she started, and found that she had overlooked nothing. It began to mist as soon as she had skirted Vegg's Heath, where Wynn used to descend – it seemed to her that she could almost hear the beat of his propellers overhead, but there was nothing to see. She hoisted her umbrella and lunged into the blind wet till she had reached the shelter of the empty village. As she came out of Mr. Kidd's shop with a bottle full of paraffin in her string shopping-bag, she met Nurse Eden, the village nurse, and fell into talk with her, as usual, about the village children. They were parting opposite the 'Royal Oak' when a gun, they fancied, was fired immediately behind the house. It was followed by a child's shriek dying into a wail.

'Accident!' said Nurse Eden promptly, and dashed through the empty bar, followed by Mary. They found Mrs. Gerritt, the publican's wife, who cold only gasp and point to the yard, where a little cart-lodge was sliding sideways amid a clatter of tiles. Nurse Eden snatched up a sheet drying before the fire, ran out, lifted something from the ground, and flung the sheet round it. The she turned scarlet and half her uniform too, as she bore the load into the kitchen. It was little Edna Gerritt, aged nine, whom Mary had known since her perambulator days.

'Am I hurted bad?' Edna asked, and died between Nurse Eden's dripping hands. The sheet fell aside and for an instant, before she could shut her eyes, Mary saw the ripped and shredded body.

'It's a wonder she spoke at all,' said Nurse Eden. 'What in God's name was it?'

'A bomb,' said Mary.

'One o' the Zeppelins?'

'No. An aeroplane. I thought I heard it on the Heath but I fancied it was one of ours. It must have shut off its engines as it came down. That's why we didn't notice it.'

'The filthy pigs!' said Nurse Eden, all white and shaken. 'see the pickle I'm in! Go and tell Dr. Hennis, Miss Postgate.' Nurse looked at the mother, who had dropped face down on the floor. `She's only in a fit. Turn her over.'

Mary heaved Mrs. Gerritt right side up, and hurried off for the doctor. When she told her tale, he asked her to sit down in the surgery till he got her something.

'But I don't need it, I assure you,' said she. 'I don't think it would be wise to tell Miss Fowler about it, do you? Her heart is so irritable in this weather.'

Dr. Hennis looked at her admiringly as he packed up his bag.

'No. Don't tell anybody till we're sure,' he said, and hastened to the 'Royal Oak,' while Mary went on with the paraffin. The village behind her was as quiet as usual, for the news had not yet spread. She frowned a little to herself, the large nostrils expanded uglily from time to time as she muttered a phrase which Wynn who had never restrained himself before his women-folk, had applied to the enemy. 'Bloody pagans! They are bloody pagans. But, 'she continued, falling back on the teaching that had made her what she was, 'one mustn't let one's mind dwell on these things.'

Before she reached the house Dr. Hennis, who was also a special constable, overtook her in his car.

'Oh, Miss Postgate,' he said, 'I wanted to tell you that that accident at the 'Royal Oak' was due to Gerritt's stable tumbling down. It's been dangerous for a long time. It ought to have been condemned.'

'I thought I heard an explosion too,' said Mary.

'You might have been misled by the beams snapping. I've been looking at 'em. They were dry-rotted through and through. Of course, as they broke, they would make a noise just like a gun.'

'Yes?' said Mary politely.

'Poor little Edna was playing underneath it,' he went on, still holding her with his eyes, 'and that and the tiles cut her to pieces, you see?'

'I saw it,' said Mary, shaking her head. 'I heard it too.'

'Well, we cannot be sure.' Dr. Hennis changed his tone completely. 'I know both you and Nurse Eden (I've been speaking to her) are perfectly trustworthy, and I can rely on you not to say anything – yet at least. It is no good to stir up people unless – '

'Oh, I never do – anyhow,' said Mary, and Dr. Hennis went on to the country town.

After all, she told herself, it might, just possibly, have been the collapse of the old stable that had done all those things to poor little Edna. She was sorry she had even hinted at other things, but Nurse Eden was discretion itself. By the time she reached home the affair seemed increasingly remote by its very monstrosity. As she came in, Miss Fowler told her that a couple of aeroplanes had passed half an hour ago.

'I though I heard them,' she replied, 'I'm going down to the garden now. I've got the paraffin.'

'Yes, but – what have you got on your boots? They're soaking wet. Change them at once.'

Not only did Mary obey, but she wrapped the boots in a newspaper, and put them into the string bag with the bottles. So, armed with the longest kitchen poker, she left.

'It's raining again,' was Miss Fowler's last word, 'but – I know you won't be happy till that's disposed of.'

'It won't take long. I've got everything down there, and I've put the lid on the destructor to keep the wet out.'

The shrubbery was filling with twilight by the same time she had completed her arrangements and sprinkled the sacrificial oil. As she lit the match that would burn her heart to ashes, she heard a groan or a grunt behind the dense Portugal laurels.

'Cheape?' she called impatiently, but Cheape, with his ancient lumbago, in his comfortable cottage would be the last man to profane the sanctuary. 'Sheep,' she concluded, and threw in the fuse. The pure went up in a roar, and the immediate flame hastened the night around her.'

'How Wynn would have loved this!' she thought, stepping back from the blaze.

By its light she saw, half hidden behind a laurel not five paces away, a bare-headed man sitting very stiffly at the foot of one of the oaks. A broken branch lay across his lap – one booted leg protruding from beneath it. His head moved ceaselessly from side to side, but his body was as still as the tree's trunk. He was dressed – she moved sideways to look more closely – in a uniform something like Lynn's with a flap buttoned across the chest. For an instant she had some idea that it might be one of the young flying men she had met at the funeral. But their heads were dark and glassy. This man's was as pale as a baby's, and so closely cropped that she could see the disgusting pink skin beneath. His lips moved.

'What do you say?' Mary moved towards him and stooped.

'Laty! Laty! Laty!' he muttered, while his hands picked at the dead wet leaves. There was no doubt as to his nationality. It made her so angry that she strode back to the destructor, though it was still too hot to use the poker there. Wynn's books seemed to be catching well. She looked up at the oak behind the man; several of the light upper and two or three rotten lower branches had broken and scattered their rubbish on the shrubbery path. On the lowest fork a helmet with dependent strings, showed like a bird's-nest in the light of a long-tongued flame. Evidently this person had fallen through the trees. Wynn had told her that it was quite possible for people to fall out of aeroplanes. Wynn told her, too, that trees were useful things to break an aviators fall, but in this case the aviator must have been broken or he would moved from his queer position. He seemed helpless except for his belt – and Mary loathed pistols. Months ago, after reading certain Belgian reports together, she and Miss Fowler had had dealings with one – a huge revolver with flat-nosed bullets, which latter, Wynn said, were forbidden by the rules of war to be used against civilised enemies. 'They're good enough for us,' Miss Fowler had replied. 'show Mary how it works.' And Wynn, laughing at the mere possibility of any such need, had led the craven winking Mary into the Rector's disused quarry, and had shown her how to fire the terrible machine. It lay now in the top-left-hand drawer of her toilet-table – a memento not included in the burning. Wynn would be pleased to see how she was not afraid.

She slipped up to the house to get it. When she came through the rain, the eyes in the head were alive with expectation. The mouth even tried to smile. But at sight of the revolver its corners went down just like Edna Gerritt's. A tear trickled from one eye, and the head rolled from shoulder to shoulder as through trying to point out something.

'Cassee. Tout cassee [Broken. All broken],' it whimpered.

'What do you say?' said Mary disgustedly, keeping well to one side, though only the head moved.

'Cassee,' it repeated. 'Che me rends. Le medicin! Toctor! [I am hurt. The doctor (French) Doctor!]'

'Nein!' said she, bringing all her small German to bear with the big pistol. 'Ich haben der todt Kinder gesehn [I have see the dead child].'

The head was still. Mary's hand dropped. She had been careful to keep her finger off the trigger for fear of acci-dents. After a few moments' waiting, she returned to the destructor, where the flames were falling, and churned up Wynn's charring books with the poker. Again the head groaned for the doctor.

'Stop that!' said Mary, and stamped her foot. 'Stop that, you bloody pagan!'

The words came quite smoothly and naturally. They were Wynn's own words, and Wynn was a gentleman who for no consideration on earth would have torn little Edna into those vividly coloured strips and strings. But this thing hunched under the oak-tree had done that thing. It was no question of reading horrors out of newspapers to Miss Fowler. Mary had seen it with her own eyes on the 'Royal Oak' kitchen table. She must not allow her mind to dwell upon it. Now Wynn was dead, and every thing connected with him was lumping and rustling and tinkling under her busy poker into red black dust and grey leaves of ash. The thing beneath the oak would die too. Mary had seen death more than once. She came of a family that had a knack of dying under, as she told Miss Fowler, 'most distressing circumstances.' She would stay where she was till she was entirely satisfied that It was dead – dead as dear papa in the late 'eighties; aunt Mary in 'eighty-nine; mamma in 'ninety-one; cousin Dick in 'ninety-five; Lady McCausland's housemaid in 'ninety-nine; Lady McCausland's sister in nineteen hundred and one; Wynn burried five days ago; and Edna Gerritt still waiting for decent earth to hide her. As she thought – her underlip caught up by one faded canine, brows knit and nostrils wide – she wielded the poker with lunges that jarred the grating at the bottom, and careful scrapes round the brick-work above. She looked at her wrist-watch. It was getting on to half-past four, and the rain was coming down in earnest. Tea would be at five. If It did not die before that time, she would be soaked and would have to change. Meantime, and this occupied her, Wynn's things were burning well in spite of the hissing wet though now and again a book-back with a quite distinguishable title would be heaved up out of the mass. The exercise of stoking had given her a glow which seemed to reach to the marrow of her bones. She hummed – Mary never had a voice – to herself. She had never believed in all those advanced views – though Miss Fowler herself leaned a little that way – of woman's work in the world; but now she saw there was much to be said for them. This, for instance, was her work – work which no man, least of all Dr. Hennis, would ever have done. A man, at such a crisis, would be what Wynn called a 'sportsman'; would leave everything to fetch help, and would certainly bring It into the house. Now a woman's business was to make a happy home for – for a husband and children. Failing these – it was not a thing one should allow one's mind to dwell upon – but –

'Stop it!' Mary cried once more across the shadows. 'Nein, I tell you! Ich haben der todt Kinder gesehn.'

But it was a fact. A woman who had missed these things could still be useful – more useful than a man in certain respects. She thumped like a paviour through the settling ashes at the secret thrill of it. The rain was damping the fire, but she could feel – it was too dark to see – that her work was done. There was a dull red glow at the bottom of the destructor, not enough to char the wooden lid if she slipped it half over against the driving wet. This arranged, she leaned on the poker and waited, while an increasing rapture laid hold on her. She ceased to think. She gave herself up to feel. Her long pleasure was broken by a sound that she had waited for in agony several times in her life. She leaned forward and listened, smiling. There could be no mistake. She closed her eyes and drank it in. Once it ceased abruptly.

'Go on,' she murmured, half aloud. 'That isn't the end.'

Then the end came very distinctly in a lull between two rain-gusts. Mary Postgate drew her breath short between her teeth and shivered from head to foot. 'That's all right,' said she contentedly, and went up to the house, where she scandalised the whole routine by taking a luxurious hot bath before tea, and came down looking, as Miss Fowler said when she saw her lying all relaxed on the other sofa, 'quite handsome!'

○○

THEY

○○

ONE VIEW CALLED ME TO ANOTHER; ONE hill top to its fellow, half across the county, and since I could answer at no more trouble than the snapping forward of a lever, I let the county flow under my wheels. The orchid-studded flats of the East gave way to the thyme, ilex, and grey grass of the Downs; these again to the rich cornland and fig-trees of the lower coast, where you carry the beat of the tide on your left hand for fifteen level miles; and when at last I turned inland through a huddle of rounded hills and woods I had run myself clean out of my known marks. Beyond that precise hamlet which stands godmother to the capital of the

United States, I found hidden villages where bees, the only things awake, boomed in eighty-foot lindens that overhung grey Norman churches; miraculous brooks diving under stone bridges built for heavier traffic than would ever vex them again; tithe-barns larger than their churches, and an old smithy that cried out aloud how it had once been a hall of the Knights of the Temple. Gipsies I found on a common where the gorse, bracken, and heath fought it out together up a mile of Roman road; and a little further on I disturbed a red fox rolling dog-fashion in the naked sunlight.

As the wooded hills closed about me I stood up in the car to take the bearings of that great Down whose ringed head is a landmark for fifty miles across the low countries. I judged that the lie of the country would bring me across some westward running road that went to his feet, but I did not allow for the confusing veils of the woods. A quick turn plunged me first into a green cutting brimful of liquid sunshine, next into a gloomy tunnel where last year's dead leaves whispered and scuffled about my tyres. The strong hazel stuff meeting overhead had not been cut for a couple of generations at least, nor had any axe helped the moss-cankered oak and beech to spring above them. Here the road changed frankly into a carpeted ride on whose brown velvet spent primrose-clumps showed like jade, and a few sickly, white-stalked blue-bells nodded together. As the slope favoured I shut off the power and slid over the whirled leaves, expecting every moment to meet a keeper; but I only heard a jay, far off, arguing against the silence under the twilight of the trees.

Still the track descended. I was on the point of reversing and working my way back on the second speed ere I ended in some swamp, when I saw sunshine through the tangle ahead and lifted the brake.

It was down again at once. As the light beat across my face my fore-wheels took the turf of a great still lawn from which sprang horsemen ten feet high with levelled lances, monstrous peacocks, and sleek round-headed maids of honour – blue, black, and glistening – all of clipped yew. Across the lawn – the marshalled woods besieged it on three sides – stood an ancient house of lichened and weather-worn stone, with mullioned windows and roofs of rose-red tile. It was flanked by semi-circular walls, also rose-red, that closed the lawn on the fourth side, and at their feet a box hedge grew man-high. There were doves on the roof about the slim brick chimneys, and I caught a glimpse of an octagonal dove-house behind the screening wall.

Here, then, I stayed; a horseman's green spear laid at my breast; held by the exceeding beauty of that jewel in that setting.

'If I am not packed off for a trespasser, or if this knight does not ride a wallop at me,' thought I, 'Shakespeare and Queen Elizabeth at least must come out of that half-open garden door and ask me to tea.'

A child appeared at an upper window, and I thought the little thing waved a friendly hand. But it was to call a companion, for presently another bright head showed. Then I heard a laugh among the yew-peacocks, and turning to make sure (till then I had been watching the house only) I saw the silver of a fountain behind a hedge thrown up against the sun. The doves on the roof cooed to the cooing water; but between the two notes I caught the utterly happy chuckle of a child absorbed in some light mischief.

The garden door – heavy oak sunk deep in the thickness of the wall – opened further: a woman in a big garden hat set her foot slowly on the time-hollowed stone step and as slowly walked across the turf. I was forming some apology when she lifted up her head and I saw that she was blind.

'I heard you,' she said. 'Isn't that a motor car?'

'I'm afraid I've made a mistake in my road. I should have turned off up above – I never dreamed –' I began.

'But I'm very glad. Fancy a motor car coming into the garden! It will be such a treat –' She turned and made as though looking about her. 'You – you haven't seen any one, have you – perhaps?'

'No one to speak to, but the children seemed interested at a distance.'

'Which?'

'I saw a couple up at the window just now, and I think I heard a little chap in the grounds.'

'Oh, lucky you!' she cried, and her face brightened. 'I hear them, of course, but that's all. You've seen them and heard them?'

'Yes,' I answered. 'And if I know anything of children one of them's having a beautiful time by the fountain yonder. Escaped, I should imagine.'

'You're fond of children?'

I gave her one or two reasons why I did not altogether hate them.

'Of course, of course,' she said. 'Then you understand. Then you won't think it foolish if I ask you to take your car through the gardens, once or twice – quite slowly. I'm sure they'd like to see it. They see so little, poor things. One tries to make their life pleasant, but –' she threw out her hands towards the woods. 'We're so out of the world here.'

'That will be splendid,' I said. 'But I can't cut up your grass.'

She faced to the right. 'Wait a minute,' she said. 'We're at the South gate, aren't we? Behind those peacocks there's a flagged path. We call it the Peacock's Walk. You can't see it from here, they tell me, but if you squeeze along by the edge of the wood you can turn at the first peacock and get on to the flags.'

It was sacrilege to wake that dreaming house-front with the clatter of machinery, but I swung the car to clear the turf, brushed along the edge of the wood and turned in on the broad stone path where the fountain-basin lay like one star-sapphire.

'May I come too?' she cried. 'No, please don't help me. They'll like it better if they see me.'

She felt her way lightly to the front of the car, and with one foot on the step she called: 'Children, oh, children! Look and see what's going to happen!'

The voice would have drawn lost souls from the Pit, for the yearning that underlay its sweetness, and I was not surprised to hear an answering shout behind the yews. It must have been the child by the fountain, but he fled at our approach, leaving a little toy boat in the water. I saw the glint of his blue blouse among the still horsemen.

Very disposedly we paraded the length of the walk and at her request backed again. This time the child had got the better of his panic, but stood far off and doubting.

'The little fellow's watching us,' I said. 'I wonder if he'd like a ride.'

'They're very shy still. Very shy. But, oh, lucky you to be able to see them! Let's listen.'

I stopped the machine at once, and the humid stillness, heavy with the scent of box, cloaked us deep. Shears I could hear where some gardener was clipping; a mumble of bees and broken voices that might have been the doves.

'Oh, unkind!' she said weariedly.

'Perhaps they're only shy of the motor. The little maid at the window looks tremendously interested.'

'Yes?' She raised her head. 'It was wrong of me to say that. They are really fond of me. It's the only thing that makes life worth living – when they're fond of you, isn't it? I daren't think what the place would be without them. By the way, is it beautiful?'

'I think it is the most beautiful place I have ever seen.'

'So they all tell me. I can feel it, of course, but that isn't quite the same thing.'

'Then have you never? – ' I began, but stopped abashed.

'Not since I can remember. It happened when I was only a few months old, they tell me. And yet I must remember something, else how could I dream about colours? I see light in my dreams, and colours, but I never see them. I only hear them just as I do when I'm awake.'

'It's difficult to see faces in dreams. Some people can, but most of us haven't the gift,' I went on, looking up at the window where the child stood all but hidden.

'I've heard that too,' she said. 'And they tell me that one never sees a dead person's face in a dream. Is that true?'

'I believe it is – now I come to think of it.'

'But how is it with yourself – yourself?' The blind eyes turned towards me.

'I have never seen the faces of my dead in any dream,' I answered.

'Then it must be as bad as being blind.'

The sun had dipped behind the woods and the long shades were possessing the insolent horsemen one by one. I saw the light die from off the top of a glossy-leaved lance and all the brave hard green turn to soft black. The house, accepting another day at end, as it had accepted one hundred thousand gone, seemed to settle deeper into its rest among the shadows.

'Have you ever wanted to?' she said after the silence.

'Very much sometimes,' I replied. The child had left the window as the shadows closed upon it.

'Ah! So've I, but I don't suppose it's allowed . . . Where d'you live?'

'Quite the other side of the county – sixty miles and more, and I must be going back. I've come without my big lamp.'

'But it's not dark yet. I can feel it.'

'I'm afraid it will be by the time I get home. Could you lend me someone to set me on my road at first? I've utterly lost myself.'

'I'll send Madden with you to the cross-roads. We are so out of the world, I don't wonder you were lost! I'll guide you round to the front of the house; but you will go slowly, won't you, till you're out of the grounds? It isn't foolish, do you think?'

'I promise you I'll go like this,' I said, and let the car start herself down the flagged path.

We skirted the left wing of the house, whose elaborately cast lead guttering alone was worth a day's journey; passed under a great rose-grown gate in the red wall, and so round to the high front of the house which in beauty and stateliness as much excelled the back as that all others I had seen.

'Is it so very beautiful?' she said wistfully when she heard my raptures. 'And you like the lead-figures too? There's the old azalea garden behind. They say that this place must have been made for children. Will you help me out, please? I should like to come with you as far as the cross-roads, but I mustn't leave them. Is that you, Madden? I want you to show this gentleman the way to the cross-roads. He has lost his way but – he has seen them.'

A butler appeared noiselessly at the miracle of old oak that must be called the front door, and slipped aside to put on his hat. She stood looking at me with open blue eyes in which no sight lay, and I saw for the first time that she was beautiful.

'Remember,' she said quietly, 'if you are fond of them you will come again,' and disappeared within the house.

The butler in the car said nothing till we were nearly at the lodge gates, where, catching a glimpse of a blue blouse in a shrubbery, I swerved amply lest the devil that leads little boys to play should drag me into child-murder.

'Excuse me,' he asked of a sudden, 'but why did you do that, Sir?'

'The child yonder.'

'Our young gentleman in blue?'

'Of course.'

'He runs about a good deal. Did you see him by the fountain, Sir?'

'Oh, yes, several times. Do we turn here?'

'Yes, Sir. And did you 'appen to see them upstairs too?'

'At the upper window? Yes.'

'Was that before the mistress come out to speak to you, Sir?'

'A little before that. Why d'you want to know?'

He paused a little. 'Only to make sure that – that they had seen the car, Sir, because with children running about, though I'm sure you're driving particularly careful, there might be an accident. That was all, Sir. Here are the cross-roads. You can't miss your way from now on. Thank you, Sir, but that isn't our custom, not with –'

'I beg your pardon,' I said, and thrust away the British silver.

'Oh, it's quite right with the rest of 'em as a rule. Good-bye, Sir.'

He retired into the armour-plated conning tower of his caste and walked away. Evidently a butler solicitous for the honour of his house, and interested, probably through a maid, in the nursery.

Once beyond the signposts at the cross-roads I looked back, but the crumpled hills interlaced so jealously that I could not see where the house had lain. When I asked its name at a cottage along the road, the fat woman who sold sweetmeats there gave me to understand that people with motor cars had small right to live – much less to 'go about talking like carriage folk.' They were not a pleasant-mannered community.

When I retraced my route on the map that evening I was little wiser. Hawkin's Old Farm appeared to be the survey title of the place, and the old County Gazetteer, generally so ample, did not allude to it. The big house of those parts was Hodnington Hall, Georgian with early Victorian embellishments, as an atrocious steel engraving attested. I carried my difficulty to a neighbour – a deep-rooted tree of that soil – and he gave me a name of a family which conveyed no meaning.

A month or so later – I went again, or it may have been that my car took the road of her own volition. She over-ran the fruitless Downs, threaded every turn of the maze of lanes below the hills, drew through the high-walled woods, impenetrable in their full leaf, came out at the cross-roads where the butler had left me, and a little further on developed an internal trouble which forced me to turn her in on a grass way-waste that cut into a summer-silent hazel wood. So far as I could make sure by the sun and a six-inch Ordnance map, this should be the road flank of that wood which I had first explored from the heights above. I made a mighty serious business of my repairs and a glittering shop of my repair kit, spanners, pump, and the like, which I spread out orderly upon a rug. It was a trap to catch all childhood, for on such a day, I argued, the children would not be far off. When I paused in my work I listened, but the wood was so full of the noises of summer (though the birds had mated) that I could not at first distinguish these from the tread of small cautious feet stealing across the dead leaves. I rang my bell in an alluring manner, but the feet fled, and I repented, for to a child a sudden noise is very real terror. I must have been at work half an hour when I heard in the wood the voice of the blind woman crying: 'Children, oh, children, where are you?' and the stillness made slow to close on the perfection of that cry. She came towards me, half feeling her way between the tree-boles, and though a child, it seemed, clung to her skirt, it swerved into the leafage like a rabbit as she drew nearer.

'Is that you?' she said, 'from the other side of the county?'

'Yes, it's me from the other side of the county.'

'Then why didn't you come through the upper woods? They were there just now.'

'They were here a few minutes ago. I expect they knew my car had broken down, and came to see the fun.'

'Nothing serious, I hope? How do cars break down?'

'In fifty different ways. Only mine has chosen the fifty-first.'

She laughed merrily at the tiny joke, cooed with delicious laughter, and pushed her hat back.

'Let me hear,' she said.

'Wait a moment,' I cried, 'and I'll get you a cushion.'

She set her foot on the rug all covered with spare parts, and stooped above it eagerly. 'What delightful things!' The hands through which she saw glanced in the chequered sunlight. 'A box here – another box! Why you've arranged them like playing shop!'

'I confess now that I put it out to attract them. I don't need half those things really.'

'How nice of you! I heard your bell in the upper wood. You say they were here before that?'

'I'm sure of it. Why are they so shy? That little fellow in blue who was with you just now ought to have got over his fright. He's been watching me like a Red Indian.'

'It must have been your bell,' she said. 'I heard one of them go past me in trouble when I was coming down. They're shy – so shy even with me.' She turned her face over her shoulder and cried again: 'Children! Oh, children! Look and see!'

'They must have gone off together on their own affairs,' I suggested, for there was a murmur behind us of lowered voices broken by the sudden squeaking giggles of childhood. I returned to my tinkerings and she leaned forward, her chin on her hand, listening interestedly.

'How many are they?' I said at last. The work was finished, but I saw no reason to go.

Her forehead puckered a little in thought. 'I don't quite know,' she said simply. 'Sometimes more – sometimes less. They come and stay with me because I love them, you see.'

'That must be very jolly,' I said, replacing a drawer, and as I spoke I heard the inanity of my answer.

'You – you aren't laughing at me,' she cried. 'I – I haven't any of my own. I never married. People laugh at me sometimes about them because – because – '

'Because they're savages,' I returned. 'It's nothing to fret for. That sort laugh at everything that isn't in their own fat lives.'

'I don't know. How should I? I only don't like being

laughed at about them. It hurts; and when one can't see . . . I don't want to seem silly,' her chin quivered like a child's as she spoke, 'but we blindies have only one skin, I think. Everything outside hits straight at our souls. It's different with you. You've such good defences in your eyes – looking out – before any one can really pain you in your soul. People forget that with us.'

I was silent, reviewing that inexhaustible matter – the more than inherited (since it is also carefully taught) brutality of the Christian peoples, beside which the mere heathendom of the West Coast nigger is clean and restrained. It led me a long distance into myself.

'Don't do that!' she said of a sudden, putting her hands before her eyes.

'What?'

She made a gesture with her hand.

'That! It's – it's all purple and black. Don't! That colour hurts.'

'But how in the world do you know about colours?' I exclaimed, for here was a revelation indeed.

'Colours as colours?' she asked.

'No. Those Colours which you saw just now.'

'You know as well as I do,' she laughed, 'else you wouldn't have asked that question. They aren't in the world at all. They're in you – when you went so angry.'

'D'you mean a dull purplish patch, like port-wine mixed with ink?' I said.

'I've never seen ink or port-wine, but the colours aren't mixed. They are separate – all separate.'

'Do you mean black streaks and jags across the purple?'

She nodded. 'Yes – if they are like this,' and zigzagged

her finger again, 'but it's more red than purple – that bad colour.'

'And what are the colours at the top of the – whatever you see?'

Slowly she leaned forward and traced on the rug the figure of the Egg itself.

'I see them so,' she said, pointing with a grass stem, 'white, green, yellow, red, purple, and when people are angry or bad, black across the red – as you were just now.'

'Who told you anything about it – in the beginning?' I demanded.

'About the colours? No one. I used to ask what colours were when I was little – in table-covers and curtains and carpets, you see – because some colours hurt me and some made me happy. People told me; and when I got older that was how I saw people.' Again she traced the outline of the Egg which it is given to very few of us to see.

'All by yourself?' I repeated.

'All by myself. There wasn't any one else. I only found out afterwards that other people did not see the Colours.'

She leaned against the tree-bole plaiting and unplaiting chance-plucked grass stems. The children in the wood had drawn nearer. I could see them with the tail of my eye frolicking like squirrels.

'Now I am sure you will never laugh at me,' she went on after a long silence. 'Nor at them.'

'Goodness! No!' I cried, jolted out of my train of thought. 'A man who laughs at a child – unless the child is laughing too – is a heathen!'

'I didn't mean that of course. You'd never laugh at

children, but I thought – I used to think – that perhaps you might laugh about them. So now I beg your pardon . . . What are you going to laugh at?'

I had made no sound, but she knew.

'At the notion of your begging my pardon. If you had done your duty as a pillar of the state and a landed proprietress you ought to have summoned me for trespass when I barged through your woods the other day. It was disgraceful of me – inexcusable.'

She looked at me, her head against the tree trunk – long and steadfastly – this woman who could see the naked soul.

'How curious,' she half whispered. 'How very curious.'

'Why, what have I done?'

'You don't understand . . . and yet you understood about the Colours. Don't you understand?'

She spoke with a passion that nothing had justified, and I faced her bewilderedly as she rose. The children had gathered themselves in a roundel behind a bramble bush. One sleek head bent over something smaller, and the set of the little shoulders told me that fingers were on lips. They, too, had some child's tremendous secret. I alone was hopelessly astray there in the broad sunlight.

'No,' I said, and shook my head as though the dead eyes could note. 'Whatever it is, I don't understand yet. Perhaps I shall later – if you'll let me come again.'

'You will come again,' she answered. 'You will surely come again and walk in the wood.'

'Perhaps the children will know me well enough by that time to let me play with them – as a favour. You know what children are like.'

'It isn't a matter of favour but of right,' she replied, and while I wondered what she meant, a dishevelled woman plunged round the bend of the road, loose-haired, purple, almost lowing with agony as she ran. It was my rude, fat friend of the sweetmeat shop. The blind woman heard and stepped forward. 'What is it, Mrs. Madehurst?' she asked.

The woman flung her apron over her head and literally grovelled in the dust, crying that her grandchild was sick to death, that the local doctor was away fishing, that Jenny the mother was at her wits' end, and so forth, with repetitions and bellowings.

'Where's the next nearest doctor?' I asked between paroxysms.

'Madden will tell you. Go round to the house and take him with you. I'll attend to this. Be quick!' She half-supported the fat woman into the shade. In two minutes I was blowing all the horns of Jericho under the front of the House Beautiful, and Madden, in the pantry, rose to the crisis like a butler and a man.

A quarter of an hour at illegal speeds caught us a doctor five miles away. Within the half-hour we had decanted him, much interested in motors, at the door of the sweetmeat shop, and drew up the road to await the verdict.

'Useful things cars,' said Madden, all man and no butler. 'If I'd had one when mine took sick she wouldn't have died.'

'How was it?' I asked.

'Croup. Mrs. Madden was away. No one knew what to do. I drove eight miles in a tax cart for the Doctor.

She was choked when we came back. This car'd ha' saved her. She'd have been close on ten now.'

'I'm sorry,' I said. 'I thought you were rather fond of children from what you told me going to the cross-roads the other day.'

'Have you seen 'em again, Sir – this mornin'?'

'Yes, but they're well broke to cars. I couldn't get any of them within twenty yards of it.'

He looked at me carefully as a scout considers a stranger – not as a menial should lift his eyes to his divinely appointed superior.

'I wonder why,' he said just above the breath that he drew.

We waited on. A light wind from the sea wandered up and down the long lines of the woods, and the wayside grasses, whitened already with summer dust, rose and bowed in sallow waves.

A woman, wiping the suds off her arms, came out of the cottage next the sweetmeat shop.

'I've be'n listenin' in de back-yard,' she said cheerily. 'He says Arthur's unaccountable bad. Did ye hear him shruck just now? Unaccountable bad. I reckon t'will come Jenny's turn to walk in de wood nex' week along, Mr. Madden.'

'Excuse me, Sir, but your lap-robe is slipping,' said Madden deferentially. The woman started, dropped a curtsey, and hurried away.

'What does she mean by 'walking in the wood'?' I asked.

'It must be some saying they use hereabouts. I'm from Norfolk myself,' said Madden. 'They're an independent lot in this county. She took you for a chauffeur, Sir.'

I saw the Doctor come out of the cottage followed by a draggle-tailed wench who clung to his arm as though he could make treaty for her with Death. 'Dat sort,' she wailed – 'dey're just as much to us dat has 'em as if dey was lawful born. Just as much – just as much! An' God he'd be just as pleased if you saved 'un, Doctor. Don't take it from me. Miss Florence will tell ye de very same. Don't leave 'im, Doctor!'

'I know. I know,' said the man, 'but he'll be quiet for a while now. We'll get the nurse and the medicine as fast as we can.' He signalled me to come forward with the car, and I strove not to be privy to what followed; but I saw the girl's face, blotched and frozen with grief, and I felt the hand without a ring clutching at my knees when we moved away.

The Doctor was a man of some humour, for I remember he claimed my car under the Oath of Aesculapius, and used it and me without mercy. First we convoyed Mrs. Madehurst and the blind woman to wait by the sick-bed till the nurse should come. Next we invaded a neat county town for prescriptions (the Doctor said the trouble was cerebro-spinal meningitis), and when the County Institute, banked and flanked with scared market cattle, reported itself out of nurses, for the moment we literally flung ourselves loose upon the county. We conferred with the owners of great houses – magnates at the ends of overarching avenues whose big-boned womenfolk strode away from their tea-tables to listen to the imperious Doctor. At last a white-haired lady sitting under a cedar of Lebanon and surrounded by a court of magnificent Borzois – all hostile to motors – gave the

Doctor, who received them as from a princess, written orders which we bore many miles at top speed, through a park, to a French nunnery, where we took over in exchange a pallid-faced and trembling Sister. She knelt at the bottom of the tonneau telling her beads without pause till, by short cuts of the Doctor's invention, we had her to the sweetmeat shop once more. It was a long afternoon crowded with mad episodes that rose and dissolved like the dust of our wheels; cross-sections of remote and incomprehensible lives through which we raced at right angles; and I went home in the dusk, wearied out, to dream of the clashing horns of cattle; round-eyed nuns walking in a garden of graves; pleasant tea-parties beneath shaded trees; the carbolic-scented, grey-painted corridors of the County Institute; the steps of shy children in the wood, and the hands that clung to my knees as the motor began to move.

★　★　★　★　★

I had intended to return in a day or two, but it pleased Fate to hold me from that side of the county, on many pretexts, till the elder and the wild rose had fruited. There came at last a brilliant day, swept clear from the southwest, that brought the hills within hand's reach – a day of unstable airs and high filmy clouds. Through no merit of my own I was free, and set the car for the third time on that known road. As I reached the crest of the Downs I felt the soft air change, saw it glaze under the sun; and, looking down at the sea, in that instant beheld the blue of the Channel turn through polished silver and dulled steel to dingy pewter. A laden collier hugging the coast steered outward for deeper water and, across copper-coloured haze, I saw sails rise one by one on the anchored fishing-fleet. In a deep dene behind me an eddy of sudden wind drummed through sheltered oaks, and spun aloft the first dry sample of autumn leaves. When I reached the beach road the sea-fog fumed over the brickfields, and the tide was telling all the groins of the gale beyond Ushant. In less than an hour summer England vanished in chill grey. We were again the shut island of the North, all the ships of the world bellowing at our perilous gates; and between their outcries ran the piping of bewildered gulls. My cap dripped moisture, the folds of the rug held it in pools or sluiced it away in runnels, and the salt-rime stuck to my lips.

Inland the smell of autumn loaded the thickened fog among the trees, and the drip became a continuous shower. Yet the late flowers — mallow of the wayside, scabious of the field, and dahlia of the garden — showed gay in the mist, and beyond the sea's breath there was little sign of decay in the leaf. Yet in the villages the house doors were all open, and bare-legged, bare-headed children sat at ease on the damp doorsteps to shout 'pip-pip' at the stranger.

I made bold to call at the sweetmeat shop, where Mrs. Madehurst met me with a fat woman's hospitable tears. Jenny's child, she said, had died two days after the nun had come. It was, she felt, best out of the way, even though insurance offices, for reasons which she did not pretend to follow, would not willingly insure such stray lives. 'Not but what Jenny didn't tend to Arthur as though he'd come all proper at de end of de first year – like Jenny herself.' Thanks to Miss Florence, the child had been buried with a pomp which, in Mrs. Madehurst's opinion, more than covered the small irregularity of its birth. She described the coffin, within and without, the glass hearse, and the evergreen lining of the grave.

'But how's the mother?' I asked.

'Jenny? Oh, she'll get over it. I've felt dat way with one or two o' my own. She'll get over. She's walkin' in de wood now.'

'In this weather?'

Mrs. Madehurst looked at me with narrowed eyes across the counter.

'I dunno but it opens de 'eart like. Yes, it opens de 'eart. Dat's where losin' and bearin' comes so alike in de long run, we do say.'

Now the wisdom of the old wives is greater than that of all the Fathers, and this last oracle sent me thinking so extendedly as I went up the road that I nearly ran over a woman and a child at the wooded corner by the lodge gates of the House Beautiful.

'Awful weather!' I cried, as I slowed dead for the turn.

'Not so bad,' she answered placidly out of the fog. 'Mine's used to 'un. You'll find yours indoors, I reckon.'

Indoors, Madden received me with professional courtesy, and kind inquiries for the health of the motor, which he would put under cover.

I waited in a still, nut-brown hall, pleasant with late flowers and warmed with a delicious wood fire – a place of good influence and great peace. (Men and women may sometimes, after great effort, achieve a creditable lie;

but the house, which is their temple, cannot say anything save the truth of those who have lived in it.) A child's cart and a doll lay on the black-and-white floor, where a rug had been kicked back. I felt that the children had only just hurried away – to hide themselves, most like – in the many turns of the great adzed staircase that climbed statelily out of the hall, or to crouch at gaze behind the lions and roses of the carven gallery above. Then I heard her voice above me, singing as the blind sing – from the soul: –

In the pleasant orchard-closes.

And all my early summer came back at the call.

In the pleasant orchard-closes,
God bless all our gains say we –
But may God bless all our losses,
Better suits with our degree.

She dropped the marring fifth line, and repeated –

Better suits with our degree!

I saw her lean over the gallery, her linked hands white as pearl against the oak.

'Is that you – from the other side of the county?' she called.

'Yes, me from the other side of the county,' I answered, laughing.

'What a long time before you had to come here again.'

She ran down the stairs, one hand lightly touching the broad rail. 'It's two months and four days. Summer's gone!'

'I meant to come before, but Fate prevented.'

'I knew it. Please do something to that fire. They won't let me play with it, but I can feel it's behaving badly. Hit it!'

I looked on either side of the deep fireplace, and found but a half-charred hedge-stake with which I punched a black log into flame.

'It never goes out, day or night,' she said, as though explaining. 'In case any one comes in with cold toes, you see.'

'It's even lovelier inside than it was out,' I murmured. The red light poured itself along the age-polished dusky panels till the Tudor roses and lions of the gallery took colour and motion. An old eagle-topped convex mirror gathered the picture into its mysterious heart, distorting afresh the distorted shadows, and curving the gallery lines into the curves of a ship. The day was shutting down in half a gale as the fog turned to stringy scud. Through the uncurtained mullions of the broad window I could see valiant horsemen of the lawn rear and recover against the wind that taunted them with legions of dead leaves.

'Yes, it must be beautiful,' she said. 'Would you like to go over it? There's still light enough upstairs.'

I followed her up the unflinching, wagon-wide staircase to the gallery, whence opened the thin fluted Elizabethan doors.

'Feel how they put the latch low down for the sake of the children.' She swung a light door inward.

'By the way, where are they?' I asked. 'I haven't even heard them today.'

She did not answer at once. Then, 'I can only hear them,' she replied softly. 'This is one of their rooms – everything ready, you see.'

She pointed into a heavily-timbered room. There were little low gate tables and children's chairs. A doll's house, its hooked front half open, faced a great dappled rocking-horse, from whose padded saddle it was but a child's scramble to the broad window-seat overlooking the lawn. A toy gun lay in a corner beside a gilt wooden cannon.

'Surely they've only just gone,' I whispered. In the failing light a door creaked cautiously. I heard the rustle of a frock and the patter of feet – quick feet through a room beyond.

'I heard that,' she cried triumphantly. 'Did you? Children, oh, children, where are you?'

The voice filled the walls that held it lovingly to the last perfect note, but there came no answering shout such as I had heard in the garden. We hurried on from room to oak-floored room; up a step here, down three steps there; among a maze of passages; always mocked by our quarry. One might as well have tried to work an unstopped warren with a single ferret. There were bolt-holes innumerable – recesses in walls, embrasures of deep slitten windows now darkened, whence they could start up behind us; and abandoned fireplaces, six feet deep in the masonry, as well as the tangle of communicating doors. Above all, they had the twilight for their helper in our game. I had caught one or two joyous chuckles of evasion, and once or twice had seen the silhouette of a child's frock against some darkening window at the end of a passage; but we returned empty-handed to the gallery, just as a middle-aged woman was setting a lamp in its niche.

'No, I haven't seen her either this evening, Miss Florence,' I heard her say, 'but that Turpin he says he wants to see you about his shed.'

'Oh, Mr. Turpin must want to see me very badly. Tell him to come to the hall, Mrs. Madden.'

I looked down into the hall whose only light was the dulled fire, and deep in the shadow I saw them at last. They must have slipped down while we were in the passages, and now thought themselves perfectly hidden behind an old gilt leather screen. By child's law, my fruitless chase was as good as an introduction, but since I had taken so much trouble I resolved to force them to come forward later by the simple trick, which children detest, of pretending not to notice them. They lay close, in a little huddle, no more than shadows except when a quick flame betrayed an outline.

'And now we'll have some tea,' she said. 'I believe I ought to have offered it you at first, but one doesn't arrive at manners, somehow, when one lives alone and is considered – h'm – peculiar.' Then with very pretty scorn, 'would you like a lamp to see to eat by?'

'The firelight's much pleasanter, I think.' We descended into that delicious gloom and Madden brought tea.

I took my chair in the direction of the screen, ready to surprise or be surprised as the game should go, and at her permission, since a hearth is always sacred, bent forward to play with the fire.

'Where do you get these beautiful short faggots from?' I asked idly. 'Why, they are tallies!'

'Of course,' she said. 'As I can't read or write I'm driven back on the early English tally for my accounts. Give me one and I'll tell you what it meant.'

I passed her an unburnt hazel-tally, about a foot long, and she ran her thumb down the nicks.

'This is the milk-record for the home farm for the month of April last year, in gallons,' said she. 'I don't know what I should have done without tallies. An old forester of mine taught me the system. It's out of date now for every one else; but my tenants respect it. One of them's coming now to see me. Oh, it doesn't matter. He has no business here out of office hours. He's a greedy, ignorant man — very greedy or — he wouldn't come here after dark.'

'Have you much land then?'

'Only a couple of hundred acres in hand, thank goodness. The other six hundred are nearly all let to folk who knew my folk before me, but this Turpin is quite a new man — and a highway robber.'

'But are you sure I sha'n't be — ?'

'Certainly not. You have the right. He hasn't any children.'

'Ah, the children!' I said, and slid my low chair back till it nearly touched the screen that hid them. 'I wonder whether they'll come out for me.'

There was a murmur of voices — Madden's and a deeper note — at the low, dark side door, and a ginger-headed, canvas-gaitered giant of the unmistakable tenant farmer type stumbled or was pushed in.

'Come to the fire, Mr. Turpin,' she said.

'If — if you please, Miss, I'll — I'll be quite as well by

the door.' He clung to the latch as he spoke, like a frightened child. Of a sudden I realised that he was in the grip of some almost overpowering fear.

'Well?'

'About that new shed for the young stock – that was all. These first autumn storms settin' in . . . but I'll come again, Miss.' His teeth did not chatter much more than the door latch.

'I think not,' she answered levelly. 'The new shed – m'm. What did my agent write you on the 15th?'

'I – fancied p'r'aps that if I came to see you – ma – man to man like, Miss – but – '

His eyes rolled into every corner of the room, wide with horror. He half opened the door through which he had entered, but I noticed it shut again – from without and firmly.

'He wrote what I told him,' she went on. 'You are overstocked already. Dunnett's Farm never carried more than fifty bullocks – even in Mr. Wright's time. And he used cake. You've sixty-seven and you don't cake. You've broken the lease in that respect. You're dragging the heart out of the farm.'

'I'm – I'm getting some minerals – superphosphates – next week. I've as good as ordered a truck-load already. I'll go down to the station tomorrow about 'em. Then I can come and see you man to man like, Miss, in the daylight . . . That gentleman's not going away, is he?' He almost shrieked.

I had only slid the chair a little further back, reaching behind me to tap on the leather of the screen, but he jumped like a rat.

'No. Please attend to me, Mr. Turpin.' She turned in her chair and faced him with his back to the door. It was an old and sordid little piece of scheming that she forced from him – his plea for the new cowshed at his landlady's expense, that he might with the covered manure pay his next year's rent out of the valuation after, as she made clear, he had bled the enriched pastures to the bone. I could not but admire the intensity of his greed, when I saw him out-facing for its sake whatever terror it was that ran wet on his forehead.

I ceased to tap the leather – was, indeed, calculating the cost of the shed – when I felt my relaxed hand taken and turned softly between the soft hands of a child. So at last I had triumphed. In a moment I would turn and acquaint myself with those quick-footed wanderers . . .

The little brushing kiss fell in the centre of my palm – as a gift on which the fingers were, once, expected to close: as the all faithful half-reproachful signal of a waiting child not used to neglect even when grown-ups were busiest – a fragment of the mute code devised very long ago.

Then I knew. And it was as though I had known from the first day when I looked across the lawn at the high window.

I heard the door shut. The woman turned to me in silence, and I felt that she knew.

What time passed after this I cannot say. I was roused by the fall of a log, and mechanically rose to put it back. Then I returned to my place in the chair very close to the screen.

'Now you understand,' she whispered, across the packed shadows.

'Yes, I understand – now. Thank you.'

'I – I only hear them.' She bowed her head in her hands. 'I have no right, you know – no other right. I have neither borne nor lost – neither borne nor lost!'

'Be very glad then,' said I, for my soul was torn open within me.

'Forgive me!'

She was still, and I went back to my sorrow and my joy.

'It was because I loved them so,' she said at last, brokenly. 'That was why it was, even from the first – even before I knew that they – they were all I should ever have. And I loved them so!'

She stretched out her arms to the shadows and the shadows within the shadow.

'They came because I loved them – because I needed them. I – I must have made them come. Was that wrong, think you?'

'No – no.'

'I – I grant you that the toys and – and all that sort of thing were nonsense, but – but I used to so hate empty rooms myself when I was little.' She pointed to the gallery. 'And the passages all empty. . . . And how could I ever bear the garden door shut? Suppose –'

'Don't! For pity's sake, don't!' I cried. The twilight had brought a cold rain with gusty squalls that plucked at the leaded windows.

'And the same thing with keeping the fire in all night. I don't think it so foolish – do you?'

I looked at the broad brick hearth, saw, through tears I believe, that there was no unpassable iron on or near it, and bowed my head.

'I did all that and lots of other things – just to make believe. Then they came. I heard them, but I didn't know that they were not mine by right till Mrs. Madden told me –'

'The butler's wife? What?'

'One of them – I heard – she saw – and knew. Hers! Not for me. I didn't know at first. Perhaps I was jealous. Afterwards, I began to understand that it was only because I loved them, not because – . . . Oh, you must bear or lose,' she said piteously. 'There is no other way – and yet they love me. They must! Don't they?'

There was no sound in the room except the lapping voices of the fire, but we two listened intently, and she at least took comfort from what she heard. She recovered herself and half rose. I sat still in my chair by the screen.

'Don't think me a wretch to whine about myself like this, but – but I'm all in the dark, you know, and you can see.'

In truth I could see, and my vision confirmed me in my resolve, though that was like the very parting of spirit and flesh. Yet a little longer I would stay since it was the last time.

'You think it is wrong, then?' she cried sharply, though I had said nothing.

'Not for you. A thousand times no. For you it is right . . . I am grateful to you beyond words. For me it would be wrong. For me only . . .'

'Why?' she said, but passed her hand before her face

as she had done at our second meeting in the wood. 'Oh, I see,' she went on simply as a child. 'For you it would be wrong.' Then with a little indrawn laugh, 'and, d'you remember, I called you lucky – once – at first. You who must never come here again!'

She left me to sit a little longer by the screen, and I heard the sound of her feet die out along the gallery above.